WHAT EVIL HIDES

A DETECTIVE KAY HUNTER CRIME THRILLER

RACHEL AMPHLETT

SAXON PUBLISHING

BOOKS IN ORDER

Discover all of Rachel Amphlett's books here:

ONE

Alexandru Popa drove his knuckles into his back and contemplated the fine mist rising over the hop bines.

It was a little after seven o'clock in the morning, and he took a moment to enjoy one of the most beautiful sunrises he had seen since returning to Kent that July. The Weald's undulating landscape was awash with different shades of green after a summer of showers and sunshine, and the hops were flourishing.

Hand-woven trellises lined the hillside hop garden in neat rows that went on for several hundred metres, broken in places by natural corridors between the trellises to allow for the tractor and trailer that would collect the harvest once Alexandru and the other pickers had snipped the bines loose. The bines wound their way up wires that had been woven that February and March, ready for the first tentative shoots to grasp come April, and then the summer months had been spent coaxing those into the eight-metre-high vines that towered over him.

They provided a modicum of shade over the parched

clay and sandstone-based soil that had been baked and cracked by the late summer's heatwave, and he took a moment to pause and take a deep breath.

There was an aroma here that defied explanation, and made Alexandru's heart soar. It depended on the hop variety he passed but could vary between an earthy, wholesome smell to citrus within a few lengths of trellis. He ran his calloused hand over the nearest ripened hop cones with a practised light touch that came from years of travelling here from Romania each season to lend his expertise and labour to the full-time staff contingent.

The farm belonged to a well-established business that provided hops to several independent craft breweries in the county, as well as one or two over the border in Sussex. By the time the September harvest was complete, Alexandru and his co-workers would work ten- to twelve-hour days picking several thousand bines, each one destined to become a part of the flourishing local craft beer industry.

He had even heard rumours about breweries from further afield placing orders for next year, depending on how well two new varieties were received at next month's green hop festival.

'Here.'

He turned at the sound of a voice to see Daniel Ionescu walking towards him, a thermal flask in his hand, and raised an eyebrow. 'Is that coffee?'

'Justin turned up with the tractor five minutes ago and brought fresh supplies.'

'I knew I liked him for a reason.'

Daniel smiled and handed over one of two tin mugs, then shrugged his daypack to the ground before uncapping the flask and pouring a generous serving. 'How's your back?'

Alexandru waggled his free hand by way of response.

'It's your age,' said Daniel.

'Piss off.' He blew across the surface of the hot liquid and closed his eyes, savouring the arabica beans before taking a tentative sip. 'Are we still picking these today?'

The younger man raised his gaze to the top of the bines, eyeing the criss-crossing wires at the top of each. 'He says they're ready.'

'I think he's right.'

'You agree with him?'

'He's not as patient as his father was, but yes – he knows what he's doing,' said Alexandru, pausing to take another sip. He pointed at the bines across the other side of the baked earth track. 'And he's not afraid to try new varieties. Those have done really well this year.'

Daniel wrinkled his nose. 'Has he found a buyer?'

'A new craft brewery in Maidstone wants half of them.' Alexandru finished the coffee and tipped the dregs onto the track, away from the bines so as not to affect the delicate balance of precious nutrients in the soil. 'They've already placed an order for next year too.'

The other man's eyes widened. 'Can they do that?'

'They didn't want to wait until the hop festival in case they lost out, but based on that I don't think he'll have a problem selling the rest once the word gets out.'

'Good.' Daniel took the mug from him and dropped both into his daypack together with the flask. 'That means we'll have work next year then.'

'Looks like it.' Alexandru paused at the sound of the

tractor a few hundred metres to his right through the bines, and jerked his thumb at the trellises beside them. 'Best get back to work.'

The two men walked to the end of the row where a pair of red tractors rumbled, one with a corn picker platform attached to its rear, the other towing a trailer.

'Ready?' called the man with the corn picker. 'Thought we'd make a start on this row before the sun gets too high – the remaining bines will give us some shade while we work.'

'Ready, Howard.' Alexandru tested the weight of the vicious-looking scythe in his calloused hand and eyed first the nearest hops, then Daniel. 'Do you want to go up again?'

'You go. We'll switch in an hour or so.'

Pulling a floppy cotton bucket hat from the back pocket of his jeans and adjusting it on his head, Alexandru lifted the safety rail and clambered into the steel picker, planted his feet on the grilled floor and waited while Howard controlled the ascent. In one fluid motion he was up in the air and able to reach out and cut the top of the bine with a single slash of the scythe.

Below, Daniel did the same, leaving a few centimetres of the bine protruding from the ground, and carried the remains over to the trailer being pulled by the second tractor before returning.

The two men repeated the exercise along the row of hops before Howard lowered the corn picker and Alexandru climbed out while the tractor was positioned to return along the next row.

The trailer was only a quarter full, and the second

tractor's engine idled while the driver waited for them to start the harvesting process once more.

As the corn picker lifted him into the air, Alexandru took a moment to admire the scenery. He would never tire of it, he was sure. From here, he could see along the bines and over towards the main dirt track that led from the field to the farmyard. An old stone wall ran the width of the hop garden, disappearing into a woodland copse of beech, oak and ash that was being regenerated with some of the profit from the farm. The gate from the field to the yard was left open for ease of access for the two tractors and the workers, and parked beyond that was a dark green four-wheel drive and a blue pick-up truck used by the owner and his wife.

The farmhouse was late Victorian, a striking building that reflected the early morning sunshine across its red brick walls and clay-tiled roof. There was movement at a door to the side of the building, and then Justin Mallory, the owner, strode across the yard towards a converted stable block on the opposite side of the yard that was used for the farm office and a rudimentary staffroom. He had his hand raised to his head, and Alexandru realised the man was on his mobile phone, the working day already underway for the busy enterprise.

In another hour or so, the first tourist group would be deposited at the main gate by minibus, eager to walk amongst the bines – and participate in an entertaining beer tasting afterwards, even if it was before lunchtime.

'Today, Alex.'

He jumped, then looked down to where Daniel was

waiting at the bottom of the bine, his scythe lowered. 'Sorry.'

Turning his attention back to his work, they moved methodically along the row, the *swish* of the scythe and the rustle of fresh hops settling in the trailer below filtering up to where he stood and setting a rhythm to the work that held an underlying urgency.

If the hops were left too long to ripen, the delicate balancing act that ensured the flavours were what the waiting brewers expected would be ruined and with it, the hop garden's reputation.

Alexandru grimaced as a familiar twinge struck the base of his spine when he let go of the next bine, and straightened for a moment, letting his gaze roam across the remaining rows that stretched out for another hundred metres or more.

And then he frowned.

There was something stuck between the bines in a row twenty metres or so away, something pale blue that flapped in the gentle breeze. Something that—

'Lower me down!' he bellowed. 'Quickly!'

Howard didn't hesitate. The corn picker boom dropped while Alexandru clutched the safety railing, his jaw set.

As soon as the boom was safe, he lifted the rail, unhitched his safety line and ran to the end of the row, Daniel and Howard at his heels.

'What's going on?' Daniel called. 'What is it?'

He didn't answer, already out of breath and ruing the amount of real ale he had enjoyed in the evenings with his compatriots in the local pub. There used to be a time in his youth when he could run a half marathon, but those days were long gone. Sweat beaded at his forehead and he was panting by the time he reached the track and slowed to a walk, peering between the rows of bines while he tried to locate what he had seen.

Howard caught up with him first, his English accent tinged with a Somerset burr that spoke of his experience in the cider fields of the West Country. 'What did you see?'

'I'm not sure. I think…' Alexandru broke off when he reached the next row, and he felt his bowels twist. 'Stay here.'

'Alex?' Daniel tried to squeeze past him, but he pushed him back.

'I said, stay here.' He could hear the fear in his own voice now, and the other man's eyes widened, seeing something in his expression that brooked no argument. 'Let me check first. I may be mistaken.'

He turned away before Daniel and Howard could protest further, and walked along the row. There was a natural curve to it caused by the topography of the hop garden. On a gentle slope that caught the sun's rays throughout the day and that drained well after heavy rains, the centre of the row of bines was hidden from view at the moment, revealing its secret as he edged closer.

Alexandru's footsteps were slower now and more hesitant as he looked up and ran his gaze over the crisscrossing trellis lines, trying to gauge how close he was to… it.

Then there was a flutter of wind amongst the bines, and the leaves parted to reveal a scrap of the same pale blue he had seen from the corn picker's platform.

Except it wasn't a scrap.

It was a man's shirt, he could see that now. It had been torn lengthways, collar to hem, and there was what looked like…

Blood.

It had soaked through the hem of the shirt, down the dark grey cargo trousers and over dirty and well-worn work boots before pooling on the floor amongst…

Alexandru reached for the silver crucifix at the nape of his neck, bile rising in this throat as he gazed up at the bloodied man who was bound by his wrists and ankles to the trellis wires, his face a rictus of agony.

There was so much blood, so much horror in the man's eyes, and his—

'My God,' Alexandru managed, and then turned on his heel and stumbled back towards Daniel and Howard.

TWO

Detective Inspector Kay Hunter climbed from the dull grey pool car and leaned her arm on the door, a faint breeze tickling the fine blonde hairs at the nape of her neck.

It was warm already, with the forecast promising a blistering heat taking a hold of the Kentish countryside for the next twenty-four hours, with no promise of rain for at least another week. As she rolled up her shirt sleeves and eyed the array of liveried Kent Police cars, a plain white van belonging to the forensic team and a silver four-door saloon car that belonged to the Home Office pathologist, Kay huffed her fringe from her eyes and wished she had remembered to bring a bottle of water with her.

Except there had been no time.

The call had been patched through by the dispatch team an hour ago, the first patrol had been on site within twenty minutes of that, and she and her detective sergeant, Ian Barnes, had been assigned to the subsequent investigation fifteen minutes later. Notwithstanding their current workload, their superiors in Gravesend had taken one look at their location – a scrap metal yard on the outskirts of Tunbridge Wells that had been under investigation for the past month – and opted to send the nearest available superior officer.

'Lucky me,' she muttered. Closing the door, she peered over the roof as Barnes emerged from the passenger seat, loosening his tie. 'What did Gavin say?'

Barnes tucked his mobile phone into his shirt pocket and shielded his eyes with his hand as he looked at three forensic specialists in white protective suits moving between their van and a building at the far end of the farmyard. 'He reckons there's never been a sniff of trouble here. The nearest recorded incident was a drink-driving crash about a mile or so down the lane towards Headcorn in February.'

'I remember that one. Three nineteen-year-olds, wasn't it?' Kay shivered. 'I think one of the traffic officers who attended that is still off sick.'

'Yeah. It was a nasty one.' Barnes dropped his hand and peered over the car roof. 'Ready?'

'As I'll ever be. Looks like Nadine's got the cordon under control.'

Kay led the way over to the far end of the yard where a young uniformed constable with brown hair tied back into a neat ponytail stood beside a metal five-bar gate. The gate had been left open, with a rusting chain looped around the top rail and its other end over a wooden post set into the drystone wall beside it.

Nadine had stretched blue and white crime scene tape between the post and a protruding lump of flint in the wall opposite, and stood with a clipboard in her hand and a black biro in the other. She straightened at the sight of the two detectives.

'Morning, guv,' she said to Kay, giving Barnes a nod by way of greeting and holding out the clipboard. 'Kyle said you were on your way over.'

Kay scrawled her signature and the time on the sign-in sheet before handing it to her colleague. 'Is he helping Gavin to set up the incident room?'

'He is, and Laura and Debbie have been assigned to this one as well,' said Nadine. 'They're ready to start processing information the moment we get anything here.'

'That's great work. Were you first on scene?'

'Myself and Tim Wallace. He's down in the hop fields at the moment, helping to coordinate with Harriet's forensic team. They got here about ten minutes ago, so they're making sure we didn't mess anything up.'

'Did you?' said Barnes.

'No, sarge. As soon as the workers showed us the crime scene, we moved all of them up to the staffroom in that barn over there. Harry Davis and Sean Gastrell got here twenty minutes ago and have started taking statements, starting with the bloke who found the body.'

'Any ID on the victim?'

'None, sarge. We'll wait until Harriet's team hand back the crime scene and then we'll organise a fingertip search with them to see if we can locate his wallet or phone or anything else.'

As Kay listened, the knowledge that everything she and her team did would be scrutinised by her superiors was tempered by the methodical calmness with which one of the youngest officers was undertaking her duties.

She smiled. 'Sounds like you're managing it all well. Do we need to suit up here?'

'No, guv.' Nadine turned and pointed past the gate to the rows of hops lining the trellises as far as Kay could see. 'If you follow the line for about two hundred metres, you'll come to a wider track between the hops the growers use to access the field beyond this one. Lucas is down there, and I believe that's where Harriet's team have based themselves too.'

'Great, thanks.'

Kay set a quick pace alongside the hops, the strong scent almost overpowering. She hadn't been this close to a fully-grown crop before, and as she looked between the rows of trellises, she shuddered at the way in which they towered above her, blocking out any light between them.

There was a stillness in the air, an anticipation that whatever had happened here would ripple out across those who worked here, as well as families, friends, locals – all of whom would be affected by the victim's death and the ensuing investigation.

There was a verge of long grass to the left of the track separating it from the trellises, and she spotted a pair of opened cardboard boxes halfway along it, together with a biohazard bin that was being managed by one of Harriet's team, the man pacing beside it with his phone to his ear.

The pathways between the four trellises either side of him were cordoned off by a second strip of crime scene tape, and a sandy-haired giant of a uniformed sergeant stood beside it, his face stoical.

'Morning, Tim,' said Kay. 'I heard it's a bit of a mess along there.'

'It is, guv,' said PS Wallace. 'It's why I thought I'd best tell Nadine to manage the first cordon while I came down here when we arrived.'

'Thanks.' Kay shot him a grateful smile, then turned to the forensic specialist as he ended his call. 'Morning, Gareth.'

'Morning, Detective Hunter.'

'Mind if we have two of those suits?'

'No problem.' The technician stooped for a moment, then pulled out two plastic-wrapped protective suits from the first box and matching gloves and booties from the other. While Kay and Barnes wriggled them over their suits, Gareth pointed along the row to Tim's left. 'We've set up a demarcated path along there. Luckily, it's quite wide because they need to get a trailer along it during harvest, so you won't risk touching anything while you're walking along. Lucas is along there now.'

'Okay, thanks.'

She waited while Tim lifted the crime scene tape for her and Barnes to duck under, then fell into step beside her colleague. 'Once we've taken a look at what we're dealing with, I'd like to interview the man who found him.'

'Alexandru Popa,' said Barnes from memory. 'He's one of the part-time Romanian workers who come here for the harvest season.'

'Visa okay?'

'Yes, all legitimate. There are four of them at this farm, and more Romanian nationals spread around other hop farms and fruit growers in the area together with a few Polish and Hungarians. This is the fifth year Alexandru has worked here.'

'Thanks,' Kay murmured, then slowed her pace as she spotted a familiar gangly figure blocking the middle of the row, waiting for them.

Simon Winter had joined Lucas Anderson's pathology team a few years ago and was a key member of that tight-knit contingent of experts. She had worked with him on a number of occasions and his calm methodical approach to his work was one that calmed the most nervous visitors to the Dartford-based mortuary.

He greeted the two detectives with a nod, then stood to one side as a burly figure joined him, the older man giving Simon a nudge before handing him a tablet computer.

'Thanks for getting here so fast, Lucas,' said Kay, then watched as Simon brushed past her and Barnes, a worried expression on his face while he stared at the tablet's screen.

'No problem. One of the forensic lot said you were on your way down from the farmyard so I thought I'd meet you here.' Lucas Anderson used a gloved finger to scratch at the plastic hood covering his head. 'I'll warn you now, it's not pretty.'

'What do you mean, not pretty?'

The pathologist peered over his mask at her, his brown eyes baleful. 'Well, I can confirm he didn't die from natural causes. And I think we can rule out an accident too.'

'Why's that?'

In reply, he beckoned to them. 'It's probably better that I show you rather than try to explain it.'

With that, Lucas led them around the slight bend in the

hop trellis before standing to one side, and pointed upwards.

Kay followed with her eyes, then gasped and took a step backwards, tasting bile at the back of her throat despite her years of experience while she stared at the man's body suspended by the trellis wires, his feet dangling above the ground.

Dried blood stained the soil beneath him, and she could see where it had stained the man's trousers. What remained of his shirt exposed a vicious open wound that started just below the victim's sternum and carved a path down his stomach and abdomen, the man's intestines snaking onto the ground where flies buzzed and crawled.

'Jesus,' said Barnes, paling. 'I guess we can rule out suicide as well.'

Kay swallowed, then cast her gaze over the bindings that held the victim in place. 'How the hell did he get up there? It's what, two, three metres off the ground?'

'And he's a decent weight for his age, too,' said Lucas. 'Harriet will have her own theories from her findings in due course, but I reckon it'd have taken at least two people to get him there.'

'Was that done to him before or after he was killed?'

'Before,' said the pathologist without hesitation. 'There's too much blood here for him to have been moved from somewhere else, and there are no traces of blood along the track leading to this trellis.'

Kay checked over her shoulder before taking a step back, then craned her neck to see along the shaded rows of bines. She could see three stooped figures in identical white protective suits at the far end. 'What are the track marks going that way?'

'Harriet and her team are already down there processing those and some footprints they found,' Lucas explained. 'She's working on an initial theory that whoever did this used the cherry picker that they use here for cutting the tops of the bines free from the trellis to lift him up there.'

'Still, that'd take some doing.' Kay looked around, taking in the baked earth and gnarled hop roots. 'Any sign of the weapon?'

Lucas sighed. 'According to the owner, there are six people on site right now all carrying hop scythes. Take your pick.'

'Please tell me Harriet's seized all of those for processing.'

'She did, the moment I told her this wound was caused by a knife or similar.'

'Okay, thanks.' Kay took one last look at the victim, committing his face to memory despite the nightmares she would have to live with. She dug her fingernails into her palms.

'When do you think you can get the post mortem done?' Barnes asked, some of his normal colour returning to his face.

'Tomorrow morning. Coming along?'

'Yes.'

'So will I,' said Kay, taking a final look around. 'Whoever did this planned it well, and that worries me. A lot.'

THREE

Kay found Alexandru Popa in a cosy living room next to the kitchen in the main farmhouse. The man's weathered features looked troubled as he sat on a sagging sofa and stared at an empty coffee mug in his hands.

The living room had a low plasterwork ceiling striped with exposed oak beams and a large stone hearth at the far end that currently housed a vase full of fresh pink oriental lilies, around which a handful of dried hop cones had been scattered. A wall-mounted television stared blankly at the room from its position above the mantelpiece, a red standby light in its lower corner the only sign of life. A scuffed rosewood upright piano took up the space between two bookshelves on the right-hand wall, and the left wall gave way to two wide sash windows that overlooked a sprawling garden. A long low coffee table was in front of the sofa, separating it from two arm chairs with well-worn cushions and frames that looked as if they had been scratched by a cat, which was currently absent from the room. On the table were a selection of farming magazines, a copy of a tour brochure for the hop garden, and a television remote with the back panel off and two batteries discarded beside it.

Sunlight dappled the rug beneath Alexandru's feet, and as Kay sat in one of the armchairs opposite him and waited while Barnes extracted a notebook and pen from his shirt pocket, she saw that grey flecked the man's thinning hair and age spots covered the backs of his hands.

'Alexandru, I'm Detective Inspector Kay Hunter, and this is Detective Sergeant Ian Barnes. We're with Kent Police,' she began. 'I know you've had a terrible shock this morning, and that you've also provided my colleagues with a statement, but I'd like to ask you some questions. Is that okay?'

The man raised his gaze to hers, his dark brown eyes framed with red where he had been crying. He sniffed, then leaned forward, placed the coffee mug on the table and uttered a shuddering sigh before speaking.

'I didn't do it.'

'Do you know who did?'

'No. I have never seen that man before in my life.'

'Any trouble back home in Romania?'

He shook his head. 'None. My wife died four years ago, my two daughters are married to wonderful men, and my three grandchildren are at school.'

'Why do you work here during the summer?'

Alexandru's eyes widened. 'Have you seen the cost of universities?'

'I have, and they're expensive. Are they the same back home?'

'They are, especially when one of your granddaughters

decides she wants to study medicine. That is why I come here – to help her save.'

'That's kind of you.'

He shrugged. 'I love my family.'

'You must miss them.'

'It's only a few more weeks.'

Kay leaned back in her seat, keeping her hands relaxed in her lap. 'How long have you been working in the hop fields here?'

'Five years. Always here.'

'How did you find out about the work?'

'Through a friend who was retiring. I came over with him the first year, and they invited me back.' A faint smile reached Alexandru's lips. 'The Mallorys are a good family to work for.'

'Tell me what happened this morning.'

Alexandru's body shuddered at the memory. 'I was up in the corn picker – it's a raised platform we use so we can reach the top of the bines. Daniel had spent the first hour up there, so we take it in turns. It gives us each a break from bending over and cutting them at the bottom and lifting them into the trailer. I was just looking over at the next rows, working out how many were left for that crop and how long it might take us when I saw something moving. It's hot out there, but there's a breeze amongst the hops, and the wind was moving... it turned out to be that man's shirt... Do you know who he is?'

'Why did you decide to investigate?' asked Kay, ignoring his question.

'I don't know. I...' Alexandru broke off, and gave a shrug before continuing. 'It felt... wrong. Out of place. I wanted to see what it was. I suppose I thought if there was a problem, we should find out about it before it caused a delay… The hops need to be picked before they lose their flavour, you see.'

'And so you went to take a look?'

'Yes. Daniel and Howard followed me, but when I saw the blood, I sent them back.' Alexandru looked at Barnes. 'I used to be in the army when I was younger. Conscripted. I saw some things back then as a medic… I didn't want them to see that man, like that. They would have nightmares.'

'And you?' said Kay, waiting until he turned his attention back to her once more. 'Will you be all right?'

'I think so.'

'Do you have access to a medical professional, a doctor while you're here?'

The man nodded. 'We all do.'

'Please speak to them if you do have trouble sleeping, or need someone to talk to,' she said. 'They'll be able to help you.'

Alexandru's head bobbed. 'Thank you.'

'When you found the man in the hop garden, did you touch anything?' Kay asked.

'No. I knew not to touch anything. I kept my hands in my pockets.'

'What did you do next?'

'As soon as I saw all the blood, I knew there was no hope for him. I could see death in his eyes. He had not lived for some time.' Alexandru ran his tongue over his lips. 'I ran away. I was sick, and then I told Howard to use his mobile phone to call for help. After that, we told Justin and he told everyone to get out of the hop garden.'

Kay watched him for a moment, and then leaned forward. 'Do you have any idea who might want to kill a man like that? Anyone at all?'

'No.' Alexandru's gaze fell to his hands. He clasped his hands together as if in silent prayer, his knuckles white. 'Whoever did that to him is a devil.'

FOUR

Detective Sergeant Ian Barnes followed Kay across the farmyard, sweat beading at his brow within seconds of leaving the coolness of the house.

He pulled a cotton handkerchief from his trouser pocket, a habit passed onto him by his late father, and dabbed at his forehead before side-stepping a young forensic technician who skittered out of his way before she hurried over to the white panel van.

There was a stillness to the yard, as if it were frozen in time. Where normally he would expect to hear the rumble of machinery from the hop picking and modern drying machines in the barn beside the old oast house and voices calling across the yard while tractors and trailers arrived with more of that season's harvest, there was nothing.

Even the birds were subdued.

Barnes eyed the converted stable block they were approaching and noted the newer clay tiles at the far end and the fresh paint that had been applied to the window and door frames at some point over the summer. The window panes were dusty, with hop husks littering the concrete hardstanding below them, but the gables above had been decorated with bright hanging baskets giving the impression that the whole property was well looked after, and that the business was thriving.

The stable block had been divided up into three separate rooms. The one at the far end, nearest to all the patrol cars and other vehicles, was the largest of the three, according to Nadine, and served as a reception office and visitor centre. Barnes wet his lips at the thought of a fresh cold beer, but turned his attention to the middle room that was used as a staffroom and kitchen. The door was open as they walked past, but nobody was inside and the stainless-steel counters on each side of a matching sink were bare.

The last room in the block had been converted into a farm office, and it was to this door that Kay turned her attention. She rapped on the oak surface, and Barnes heard a muffled "come in" before she opened the door and they stepped inside.

Barnes peered around his DI to see a man in his late thirties sitting in a leather chair behind a pine desk, his head in his hands while he stared at a sheaf of reports that had been laid out before him.

He looked up with a weary expression, and waved the two detectives to a pair of visitor chairs under the window on each side of a small occasional table with a water stain in the middle of it. 'I take it you're the two detectives they said would be turning up.'

Barnes made the introductions, and took out his notebook. 'Can you confirm your name please?'

'Justin Mallory,' said the man. He leaned back in the

chair and sighed, the creak from the worn leather echoing the sentiment. 'I'm the owner of the farm, along with my wife, Cassandra. Have you met her?'

'We found her in the kitchen, doling out coffee to everybody. She said we'd find you here,' said Barnes.

'That sounds like Cassandra.' The farmer gave a sad smile. 'Always the one to face any crisis head-on.'

'How long have you had the farm?'

'It belonged to my grandfather,' Justin said, gathering up the reports and stacking them into a tray to the left of a computer screen. That done, he pushed away the keyboard and mouse and folded his arms on the desk, tanned skin emphasised by the light green polo shirt he wore. 'It was an arable farm until my father decided to experiment with hops. We haven't looked back since.'

'When did your father retire?'

The farmer's mouth quirked. 'He says two years ago, although he's never really given up. He likes to keep his hand in.'

'Oh?' Barnes cocked an eyebrow. 'Does that cause problems around here?'

'Not often. He still holds sway with some of the long-time employees but they're good enough to humour him without insulting him, and then we find a workaround between us.' Justin gave a sad smile. 'He kept this place going through some really rough times over the years, so I don't want him to feel left out.'

'Is it just you and your wife here?'

'We've got teenaged girls — they're away at Cassandra's parents' house in Wiltshire at the moment, thank Christ. Dad's got the cottage on the other side of the farm, closer to a neighbouring property – there're two there, and we rent the other one out over the summer to provide some extra income, and we have three full-time staff who live nearby. Gloria manages the tourism side of things – bookings for the guided tours, the cottage I just mentioned and our website and blog. Howard's our full-time farmhand, who's been with us for over a decade now, and then there's Trevor, who runs the production side of things with me – processing and drying the hops, things like that.'

'You have a lot of vines out there,' said Barnes. 'How long does it take to harvest everything?'

Justin gave a patient smile. 'We call them "bines" in the industry. Vines for vino, bines for beer is how we tell it to the tour groups. We start in August, depending on the variety, and can be harvesting through to early October.'

'Any problems in the business?'

'No.' The man's answer was emphatic. 'I've just signed a contract with a new local brewer for a variety we've trialled since last year and they've already placed an order assigning fifty percent of next year's harvest of that to them. As for the rest of this year's hops, we're up to capacity and preparing for next month's green hop festivals.'

'Green hops?' Kay asked.

'New brews, very young and an acquired taste,' Justin explained. 'But integral to our marketing – it gets the brewers excited about the potential of new and existing varieties and helps us sell the hops we harvest as well as laying the foundations for next year's. It's what helps drive our balance sheet. By getting a feel for what's trending or what might be the next big thing, we can tailor our planting in February and March to suit those needs.'

'Have you received any threats that might explain what happened here this morning?' said Barnes. 'And I mean *anything*. Even if you think it's insignificant.'

'Nothing,' the man said. He waved a hand towards the reports in the tray. 'I've been thinking about that while I was going through the orders. There've been no threats, nothing said – as far as I know – in the local pubs... So no, I've got no idea why there's a dead man hanging in my hop garden.'

'Did you see him?'

'I accompanied your sergeant, Wallace, when he arrived here.' Justin shuddered. 'I didn't walk all the way down to... it... but it was obvious whoever it was, he was dead.'

'Do you know who he was?'

'I didn't see his face.'

'If we obtained a photograph, would you be willing to take a look to see if you recognise him?' said Barnes.

'Maybe...' Justin's tone was wary.

'Don't worry – it'll be after he's been cleaned up, and I'll make sure I'm the one to show you. That all right?'

'Okay. I guess, if it helps.'

'Thanks, it would.' Barnes updated his notes before continuing. 'You said that you have tour groups visit the farm – how often does that take place?'

'Tuesdays, Thursdays and the weekends. Mondays, if it's a public holiday,' said Justin, his shoulders relaxing a little at the change in topic. 'Gloria organises them through our website, and myself or Trevor do the tours. We also offer business conference facilities, weddings, private tastings in the evenings over the summer with a hop garden picnic – we bring in a catering contractor to help with those. It's run by someone in the village – we try to pass on the success of the farm to other local businesses wherever we can.'

'Sounds good. Any issues with members of the public on any of those visits?'

'None.' Justin shook his head. 'We're very careful how much alcohol we serve – I've got to be, to keep my licence after all, and we make it very clear in our marketing that we're not interested in hosting stag groups or hen parties, that sort of thing. Some of the corporate and wedding gatherings can get a bit rowdy, but nothing untoward. The weddings are typically small groups compared to some of the parties the hotels around here cater for. We market ourselves for the exclusivity of the setting, you see.'

'What effect is today going to have on your business, Mr Mallory?' Kay asked.

His attention snapped to her, as if he had forgotten she was there, and Barnes saw fear in his eyes.

'Apart from the tours that've just been cancelled at the last minute? Timing is everything in hop growing,' Justin said, his clasped hands tapping the table for emphasis as he spoke. 'In fact, in any arable farming system. Too early, and the taste will be too bitter. Too late, and all the aromas and flavours will be lost. If the hops aren't harvested on time, they'll be ruined. If I don't harvest that new variety this week, everything we've worked for over the last two years will be up in smoke.'

'And how much money will you lose?' she said.

'Hundreds of thousands of pounds,' Justin replied. 'I realise some poor bloke has been tortured and killed out there, but if you don't find out who did this, I could lose my business – and my home.'

Detective Constable Gavin Piper took a sip from his can of energy drink and surveyed the bustling incident room with a familiar sense of anticipation.

Two floors up and along a corridor from the main reception for Maidstone Police station, he could hear the roar and honk of traffic along Palace Avenue beyond the double-glazed windows, an ambulance siren adding a mournful refrain in the distance. Across the room, over where a group of four administrative staff sat at a pod of desks, an enormous printer and photocopier machine belched out page after page of reports and updates from early enquiries, the smell of burning toner mixing with the aroma of stale coffee from the small kitchenette off to one side of the room.

Two more detectives sat at desks that were positioned outside an abandoned office, its door closed and the blinds down. He had tasked Laura Hanway and Kyle Walker with drawing up a list of the hop farm's neighbouring properties and sourcing contact details for the owners twenty minutes ago, and they now stood with their heads bowed over a map that would eventually be pinned to the cork board at his back.

Turning, he put down the energy drink can and selected a black pen from a collection tucked into an old chipped coffee mug and began a list of bullet points on the whiteboard that summarised the known facts.

They were scant at best.

Gavin knew better than to posit any theories at this stage – Kay would ask for those during the briefing when she arrived from the crime scene – but they were already tumbling around in his head.

A single photograph was pinned to the top right-hand corner of the board taken by Kay at the crime scene, which showed the face of the man who had been found slaughtered in amongst the hop trellises. It would be replaced in time with one taken by Lucas Anderson after he had performed the post mortem and a cleaner version was made available to the team, but it now served as a reminder to all of them about the urgency of the investigation.

Gavin grimaced, then tore his gaze away and clenched his jaw.

Even experienced Tim Wallace had sounded shaken when he had phoned five minutes ago to tell him that Kay and Ian Barnes were on their way back, and when Gavin had asked for details about the victim's injuries, the uniformed sergeant had been curt, his disgust apparent.

As much as he would have liked to have been at the crime scene and listened first-hand to the initial crucial witness statements, Gavin's regret was tempered with relief that he would have one less nightmare to worry about.

'Gav, we've got six properties bordering the hop farm, and three of those are smallholdings,' said Laura, interrupting his thoughts. 'The others are private dwellings.'

He looked over his shoulder, the pen frozen above the board. 'Are there enough patrols already out there to start the interviews today?'

'No, but Kyle's onto headquarters at the moment to ask them to find some more.' She held the map in one hand and jiggled some drawing pins in the other, before aiming her fist at the cork board. 'Do you want me to put this up?'

'Please, and thanks. It'd be good if we could interview the closest neighbours today to see if they've noticed anything unusual around there over the past few days. At least that way, if they have, we can send forensics over there.'

Laura nodded by way of response, then smoothed down the map and took a step back before reading his notes. 'There's not a lot to go on, is there?'

'Not yet.' He sighed, then recapped the pen and dropped it onto the table beside the whiteboard. 'What do you think?'

Her gaze travelled to the photograph, and she bit her lip before speaking. 'Well, premeditated I reckon, given the logistics of getting him up there. That's a two-man lift at least, right? And from what you said Tim told you about the wounds, somebody tortured him before he died, which to me means they wanted him to suffer – but why?'

'Aaron Stewart is coordinating with the lab who've

been sent copies of the victim's fingerprints,' said Gavin. 'But unless he's in our system, it won't help us from that perspective.'

'Fingers crossed then,' said Laura. 'Pun unintended.'

'You've been spending too much time with Barnes,' Gavin replied, his mouth quirking. 'You'll be telling dad jokes next.'

'Perish the thought.'

They turned at the sound of the incident room door squeaking on its hinges and Gavin saw Kay and Barnes walk in.

The DI's eyes were haunted as she moved towards the whiteboard, leaving Barnes to round up the rest of the team. 'Everything under control, Gav?'

'Yes, guv.' He moved to one side and gestured to the bullet points. 'It's not much at the moment, but—'

'Don't worry. It's early days, and we've got some long hours ahead of us.' Kay turned to Laura. 'I don't suppose you've had a chance to see what surveillance footage might be around the area?'

'Debbie's doing that, guv,' said her younger colleague. 'I asked her to start with petrol stations, that construction supplier that's up the road from the farm – the pub I was thinking of shut down three months ago, but Debbie's going to get in touch with the leasehold agent whose signboard is in the window to see if they've got cameras on site. After that, we'll start speaking to local residents.' She indicated the map. 'And we've identified the owners of the six properties surrounding the hop farm.'

Gavin grabbed the pen and updated his notes while she

spoke, then handed it to Kay. 'Reckon we're about ready for that briefing, guv.'

'Good work, all of you.' Kay glanced over her shoulder at the sound of chairs being wheeled over to them by the rest of the investigation team, then turned back to him. 'And thanks, Gavin – I appreciate the head start.'

He shot her a grim smile. 'Let's just make sure we catch the bastards who did this to him, guv.'

SIX

Kay swept her gaze over the assembled officers and administrative staff while they settled into their seats.

There was a heightened sense of anticipation in the incident room that was accompanied by a familiar surge of adrenaline coursing through her body, and she took a moment to concentrate on her breathing to calm her heart rate.

The mid-morning traffic beyond the windows had reduced to a subdued hum, and above her head the air conditioning vents purred while a constant cool breeze graced her shoulders. Beyond the incident room, she heard a door slam further along the corridor from where another investigation was being managed, and footsteps pounded the staircase between this floor and the lower two levels as administration staff delivered equipment and stationery supplies, placing it all on three desks at the far end of the incident room, ready to be set up after the briefing.

As she looked around at the familiar faces, some of Kay's initial concerns about the enormity of the task ahead of her began to dissipate. There were a number of uniformed constables and two or three sergeants who had provided their experience on previous investigations, and who had often been the ones to have key breakthroughs that secured suspects' arrests.

Her team of detectives sat in the front row, wearing stoic expressions while bracing themselves for what would be several days of long hours and frustration. Kyle Walker hurried over from his desk and sat beside Barnes, leaning behind the older detective to tap Laura on the shoulder and giving her a slight shake of his head before pulling his mobile from his pocket and tweaking the volume.

Kay glanced to her left as PC Debbie West approached, carrying a sheaf of documents in one hand and a fresh mug of coffee in the other.

Debbie handed Kay the coffee then swept one of the stapled documents from the top of the pile and handed it to her. 'That's the suggested agenda, guv, based on what we've got so far. I'll update the system again after the briefing.'

'Brilliant, thanks.' Kay raised the coffee mug in salute and took a sip, waiting while the experienced exhibits officer took a seat near the front and passed around the agendas. Using her thumb to trace the items listed, Kay listened while the remaining team members found seats or leaned against desks and filing cabinets, and took another sip of coffee before beginning. 'Right, everyone — let's make a start.'

As one, they all turned to her. There was the rustle of notebooks being opened, faint murmurs while one or two of the younger uniformed officers scrabbled around for pens that worked, and then a rapt silence descended on the incident room.

'Thank you,' said Kay. 'I'll begin this briefing by saying that this will be one of the most confronting homicide investigations some of you will have ever worked on. Our victim, currently unidentified, was crucified between two hop trellises before his killer or killers used a sharp implement to torture and then disembowel him. The full set of crime scene photos will not be made available to any admin staff, nor anyone who isn't directly involved in this investigation. If you haven't got access to them and think you should, then speak to myself or DS Ian Barnes.'

Barnes rose to his feet and turned, acknowledging those team members who were unfamiliar with him, then sat once more.

'Next, most of you know Debbie West. Debbie will be our exhibits officer for this investigation, but she's also in charge of your rosters and oversees any administrative or equipment issues you might encounter.' Kay shot them a sly smile. 'And watch yourselves – her reputation for guarding the stationery cupboard is legendary around here.'

There was a smattering of polite laughter that eased the strained atmosphere a little, and Kay saw some of the younger team members relax in their seats.

'On to business,' she continued, 'starting with a quick review of what we have so far. Lucas Anderson has advised that our victim died at the scene sometime between Sunday evening and yesterday afternoon. He'll be able to give us a better timeframe once he's completed the post mortem tomorrow. Nobody was working in that area of the hop garden yesterday because according to the farmer, Justin Mallory, the hops weren't quite ready, which is why our victim wasn't discovered until this morning.'

She turned to look at the victim's photograph, a shiver crossing her shoulders at the thought that even the image failed to capture the true horror of the man's torture and death. 'At the present time, we don't know who he is. His fingerprints aren't in our system, and he has no criminal record. Has anyone had a chance to take a look at missing persons?'

'I did.' PS Harry Davis raised himself from a seat towards the back of the group. 'I started with the most recent names and photographs, working backwards. There's no one matching his description who's gone missing in the last four months, but I'll keep looking.'

'Thanks, Harry. Although his killers had cut open his shirt, Lucas took a look at the label – it's not a cheap brand, and was otherwise in good condition, so pause your search when you get to six months and come and have a word with me,' said Kay. 'We'll make a decision whether to continue down that route or not. In the meantime, can you get in touch with headquarters and make sure they let you know if any new missing persons reports come in over the next forty-eight hours?'

'No problem, guv.'

'Lucas is going to do the post mortem in the morning and Barnes and I will attend, so if we find out anything we can share with you all, I'll do so during tomorrow afternoon's briefing.' Kay paused to take another sip of coffee, knowing it could well be her last for a few hours.

'There have been no signs of a break-in at the farm, and the security cameras facing the yard from the past two nights don't show any of the farm machinery being moved without the owner's knowledge, nor are there any signs of intruders. Sean Gastrell has completed the initial review with Justin Mallory but has requested copies of that footage and plans to go through it again in case he missed something.'

'Do you think Mallory may have distracted him or something, guv?' Gavin asked.

Kay shrugged. 'I think it's just a case of Sean wanting to make sure he's been as thorough as possible. Put it down to his military training. In the meantime, Harriet's forensic team are still working at the hop garden to try to work out how our victim's killer or killers managed to get him into the field and up onto that trellis without being seen or heard. Six scythes have been confiscated from farm workers, including the man who found the body, Alexandru Popa. He and a few others are over from Romania to help with the harvest but have a working history with Justin Mallory's farm, and haven't caused any trouble before. Mallory himself is at a loss to explain who the man is or why he's in his field. Kyle – can you start looking into Mallory's background? He took over from his father full-time two years ago but has a history working with the farm before that. I'd like to know what else he's been up to.'

'Will do, guv.' The detective constable updated his notes, then frowned. 'What about his wife?'

'Cassandra Mallory does the book-keeping for the farm and liaises with all their suppliers,' said Kay. 'She's also the one who sources seasonal workers through an employment agency based here in Maidstone. The farm has used the same workers for the past five years. Gavin, can you arrange to speak to the agency and get all the information we'll need about those workers please?'

'No problem, guv,' said Gavin. 'I'll also find out if those workers have helped out with any other harvests in the area outside of the hop-picking season.'

'Good thinking. Have any of their names appeared in our system?'

'None,' he said, shooting her a wolfish grin. 'But that doesn't mean they haven't got a previous history of violence…'

'It just means they haven't been caught,' Kay finished. 'If you find out anything, even a rumour, let me know.'

'Will do.'

'Okay, finally for now, the hop farm hosts regular tours over the summer,' said Kay. 'Laura – can you get a list of all the attendees from the past four months from Gloria, the woman who runs the farm's website and marketing, and start looking into their backgrounds?'

'Yes, guv.'

'Kyle, Laura said you were speaking to headquarters about sourcing some additional staff to help with interviewing the neighbours and all these other tasks – how are you getting on?'

The newest addition to her detective team grimaced. 'Not good, sorry guv. They've said there won't be any reinforcements available this week, and they might only be able to spare two junior constables next week if some riot training gets cancelled.'

'Dammit.' Kay sighed, eyed the rest of her coffee, then drained it in one gulp. 'Okay, it is what it is. Debbie, best you have Nadine and Sean give you a hand with tracking down the rest of that security camera footage from around the area when they've been released from the crime scene.'

'No problem, guv.' The uniformed constable updated her notes. 'While we're on that, may I ask if everyone could make sure they update HOLMES2 with their tasks by the end of each day so I can keep the reporting consistent? That way, we'll be able to identify any potential connections or anomalies faster.'

'Thanks, and yes.' Kay cast her gaze around at her colleagues. 'You heard Debbie, everyone. I know some of you are behind on your admin tasks, but you're going to have to make it a priority on this one. I'm depending on you, all right?'

There were murmurs of assent, and then she glanced at the board for a moment and looked at the victim's photograph. 'It's too early to get a full report from forensics yet, but Harriet has requested fingerprints of all the farm workers whose scythes have been taken for further investigation. Any news on whether we've got any matches to our database yet?'

'There's nobody on record, guv,' said Kyle, 'but we're missing one person – Roland Hammerton. Justin Mallory has confirmed he's off sick this week with a bad back, so as soon as he's available…'

'A bad back?' Kay spun round to face him, then saw Barnes staring at her, his hand already pulling the car keys from his trouser pocket. 'Have you got an address for him?'

SEVEN

Kay held her phone in one hand and clung to the strap above the car's passenger door as Barnes floored the accelerator and sent them flying over a narrow stone bridge crossing the River Medway.

The route out of Maidstone was along a back road that was unsuitable for heavy goods vehicles, and at this time of day there were no commuters and very little by way of local traffic. Despite the windows being shut and the air conditioning on, she could smell the sweet scent from the freshly cut grass verges on either side of the lane, and spotted the telltale flashes of yellow from castor oil crops between the fringes of oak and beech trees.

Turning her attention back to her phone, she felt the car surge forward again while Barnes's hand rested on the gear stick, his poise relaxed as the vehicle swayed around a curving left-hand turn and emerged at the top of a hill, the tree canopy giving way to bright sunlight that pooled through the windscreen.

She glanced up to see a white plaster-rendered pub

flash by, and then her colleague braked hard as a horse and its rider came into view, and she felt the seatbelt dig into her shoulder.

'Bloody hell, Ian,' she said, lowering her phone to her lap while he turned down the volume on the police radio. 'If he's really got a bad back, he's not going to be going anywhere in a hurry.'

'And if he hasn't?' Barnes shot her a glance, then turned his attention back to the winding lane through the village. 'What does his personnel file say, anyway? Did they send it through?'

'Laura managed to get a copy from Cassandra Mallory.' Kay peered at her phone screen. 'Roland Hammerton is fifty-two years old, divorced with two girls, both of whom are at university. He started working for the Mallorys four years ago after being made redundant from his previous job as a sheet metal worker at a place outside Orpington. He and his current girlfriend rent the house we're going to.'

'Any trouble?'

'Not at work, and Laura can't find him in our system.' Kay dropped the phone back into her bag and settled into her seat as Barnes adopted a more sedate approach to his driving while he listened. 'He hasn't taken any annual leave since Easter when he drove up to Manchester to see one of his daughters, but he's got a week booked off at the beginning of December, and told Cassandra he and his girlfriend are going to the Canary Islands.'

'What does his girlfriend do?'

'No idea. When Laura asked, Cassandra said she

thought Roland had only been seeing her for about four or five months.'

'And they've moved in together?'

Kay shrugged, then opened the maps app on her phone. 'Renting isn't cheap around here, and if they're getting on all right…'

'Might as well move in and save money.' Barnes shrugged. 'Makes sense.'

'Take the next left in about two hundred metres,' said Kay, tensing while he braked, 'their place is up here on the right-hand side.'

Barnes slowed to a crawl before he reached the row of four brick terraced farm cottages.

They were plain buildings with no front gardens and a simple dirt lay-by in front of them. There were four cars parked facing the houses, two ancient hatchbacks at the far end that looked as if they would fall apart at any minute, a dark green four-wheel drive outside the third terraced cottage, and a dirty white pick-up parked in front of the nearest house.

The slate-tiled roof had been battered over the years, and Kay saw blue plastic tarpaulin in places where some tiles had blown away in storms or had fallen out due to negligence. Paint peeled from the windowsills of the property too, in contrast to the neighbouring houses that had flowering baskets hanging from the shallow porches over their front doors, and appeared to be in much better condition. There was a wilted shrub in a chipped and stained terracotta pot beside the front door, and when Kay walked up the path towards it, she felt the concrete pavers rocking beneath her shoes.

Barnes rang the bell and then snatched his hand away as an electrical buzzing sounded from the wires protruding underneath it. 'Bloody hell.'

Taking a step back to look at the upper floor windows, Kay ran her gaze over the house. 'The place is falling apart. You'd think their landlord would do something about it, wouldn't you?'

'You're kidding. This place is a palace compared to some of the ones around here.' Barnes jerked his chin towards the neighbouring homes. 'Present company excepted.'

'Keep an eye out in case you see any of the neighbours,' said Kay. 'I might want to talk to them after this.'

He nodded, but said nothing as the rattle of a chain resonated through the wooden door, and then it opened to reveal a woman in her early forties, her lined mouth alluding to a decades-old smoking habit that had done nothing for her skin.

Kay held up her warrant card. 'Detective Inspector Kay Hunter, and my colleague, Detective Sergeant Ian Barnes. Is Roland Hammerton here?'

The woman's eyes narrowed. 'What do you want?'

'A word.' Kay craned her neck to see over the woman's head and along the hallway behind her. 'Is he in?'

'No.' The woman started to shut the door, but Kay stuck her foot in the way. 'Oi.'

'Where is he?'

'I dunno.'

'What's your name?'

'Not telling.'

'Look, we can do this here, or down the station,' said Kay, losing patience. 'I'm in the middle of a homicide investigation, and I'm in no mood for your attitude. It's up to you.'

The woman pouted, then let go of the door and crossed her arms over her skinny chest. 'He went down the shop for some ciggies.'

'Why didn't you go?'

'The bitch who runs it doesn't like me.'

'Why not?'

'I might've said a few things to her the last time I was in there.' Her frown deepened. 'What's this about anyway?'

'Can we come in?' Kay nodded towards the neighbouring houses, and saw a curtain twitch back into place. 'Unless you want your neighbours to get a front-seat view.'

'Bastards.' The woman stood aside and almost dragged Kay over the threshold. 'Can't mind their own business. Close the door behind you.'

With that, she turned and led the way through to a dingy living room that faced the lane. There were yellowing net curtains at the window, and thick velvet ones that reeked of cigarette smoke pulled back to let in a modicum of light.

Kay felt her shoes sticking to the carpet as she walked towards an armchair, then thought better of sitting down when she spotted the amount of white dog hair clinging to the cushions. Instead, she turned her back to the window and waited while the woman sank onto a sagging sofa against the opposite wall. Barnes stood in front of a low-slung cabinet that had a large television balanced on top of it, the screen covered in dust.

'Right,' Kay said. 'What's your name?'

'Jenna Corey.'

'And your relationship to Roland is…?'

'Complicated.' Jenna rolled her eyes, reached out for a crumpled packet of cigarettes and a red plastic lighter on the coffee table in front of her, then changed her mind and pushed them away with a scowl. 'He was a lot more fun before we moved in together.'

'Where did you meet him?'

'At that pub on the back road out of Smarden.'

'The one that's closed down?'

'Yeah.'

'How did you meet?'

Jenna shrugged. 'I was in there waiting for a friend one Friday night. My friend didn't show up, and Roland and I got talking. We hit it off straight away.'

'Has he mentioned any problems at work recently?'

'No. Why?'

'We heard he was off sick with a bad back at the moment.'

'Yeah, he hurt himself a few days ago.'

'Doing what?'

'I don't know.'

'Where were you?'

'What?'

'Where were you?' Kay repeated, watching the woman with interest while she squirmed in her seat.

'I… I went over to Tunbridge Wells in the afternoon to

meet a friend. We had a few drinks too many so I crashed on his sofa for the night.'

'He?'

Jenna's eyes narrowed. 'There's nothing going on between him and me. It was just drinks, all right?'

'And Roland didn't have a problem with that?'

'I didn't ask.' The woman lunged for the cigarettes, pulled one from the packet and lit it in one fluid motion. 'He wasn't here at the time.'

'Where was he?'

'Out.'

'Where?'

'I don't know.' Jenna took a long drag on the cigarette, then angled her chin and blew smoke at the ceiling where it joined a myriad of yellowing stains. 'He went out Saturday morning, while I was still asleep.'

'We'll need the name and address of your friend in Tunbridge Wells.'

'Why?'

'Because, as I've already told you, I'm in the middle of a murder investigation, Ms Corey, and at the moment everybody I speak to is a suspect until I'm satisfied they aren't involved.' Kay glared at her, watching the cigarette end burn to ash as Jenna's mouth fell open in a surprised "o" of shock.

'Murder?' she spluttered. 'I don't know anything about no murder.'

'Your friend's name and address?' Barnes prompted, his pen poised.

Jenna told him, then turned her attention back to Kay. 'Roland wouldn't hurt anyone.'

'But he's lying about having a bad back, isn't he?'

'It was really bad yesterday. He took some painkillers.'

Kay tried again. 'How did he hurt himself?'

'I told you, I don't know. He was in agony by the time I got back on Sunday afternoon though, I can tell you.'

Kay watched the woman, letting her squirm uncontrollably under her gaze for a few moments, then looked out the window at the sound of a car pulling up outside.

A large man in his early fifties with thinning light brown hair got out, his large stomach protruding over the waistline of his jeans. Despite his size, he moved with ease as he pulled two laden plastic shopping bags from the back seat and locked the vehicle.

Then he turned and stared at the unfamiliar silver hatchback parked further along the lay-by, his brow creasing.

'He looks okay to me,' said Kay, then took a step forward as Jenna launched herself from the sofa and tried to run towards the living room door. 'Sit down, and be quiet. Barnes?'

'Leave him to me.'

EIGHT

The detective sergeant hurried to the front door before Jenna could call out a warning, leaving Kay to glare at the woman while she listened to the door opening and Barnes ordering the man inside.

Risking a glance through the window, she watched as Roland Hammerton seemed to debate the sense in returning to the car or not, before his shoulders slumped and he trudged towards the house with the two bags.

'Don't go anywhere,' she ordered Jenna, then left the room, pulled the door closed and followed Barnes and Roland along the short hallway.

There was a strong stench of body odour emanating from Hammerton, and she saw sweat patches spreading under the arms of his pale blue T-shirt that she reckoned had nothing to do with the warm temperature outside. His breathing was heavy, and a wheezing cough had spluttered into existence by the time he reached the door at the end.

He opened it and stood to one side to let Barnes through first, but her sergeant had more sense — and experience – and waved the other man ahead of him, then turned and beckoned to her.

'It's the kitchen, guv. All clear.'

'Thanks.' She left him on the threshold and entered the room to see Roland standing with his back to the sink, his fingers busy while he broke open a cigarette packet's plastic wrapping with shaking fingers. The carrier bags were on a small chipped Formica-covered table, another packet of cigarettes and a loaf of bread tumbling out onto the surface. Two chairs were tucked under the table, with two more stacked in the corner of the kitchen beside an upright vacuum cleaner, out of the way.

Kay pulled out one of the chairs from the table and pointed to it. 'Sit down please, Mr Hammerton. You can have one of those when we've finished.'

He grunted, then winced and put a hand to his back before shuffling across to the seat and easing into it. He slid the cigarette packet and discarded plastic wrapper towards the shopping bags, then knitted his eyebrows as Kay took the seat opposite him and smiled.

She said nothing.

After a few moments of awkward silence, Roland cleared his throat with a phlegmy cough, then swallowed. 'I was going to get a sick note from me doctor today, but they haven't got any spare appointments.'

'I'm sure that's because there are people in more pain than you, Mr Hammerton, who are in more need of a doctor,' she said. 'How did you hurt yourself?'

'At work, on Friday afternoon.'

'And where is work?'

'If you're here, you know. Mallory's farm.'

'How did you hurt yourself?'

'I twisted wrong when I was moving some sacks of fertiliser.'

'And if I check the farm's accident book, I'll find a note of this incident, will I?'

'Yes, I made sure Mrs Mallory wrote it in the accident book for me but it didn't hurt so much then. It wasn't until I got home that I realised how bad it was.' Roland went to lean his elbows on his knees, then thought better of it and affected another wince. 'It's really bad.'

'And yet you can drive.'

'I have to, to get painkillers.'

'And cigarettes.' Kay watched while he eased back into his seat and avoided her gaze. 'Why didn't you ask Jenna to get them for you?'

'Jenna can't drive at the moment. She lost her licence last month.' Roland's lower lip stuck out. 'Stupid bitch.'

'How did you hurt yourself?'

'A sack of fertiliser shifted its weight on a telehandler while I was checking the straps. It knocked me to the ground, and I landed badly.'

'What time did you leave Mallory's farm on Friday?'

'Half past three, same as usual. It took until then to do the paperwork and tell her what happened.'

'Where did you go after that?'

'Why?' He narrowed his eyes.

'Just answer the question, please.'

'I came here.'

'Did you stop anywhere on the way?'

'No.'

'Not even to buy cigarettes?'

He squirmed. 'Okay, I did buy cigarettes.'

'From where?'

'Um, that convenience shop in the village down the road here.'

Kay frowned. 'That's out of your way, coming from the Mallorys' place.'

'I didn't want to go to the big supermarket in Staplehurst. Too busy at that time of day, innit?'

'Where did you go after the convenience shop?'

'Nowhere. I came here.'

'Can anyone corroborate that?'

Roland nudged his chin towards the door. 'She will.'

'Ian?' Kay looked over her shoulder. 'Would you mind asking Ms Corey to confirm that please?'

'Guv.'

She turned back to the man. 'Where did you go on Saturday morning?'

'What do you mean?'

'Ms Corey states that when she woke up on Saturday morning, you weren't here. Where were you?'

Roland's jaw tightened, and his gaze moved past Kay at the sound of footsteps.

'Guv, Jenna says he got back here at about four thirty on Friday afternoon,' said Barnes.

'Thank you,' she said, watching Roland. 'So, where were you on Saturday morning?'

'I tried to get to see a doctor...'

'Which surgery?'

He told her, and then rested his hands on the small of his back and stretched, closing his eyes and groaning.

'Mr Hammerton, if you're in pain, why didn't you

phone the surgery on Saturday morning instead of driving there?'

Opening his eyes, he dropped his hands to his lap and shrugged. 'I thought maybe if they could see me, see how much pain I was in, they'd let me have an appointment.'

'And did they?'

'No,' he said sulkily. 'They told me to take some painkillers and that if it wasn't better by today, to phone up.'

'And have you? Phoned them, that is.'

'I was going to do it when I got back.' He glared at her. 'But now I'm talking to you, and I'll probably miss their opening hours for phone calls.'

'Have you arranged to see a chiropractor or osteopath?'

'Can't afford one,' he said. 'Which is why I want a doctor's appointment so they can send me to one of theirs. Free, like.'

'Okay, Roland. So you say you injured yourself at work on Friday. Have you been back to the farm since?'

'Eh? No, why would I?'

'Have you?'

'No. I won't go there until my back's better. No point. I can't work like this, can I?' Roland rubbed his temple. 'I've been getting flashbacks, too. Nightmares.'

'What will you do for money?'

'I'll have to sign on the dole or something if the Mallorys don't give me anything I suppose. Until I'm better, anyway.'

'How long were you at the doctor's?'

'What?'

'You said you went to the doctor's surgery on Saturday morning. How long were you there for?'

'I dunno, a while.'

'Five hours?'

He shrugged again by way of response.

'Because Jenna says you weren't here when she woke up, and she left the house at two o'clock,' Kay explained. 'I don't imagine the doctor's surgery is open much past twelve on a Saturday, either. Where did you go?'

'I waited there for ages,' Roland said, his voice insistent.

'Where did you go when you left there?'

'I figured I might as well go and buy some more painkillers, to keep me going, like. Then I came back here. Jenna was out by then, so I fell asleep on the sofa watching the telly.'

Kay arched an eyebrow. 'I'd be careful if I were you, Mr Hammerton. The way you're taking painkillers, you could end up with a very nasty stomach problem.'

NINE

Laura drove the pale blue hatchback between the two brick pillars at the entrance to the Mallorys' hop farm, the dashboard vents roaring and the windows down.

Ruing the fact that she had drawn the short straw and been allocated a pool car with no working air conditioning for the week, she raised a hand in greeting to the young uniformed constable who stood at the open gate to ward off unwanted guests, then followed his directions to park over on the left-hand side of the farmyard.

She found a space beside one of the forensic team's vans, switched off the engine, and pulled her bag from the passenger footwell before rummaging in it until she found a small spray bottle of eau de parfum. She dabbed a little on her wrists and collarbone, checked she didn't need to apply more deodorant, then climbed out.

There was no breeze here, no relief from the stifling warmth that reflected off the concrete hardstanding or the stone wall that surrounded the yard. The weeds that poked up from the cracks were wilting, and she spotted a pair of sparrows a few metres along the wall, their beaks open to offset the heat while they searched for ants and beetles.

Laura didn't recognise the constable, and wandered over to introduce herself. That done, she cast her gaze around the farmyard. 'Where would I find Gloria Barkham?'

'Over there, in that converted stable block,' he said. 'Nearest office to us.'

'Thanks.'

Pushing her sunglasses onto her head, Laura approached the door marked with a sign for the visitor centre. It was closed, and somewhere nearby a motor whirred. To her relief, when she knocked and then opened the door, a cool blast of air enveloped her.

She stepped over the threshold and entered a large space that had a bar in the far corner with four pumps, and four tables and chair sets in front of it. Closing the door behind her, she eyed the marketing paraphernalia that covered the left-hand wall, its photos depicting the history of hop-picking in Kent, and then the establishment of Mallory's farm.

To her right was an oak table that served as a desk, its surface obscured by paperwork, marketing brochures and beige manila folders. The air conditioning unit was fixed to the wall behind it, its speed set to a low purr.

A woman peered over a computer screen at her with a harried expression. 'We're not open today, I'm sorry.'

'I know.' Laura extracted her warrant card and held it out. 'Detective Constable Laura Hanway, Kent Police. Are you Gloria Barkham?'

'Yes,' said the woman. 'I've already spoken to

someone and given a statement. What else do you need? I'm really busy.'

'May I sit?'

Gloria gestured to one of the chairs near the bar with a resigned sigh. 'Help yourself to one of those.'

Once she had dragged a chair over to the desk and organised herself with her notebook and pen, Laura cast her gaze over the documents and folders. 'How many tours were booked for today?'

'Three. Two, plus a private corporate event later today.' Gloria reached out and angled her screen such that she could better see Laura and sat back in her chair, eyeing the paperwork. 'They'll all be refunded of course, and according to your colleagues we need to cancel the rest of the tours this week. As for next week…'

With that, the woman sniffed, and then reached into a desk drawer and plucked a paper tissue from a crinkled packet, dabbing at her eyes before leaning back in her seat. 'This is awful, just awful.'

'How long have you worked here?' said Laura.

'Six years. I started out helping Justin's father with the day-to-day admin for the farm. I was only part-time to start with, while my kids were at school, and once they were doing their A-levels I went full-time. Justin asked me to stay on when he took over the business.'

'And how long have you been organising the tours?'

'Since the start.' Gloria straightened a little, pride in her voice. 'It was my idea, actually.'

'Oh?'

'Well, there was a bit of a lull the year before Justin took over, and – don't tell anyone I said this – but I think

Joseph, his father, was getting tired of all the work involved. He just couldn't bear to give it up though. This farm has been in the family since the late eighteen hundreds, and that got me thinking that maybe we could share that family history with craft beer enthusiasts and other tourists to the area.'

'What did Joseph think when you first mentioned it to him?'

'He wasn't too keen at first,' Gloria admitted. 'His primary concern was what that would do to his insurance – you can just imagine what that costs every year. But I spoke to some local tourism industry experts and put together a business plan to show him. Once he saw how that income could benefit other areas of the farm, he agreed to trial it over that summer. We haven't looked back since.'

Laura heard the pride in the woman's voice and smiled. 'They're obviously very lucky to have you here. Any problems with the tours lately?'

'What do you mean?'

'Well, you're serving alcohol on the premises.' Laura jerked her thumb over her shoulder towards the bar area. 'Do you ever get any issues with drunken behaviour, or anything like that?'

Gloria's nose wrinkled. 'Sometimes, but it's rare. If it does happen, it's usually because they've been to one or two of the neighbouring hop farms or vineyards before coming here. Justin and Trevor are pretty good at handling that sort of thing though, and in a way that the clients don't feel put out.'

'Any other issues you can think of?'

'No, not that I'm aware.' Gloria leaned forward and wiggled her computer mouse to wake up her screen. 'And I have no idea why there's a dead man in our hop garden.'

Laura tucked her notebook and pen into her bag. 'Thanks for your time. Before I go, I'd like a list of all the names of people who visited the farm for the past four months please. Tour groups, corporate events, private tastings, anything like that.'

The woman's eyebrows shot upwards. 'But that's private information.'

'It is, until it's requested for a formal police investigation,' Laura replied. She unzipped a compartment in her bag and pulled out a new USB stick. 'Here you go. It'll save you emailing everything.'

Gloria sighed, but took the USB from her and plugged it into her computer. 'I suppose so. You'll have to wait while I export everything from our booking system.'

'No problem.'

Laura dragged the chair back to the bar area, then walked over to the photo montage that stretched along the wall. She ran her gaze over the most recent images that showed the modernisation of hop drying methods, and spent a few moments admiring the professionalism of the photographer who had captured touching images of Justin and Cassandra Mallory walking and laughing between the hop bines while the caption stated they were inspecting last year's crop.

Tracing the year backwards, she paused when she reached the point at which the farm had transferred to Justin from his father. A posed photograph credited to a national business magazine showed the two men in the hop garden standing side by side, the elder Mallory resting his hand on his son's shoulder and smiling.

Justin had his arms folded across his chest and his feet hip-wide, giving the impression he was ready to make his mark on the business in his own right, and seemed to be ignoring his father's attempts at displaying a tight-knit generation of farmers.

'Here you go.'

Laura turned at the sound of Gloria's voice to see the woman holding out the USB stick, and hurried over. 'Thanks.'

'I really must get on, sorry.' The woman gestured to the manila folders. 'I've still got to phone all of these clients and explain the tours have to be rescheduled. I don't suppose you know when we might be able to open again?'

'I don't, sorry.' Laura said, dropping the USB into her bag. 'You'll have to speak to DI Hunter about that, or Mr Mallory will.'

Gloria bit her lip. 'Okay.'

'Thanks for your help.' Laura walked to the door, then paused and looked back. 'One more question. What was it like here, when Justin first took over the farm? Was Joseph okay with it?'

'Oh, I think Joseph struggled at first,' said Gloria. 'I think it hurt his pride more than anything, having to give up the place. I mean, he's still nearby – he lives in one of the farm cottages on the far side of the fields and drops by occasionally, but I think there was part of him that hoped Justin wouldn't do so well.'

Laura frowned. 'Why?'

'Because he wanted to sell the place four years ago,' said Gloria. 'He reckoned at the time it was worth millions, but Justin persuaded him to hang on to it because of the family history. I think he's been resentful about that ever since.'

Laura glanced over her shoulder at the photograph of the two men. 'He looks happy enough about it there.'

'That photograph was taken the year before Justin took over,' Gloria explained. 'They hardly talk to each other these days.'

TEN

The next morning was overcast and at least eight degrees cooler.

The sound of sirens pierced the air, mingling with the roar of traffic from both the dual carriageway to the south of Darent Valley Hospital and Watling Street to the north, where a steady stream of traffic was heading towards the enormous shopping centre. A helicopter flew overhead for the third time, its bright liveried paintwork identifying it as belonging to a twenty-four-hour news channel while it circled the Dartford Bridge.

Grey clouds smudged the sky as Kay leaned against the pool car and looked up at the glass frontage of the hospital, wondering if she would leave the place with the answers she sought, or whether the post mortem was about to add more questions to those already going around in her head.

She ignored the delivery vans and visitors' cars that choked the service road next to the parking bays, and instead turned her attention to her phone before scrolling through the latest emails that had arrived. With a sigh, she noted that her attempts at finding more officers to help with the enormity of the investigation ahead had been passed up the chain of command for "consideration". A shiver crossed her shoulders as she wondered what crimes had been committed that warranted more manpower than hers, and then looked up at a short, sharp whistle.

Barnes was walking towards her, a paper ticket in his hand and a grin on his face. 'It's your lucky day, guv.'

'Is it?'

'The attendant over there just gave us a free pass. Apparently they're having some remedial works done to the other car park, which is why we couldn't get in there. I showed him my warrant card, and he told me not to worry.' His grin turned to a scowl. 'Just as well, given what they usually charge.'

Kay looked up at the sign above the car that identified it as a delivery bay. 'But…'

'Don't worry – they're sending all the deliveries around to the other entrance. We're not inconveniencing anybody else.' Barnes slapped the parking pass on the car dashboard, then locked the doors. 'How are we doing for time?'

'We're ten minutes early.' She followed her colleague across the service road to the hospital's front doors, the familiar smell of disinfectant and floor cleaning fluid greeting them as they entered the main reception area.

Sidestepping a pair of paramedics carrying response bags and an elderly man steering a woman of similar age in a wheelchair, Kay crossed the space to a doorway and up a flight of stairs to the next floor. A fire door led into a long, tiled corridor with plain walls and signs hanging from the ceiling for the X-ray, MRI and ultrasound departments, but Kay ignored these and kept walking until she reached a door at the end, pushing it open to reveal a small reception desk and a door leading off to the right of that.

A man rose from a chair behind the desk and pushed a visitor sign-in sheet towards them. 'Morning, detectives. On time, too – he'll appreciate that.'

'Morning, Simon,' said Kay, scrawling her signature on the page before handing the pen to Barnes. 'Got a busy morning ahead?'

'Five today, three from the hospital, yours, and a suspected drugs overdose from another hospital,' said the pathologist's assistant. 'Yours first, given the circumstances.'

Simon Winter's calm demeanour belied a sharp mind and a penchant for procedure that complemented the skills of the Home Office pathologist and had led to several breakthroughs for Kay and her team. As she watched him complete the last of the paperwork required to enable the post mortem to go ahead, some of the tension eased from her shoulders.

'Do you want us to suit up while you're finishing that and we'll see you in there?' she said. 'After all, we're housetrained.'

Simon gave a brief smile, then stabbed his pen over his right shoulder to a second door. 'You know where to find them. He'll be starting on time, mind.'

'We won't hang about, don't worry,' said Barnes, and

stood aside to let Kay through the door before him. 'Meet you out there, guv.'

'Okay.'

She pushed open the door into the ladies' changing room and automatically reached out for one of the bagged protective suits from a pile on a bench she passed before placing her bag and jacket into one of the lockers. The bulky suit went over her suit trousers and blouse, and then she pulled the matching protective bootees over her shoes and shuffled out the door, tying her hair back while holding the string of the face mask between her teeth.

Barnes was already out in the reception area, twirling his mask around his forefinger, his hair obscured by the hood of his protective suit. He turned at the sound of her approach and raised an eyebrow. 'Ready?'

'Let's find some answers, Ian,' she said, tucking her hair under her hood and wiggling her mask into place. 'Because the longer it takes, the more time whoever did this has got to cover their tracks.'

'Nothing from Harriet's team yet?'

'Not yet. Hopefully by the time we get back to the station…'

They fell silent as Barnes pushed open the steel door to the examination room and a blast of cool air washed over them.

Simon was now standing at the far end next to a workspace filled with empty glass vials and other collecting vessels, his head bowed while he worked at a laptop that would capture the pathologist's commentary and track where various samples would be sent for further testing to different specialist laboratories.

The smell of disinfectant was stronger in here, and Kay wrinkled her nose as she and Barnes crossed to where Lucas Anderson was standing beside one of two examination tables, adjusting a microphone that was fixed to a cable above.

'Nearly there,' he said, then turned his attention to Simon. 'Is that volume okay?'

'Loud and clear,' came the reply. 'Ready when you are.'

'Thank you. Right, you two – you know the drill. Listen, observe and learn.'

'Is that what you're telling all the new recruits these days?' said Barnes.

'We *are* recording this,' said Simon.

'Right you are.' Lucas turned his attention back to the table, his demeanour returning to one of professional empathy as he waved his hand over the victim who had been laid out and washed. 'So let us turn our attention to this poor soul, and try to work out why on earth someone would want to do this to him.'

Kay circled the table, taking in the man's bruised face, the cuts and scratches to his arms and hands, and then the terrible jagged wound that had ripped apart his torso.

She swallowed. 'Where are his…?'

'Intestines?' said Lucas. 'Already over at the lab undergoing some tests. With any luck we'll have those results through in the morning. Simon put in an urgent request for them. Stand over there, both of you, and I'll make a start.'

Kay walked back to where Barnes had moved to a space beside a wheeled trolley laden with scalpels and knives, an involuntary shiver crossing her shoulders as the post mortem continued.

Lucas ran his gloved hands over the victim's arms, turning them to expose a criss-cross pattern of cuts that had been made to the skin. 'For the record, none of the cuts are deep and appear to have been inflicted as a means of torture.'

Kay winced, following Lucas's movements as he inspected the man's legs and feet next, the pathologist shaking his head as he circled the table and returned to the man's chest, his gaze resting on the gaping hole before he began removing the vital organs.

'His lungs are in good condition,' Lucas commented a while later, 'and his heart is healthy. Looking at his general physique, I'd say he worked out quite regularly, even though there's some remnant fatty tissue around his liver that would suggest he enjoyed his food on the rich side. A few more years, and that might've started causing him some issues.'

'What about his age?' said Kay.

'I'd suggest mid- to late twenties, no more than thirty.' Lucas moved to the man's shoulders, then frowned and bent over to take a closer look before beckoning to Simon. 'Could you come over here and take some photographs for me before I continue?'

'Something wrong?' Barnes asked.

'I'm not sure.' Lucas flashed them a brief smile. 'Always better to document as we go, just in case.'

The pathologist moved aside while indicating to Simon the areas he wanted photographed, then continued to examine the man's jaw and teeth.

Both detectives studied their feet while Lucas wielded a mechanical saw, and despite the number of times she had witnessed this process, Kay's stomach turned at the stench that arose from the victim's remains.

Digging her nails into the soft skin of her palms, she focused on the investigation instead, listening to Lucas as he listed the victim's injuries, and vowed to find his killers.

There was a final whirring sound from the direction of the examination table, and then Lucas set the saw aside and began passing samples to Simon for cataloguing and sending to the laboratory. Once that was done, he moved over to a stainless-steel sink and began disinfecting his hands and arms before glancing over his shoulder at the man's remains, and then at Kay. 'Shall we meet in my office in, say, fifteen minutes?'

'Okay.' She frowned, seeing a troubled expression in his eyes. 'Is there a problem?'

'No, no problem,' he said. 'I won't keep you too long.'

Dismissed, Barnes led the way out of the examination room then turned to her next to the door to the men's changing rooms. 'What was that all about?'

'I don't know. It's not like Lucas to be cagey about his findings, even in front of Simon.'

'Guess we'll have to wait and find out then.'

ELEVEN

Kay changed out of her protective coveralls and threw those and her mask and bootees into a biohazard bin before retrieving her bag and jacket from the locker, then hurried through the door to find Barnes pacing the corridor outside the mortuary entrance.

A junior nurse hurried past with a clipboard in her hand, disappearing into a room signposted for the X-ray department, and a porter wheeled a large metal cage filled with clean bedsheets and blankets further along the corridor, but there was nobody else in sight as the two detectives made their way towards Lucas's office.

The pathologist had been allocated a box-like space at the other end of the east wing as a temporary measure that was starting to look permanent given the number of files and books now lining the shelving units on each side of his desk, and when Kay pulled a spare seat from the far corner of the room, she noticed a fine layer of dust coating the computer screen.

Setting the chair beside Barnes, she pulled out her

phone and scrolled through her emails while her colleague checked his voicemail. She cast a sideways glance his way as he gave a surprised grunt at one of the messages, then an email from Detective Chief Inspector Devon Sharp caught her attention, and she bit back her frustration at the news that her old mentor was unable to source more manpower for the investigation, despite her pleas.

She dropped her phone back into her bag as Barnes finished writing in his notebook.

'Did you know Harry Davis was retiring?' he said.

'Is he?' She straightened with a start. 'I hadn't heard that.'

'It's only just been made official. Apparently he's leaving at the end of the month.'

'But that's only two weeks away.'

Barnes shrugged. 'He had some long service leave due to him, so he and the missus are going to use it so he can retire early on full pay before they go and spend a month in Australia visiting family.'

'But we haven't got anyone to replace him.' Kay heard the panic in her voice. 'Sharp's just emailed me to tell me he's still having problems finding us some more bums on seats.'

'I don't suppose it's any consolation to know we're both invited to Harry's retirement party then?'

'Detectives, sorry to keep you.'

Kay turned at the sound of Lucas's voice, her mind still racing at the news she was going to lose a key member of her team, a senior sergeant with a wealth of experience, with no plans for someone of the same calibre to help once he had gone. She blinked, reached down for her notebook and pen, and tried to refocus her attention on the current investigation as the pathologist squeezed between a bookshelf and his desk and sank into his seat with a sigh.

Lucas wiggled his computer mouse to wake up the screen, keyed in his password with a flourish, and then turned the screen to face them both while he clicked through a sequence of folders in the hospital's directory system. 'I didn't want to say anything downstairs while we were still on the record, hence the suggestion we meet here.'

'What's going on?' said Kay. 'It's not like you to be cagey.'

'I'll explain in a minute. It doesn't look like Simon's finished uploading the photos yet.' Lucas leaned back in his chair and folded his hands on the desk. 'While we're waiting for those though, I can tell you that I'm of the opinion that your victim died sometime between eleven o'clock and four o'clock on Sunday night. I don't think it would've been any later than that because it gets light at around six thirty to seven, and whoever did this managed to get him to the hop garden and kill him without being seen or heard.'

'Even so, that took some doing,' Kay mused. 'Because he would've put up a fight. Unless he was drugged?'

'Hard to tell, I'm afraid. The initial toxicology tests we ran here were inconclusive. Simon's sending some samples off to the lab for further testing, but…'

'Chances are, those will come back inconclusive as well,' said Barnes.

'Indeed.' Lucas refreshed the directory listing and then clicked on the first images that appeared. 'You see these scratches and cuts to his arms? His fingernails are torn too, look. That does lead me to believe that he was conscious when they got him to the hop field.'

Kay felt a chill across her shoulders that had nothing to do with the air conditioning vent above the door. 'So you think he was fully aware of what they were going to do to him?'

Lucas nodded. 'I'll wait for the lab results to come in before finalising my report of course, but I've seen it before with signs of a struggle. Remember that case from a year or so ago, the young woman?'

'All too well.' Kay looked at the photograph again. 'But that's not what you wanted to talk to us about, is it?'

By way of response, the pathologist started scrolling through the other images that Simon had uploaded, until he paused halfway down the directory, his mouse arrow hovering above the next photograph. 'I may be wrong, but one of my colleagues wrote a paper some time ago about a particularly nasty case he worked on in the West Country. I don't believe your investigation is related to that – all the perpetrators are serving long sentences with little hope of parole – but there are similarities between that case and some of the markings made post-mortem that I'm seeing on your victim.'

Kay saw Barnes lean closer to the computer screen and inched forward in her chair, the fine hairs on the back of her neck prickling with tension. 'What markings?'

Lucas opened the image and increased the magnification before using the mouse cursor to indicate his findings. 'See here? Initially I thought he was tortured, but upon reflection and given the evidence from my examination, I'm more inclined to believe these were made post mortem. But this pattern of cuts on the back of his neck isn't random. And then…' He paused while he selected another image from the directory. 'Ah, this one. The same marking appears on our victim's chest, in the skin above his heart – I didn't spot it yesterday at the crime scene because it was obscured by all the blood from the knife wounds to his chest and abdomen, but once Simon got him cleaned up, it stood out straight away. And here's another, near his groin… And a final one, on the sole of his left foot. I believe these were all made after he was disembowelled.'

Kay frowned, her mind spiralling.

'What the hell?' Barnes muttered.

'Closer than you think,' said Lucas, closing the last image. 'The phrase used to describe the West Country murders was that the killer was "deranged". My colleague was reprimanded for it of course – it wasn't his place to comment on the killer's state of mind in his paper – but it's stayed with me.'

'You said the killer in that investigation was under lock and key,' said Kay.

'I did, however the markings are quite well known in certain circles,' said Lucas, 'but until you find some more evidence to support this notion, I don't feel I'm able to conclusively summarise that in my report.'

'What notion?' said Barnes.

Lucas looked at each of them, and then exhaled. 'That this poor man might have been slaughtered as part of a ritualistic killing.'

TWELVE

Gavin pushed through the glass reception door of the police station and squinted in the bright sunlight that reflected off the buildings opposite while he waited for a gap in the traffic that streamed along Palace Avenue.

A fresh breeze tugged at his shirt sleeves, bringing with it a pungent odour from the River Len that flowed through a wide channel on the other side of the road before joining the larger Medway a few hundred metres to his left. The smell mingled with the fatty stench from a café serving fast food further along the street and diesel fumes from an articulated truck that rumbled past.

He spotted a gap between a small white hatchback and a moped and jogged across, his jacket gripped firmly in one hand while he held down his tie with the other before following the pavement around to Mill Street and towards the town centre.

The recruitment agency that provided the temporary workers for Justin Mallory's farm and other local agricultural businesses was located in a third-floor office above an artisan bakery halfway up the slight incline. The doorway for the agency was to the left of the bakery's window and after Gavin rang the bell on a grubby keypad with electrical wires protruding from the bottom of it, he stood back to admire the display of fresh bread, cakes and pastries. His stomach rumbled when the door to the shop swung open and a young office worker emerged with greasy bags, steam rising from them as she hurried past.

He turned his attention back to the shared door for the agency at a buzzing sound from the keypad, and then heard a metallic *click* as the lock disengaged. Glancing at the faded signs below that of the recruitment agency for a charity on the second floor and a marketing company on the first, he pushed the door open and frowned when it dragged across a coir mat.

Pushing it closed, he turned to see a pile of junk mail and free newspapers cluttering the threadbare carpet that had been laid in the ground floor hallway, and looked up to see dusty cobwebs clinging to the corners of the ceiling.

After shrugging his jacket over his shoulders, Gavin climbed the stairs, taking one look at the dirt-streaked bannister before he snatched his hand away and decided to chance the uneven treads instead. The first-floor landing had two doors on it, one for the marketing agency that remained resolutely closed with a second security panel fixed to it, and one marked "WC". He shivered at the thought of what cleaning horrors might exist beyond that door, and continued up to the second floor, passing the door to the charity and the sound of phones ringing and harried voices to the third floor.

A woman was waiting for him on the landing, peering

over the bannister as he approached. 'Found us all right, then?'

'Yes, thanks.' He held up his warrant card. 'DC Gavin Piper, I think we spoke on the phone?'

'Eleanor Wickham,' she said, and waved her hand towards an open door. 'Come on through. Would you like a coffee or anything?'

'No, I'm fine thanks.' Gavin followed her though to a surprisingly airy reception area that was sparkling compared with the rest of the offices off the stairwell.

The walls had been painted a pale yellow and offset with fake ferns that were displayed in pots of varying sizes, and tasteful artwork had been hung on three of the walls. The reception desk was a white Formica-like surface that gleamed in the light from the windows, and two frosted glass doors led off from the room, the chrome handles polished and free from grime.

Eleanor paused to gather a small collection of manila folders from the desk and a half-full glass of water, then angled her head towards one of the frosted glass doors. 'Would you mind leading the way? The one on the right – I use it for interviews. Much nicer than out here. It's got air conditioning, for a start.'

Gavin walked into a large room with three double-glazed windows that overlooked Mill Street and afforded a view over some of the jumbled rooftops of the shorter buildings opposite. An oval beech-coloured table with six matching chairs around it took up the centre of the room, while a low rectangular cabinet stretched' along the left side of the room looked as if it doubled as a stationery cupboard, given the reams of paper he could see on one of the shelves, and a TV stand for a large screen that took up most of its surface. A camera had been fixed to the top of the screen, and when he looked up, he spotted speakers in two corners of the ceiling.

'We do a lot of our meetings and interviews via video link wherever possible,' Eleanor explained, placing the folders on the table and gesturing for him to take a seat. 'Although my two kids tend to use it for games and films if I have to come in here at weekends.'

'I don't blame them.' Gavin unbuttoned his jacket, and watched while she adjusted the air conditioning as he removed his notebook and pen. 'Thanks for seeing me at short notice.'

'Not a problem, not in the circumstances.' Eleanor's face turned troubled. 'Do you have any idea who was killed yet?'

'It's an ongoing investigation,' he replied. 'However, I'm able to confirm none of your contractors were harmed.'

Her shoulders relaxed. 'That's good. I've known all of them for a while now. Speaking of which, I've taken the liberty of copying the personnel files for the contractors who are working for Justin Mallory. I take it you'll get the appropriate formal request to me? Obviously I can't go around handing out this sort of information, but I'm guessing as it's part of a police investigation...'

'You'd be right, and yes, one of my colleagues is sorting out the paperwork.' Gavin thought of the pile of requests he had seen Debbie West working her way through as he left the incident room ten minutes ago, and hoped his was near the top. He eyed the folders under Eleanor's arm. 'Any problems with your contractors?'

'None whatsoever,' she said without hesitation. 'I've known Alexandru and Daniel for a number of years, and the other two who work for Justin.'

'How do you recruit seasonal workers?'

'We advertise in groups and pages on social media, but most of the time – as with Alexandru – we're recommended by other workers. Alexandru's friend wanted to retire, so he encouraged Alexandru to message me at the start of that season,' said Eleanor. 'I spoke to him on the phone, and after he emailed over all his paperwork, I agreed to source some work for him. Given that his friend worked for the Mallorys, I suggested to them that they give Alexandru a trial run of two weeks, and he's been with them ever since.'

'I understand that Justin took over the farm from his father…'

'Two years ago, yes.'

'And did you liaise directly with Joseph Mallory, or…?'

'Always with Joseph. He was… more hands on than Justin.' Eleanor's mouth quirked. 'Less likely to delegate, that is.'

'Did you get on with him? Joseph, that is.'

'Have you met him?'

'No.'

'He's a bit of a rogue,' she explained. 'I always got the impression he would bend the rules, given half the chance – not that I'm saying he did, but I don't think he liked the admin side of farming. I was always having to chase him up for paperwork – and payments. If it wasn't for Gloria, Joseph would never have thought to open up the doors to tourists, for instance. Justin, on the other hand, is very much a modern farmer – he's got a good team around him, he's very forward-thinking and constantly seeking ways to improve the farm beyond its normal remit of growing crops.'

'Back to the seasonal workers you employ,' said Gavin. 'What about the others who you provide as contractors? What can you tell me about them?'

Eleanor tapped the top of the manila folders with a manicured nail. 'All in here. Daniel Ionescu and the others have been at the Mallorys for at least two seasons, which I think says a lot about their work ethic. Like Alexandru, they work here in the summer to subsidise the local workers we can find – a lot of people around here would rather work in retail than in fields for minimum wage, which is why agencies like mine are so important. I also source seasonal workers for local fruit farms, food distribution warehouses, the lot.'

'Any problems amongst any of your other contractors?'

'Only one lad who decided to steal from one of my longest-standing clients back in May. He's currently doing community service.' Eleanor sighed. 'And I've lost a valued client because of him. Apart from that, no, no problems. Most people who work for me are very dependable.'

'One final question,' said Gavin. 'The four workers who are at the Mallorys' farm – do they help out with any other harvests in the area?'

'Not for hops, no – that would be impossible timing-wise. It's just too busy. Once the crop's ripe, it needs to be picked, otherwise it'll be ruined.'

Gavin gathered up the files, pushing back his chair. 'Thanks for your time, Ms Wickham. I'll be in touch if I need anything else.'

He hurried down the stairs, pulling out his mobile phone from his pocket as he strode back towards the police station. 'Kyle? Do me a favour. Find out who Justin Mallory's nearest competitor is. I think we might just have a motive for our murder.'

THIRTEEN

Kyle drummed his fingers on the top of the steering wheel and counted to ten under his breath while the junior constable at the gate to the Mallorys' farm checked his ID against the clipboard in his hand.

It was almost noon, and the sun was baking the grass verges on either side of the farm entrance, and carving cracks through the packed soil that lined the edges of the asphalt. Even the birds had grown quiet in the hedgerow nearest to Kyle's open window, and there was only the sound of a lone bumblebee carried on a gentle breeze that did nothing to alleviate the stifling heat.

Nadine and Sean had been relieved of their duties late the previous day and were now back at the incident room, and Kyle didn't recognise the twenty-something who muttered under his breath while sweat beaded at his brow.

'I should be on the list,' said Kyle. 'Debbie West added me to it yesterday.'

'Oh.' The constable's eyes widened, and he paused to flip over the page. 'Got you. Sorry. Different list.'

'No problem.' Kyle took back his warrant card, then handed over a fresh bottle of water from a pack he had bought at a garage on the way from the police station. 'I used to be stuck on enough perimeters when I was in uniform.'

The constable's eyes lit up, and he cracked open the drink. 'Awesome. Thanks.'

Kyle nodded, wound up the window and turned up the air conditioning to high while he inched the car forward and found a space beside one of the forensic team's vans.

Taking a moment to let the cold air wash over him, he watched while one of Harriet's protégées appeared from the far end of the farmyard, her hands full of sealed evidence bags from the hop garden. There was still a strip of crime scene tape stretched across the gateway leading to that with a second uniformed constable on cordon duty beside it, and Kyle wondered how many more days the SOCOs would be scouring the field and those surrounding it in a desperate search for evidence.

So far, there had been no reports of a significant find, and when he climbed out of the car and nodded to the forensic technician as he made his way over to the main farmhouse, she gave him a wary look as if daring him to ask her how the search was progressing.

He found Cassandra Mallory in the kitchen.

She was sitting at a granite-topped breakfast bar, one hand wrapped around a ceramic mug and the other resting on the open page of a magazine. Her head was turned away from the door, so that she faced large French windows that had been opened out onto the garden beyond.

He cleared his throat, and she visibly jumped in her seat before turning to face him, her eyes wide.

'Mrs Mallory?' He held out his warrant card. 'DC Kyle Walker. Sorry to disturb you. Could I have a word?'

She nodded, then gestured to one of the other stools. 'Do you want a coffee?'

'No, but thank you.'

'A glass of water perhaps?'

'Really, I'm fine. Thanks.'

'More questions?'

'Sorry, yes. Do you have a moment?'

'I suppose so.' She let go of the mug and closed her eyes, pinching the bridge of her nose before dropping her hand to the worktop. 'What a fucking mess.'

'Where's your husband?'

'Over in the office, going through the figures. We were meant to be delivering hops to a new client on Friday – he's trying to work out if we've got enough, or…'

Kyle pulled out his notebook. 'I wanted to ask you about Roland Hammerton, one of your employees. My inspector, Kay Hunter, spoke to him yesterday as part of our initial enquiries and he mentioned he wasn't at work on Monday because he hurt himself here on Friday. Am I right in saying you're responsible for the welfare of your employees at the farm?'

'I am, and unfortunately that includes Roland, yes.' Cassandra shook her head, closed the magazine and pushed the coffee mug away before twisting in her seat to face him. 'What do you need to know?'

'What happened on Friday?'

'Didn't Roland tell DI Hunter?'

'I'd like to hear it in your own words.'

'Okay. Roland wandered in here at about two thirty on Friday afternoon saying he'd hurt his back while he was moving some sacks of fertiliser. He was holding his hand to his back like this,' she said, resting her palm against the base of her spine. 'And he was shuffling, like you do if your back hurts. I asked him if anything else hurt – obviously here on a farm, everything we do carries risk and I've heard some horror stories in my time – but he said no, just his back. I got him to sit on one of the chairs over there next to the dining table while I got him a glass of water, and then I went and got the accident book for him to fill out. You wouldn't believe the amount of paperwork we have to complete around here, especially when someone gets hurt.'

'What happened next?'

'He left. I offered to drive him home in his car and get a taxi back, but he reckoned he was just about okay enough to drive, and said he wanted to go to the doctor's surgery on the way.' Cassandra slid off the stool and wandered over to a large rectangular pine table in the corner. 'I haven't had a chance to put the book back in the office yet, so you can have a look if you like.'

'Thanks.' Kyle took the ledger from her, and flicked through the pages to the last entry, the paper flimsy to his touch. Cassandra's neat writing had completed the different boxes and her signature appeared at the end. Satisfied, he handed it back. 'Any problems with Roland prior to the accident?'

'What do you mean?'

Kyle said nothing, and raised an eyebrow in response.

Cassandra slid the book onto the worktop and sighed. 'He's… difficult, sometimes. He gets the work done, yes, and he's been with us a number of years, but he's got a heightened sense of entitlement. He didn't like it when Justin made Trevor our farm manager – in fact, he was very vocal about it, saying that he had more experience, and should've been promoted instead. Justin and I tried to explain to him that Trevor's background in the military made him a better candidate – he was in the logistics corps, and honestly he's been a godsend these past two years. Roland's been resentful ever since, I think.'

'Do you think that resentment would make him harm your reputation?'

'Like what?'

'Have you had any issues around the farm prior to his accident on Friday?'

'Not to my knowledge, no.'

'Has he ever injured himself before?'

'No, we've been very lucky actually. If you go through the accident book there, you'll see that most of our injuries are minor concussions or cuts and bruises, nothing more serious than that.'

'And has Roland had previous experience using the telehandler he said he was using when he hurt himself?'

'Oh yes, he's the main driver of that. Justin paid him a compliment the other week in fact, saying he handles the machinery better than anyone else around here.'

'Was anything said between you and Roland before he left here on Friday, anything at all that might give you cause for concern?'

'No, once the accident report was complete, I told him

he should make an appointment to see his GP as soon as possible, to make sure there was no damage, and I wished him a speedy recovery. After he left, I met with Trevor to see who was available over the weekend to cover Roland's shifts. Thankfully, Trevor's son is visiting him at the moment and he's got a bit of experience with that sort of machinery, and so we gave him the work.' Cassandra's eyes narrowed. 'Look, what's going on?'

'Just routine enquiries, that's all,' said Kyle. 'One final question – has Roland been back to the farm since you last saw him on Friday?'

'No, not to my knowledge.' She frowned. 'At least, I haven't seen his car here. If he got a lift or something, I wouldn't know. But why would he? He'd be resting, wouldn't he, trying to get better?'

'You'd think so,' said Kyle, and put his notebook away. 'Thanks for your time, Mrs Mallory. I'll see myself out.'

FOURTEEN

An afternoon haze clung to the rooftops of Maidstone town centre and a purpling cluster of clouds crowded the horizon. The air was heavy with the scent of ozone.

Kay glanced out the window before turning her attention back to the whiteboard at the front of the incident room. She spun a black marker pen between her fingers while her gaze roamed the notes capturing the team's early assessment of the investigation that had now gathered pace.

The sound of telephones ringing and voices talking over one another carried across to where she stood with her back to the desks, and she could hear footsteps pacing back and forth across the threadbare carpet tiles interspersed with the door opening and slamming shut as her officers processed all the leads that had been gathered so far.

She looked down and eyed the latest briefing agenda in her hand.

There were so many outstanding tasks, so many new

tasks generated from today's enquiries, and then there was Lucas's findings at the post mortem.

Kay turned to face the room and raised her voice. 'Has anybody heard from Harriet yet?'

'She phoned fifteen minutes ago, guv,' said Nadine. 'She's got some people still working through cataloguing evidence at the farm, but says they'll be finished with their initial assessment tonight. She said she's going to call you as soon as she's back in the office.'

'Thanks.' Kay checked her watch. By her estimation, that left her with twenty minutes. 'Right, everyone – briefing in five minutes please. Debs, I've made some amendments to this draft. Could you take those in and circulate it to everyone for me?'

There was a scramble for phones, notebooks and pens and then an organised stampede towards the whiteboard while her team assembled, with two or three elbowing each other out of the way to reach the printer before Debbie commandeered it to photocopy the revised agenda.

Gavin wandered across to Kay, an opened can of energy drink in his hand. 'Guv, rather than waste your time in the briefing, Sean Gastrell's just told me there's nothing untoward on the security footage around the farmyard. He had Andy over at headquarters take a look as well, but he didn't spot anything suspicious, either.'

'Okay, thanks Gav, I appreciate that.' She waited while a few last-minute stragglers joined the throng in front of the whiteboard, then lowered the agenda. 'Thanks, everyone. Before we begin, if you haven't heard already, one of our team has announced his retirement and will be leaving us at the end of next week. Harry, I'm going to be honest – I don't know what I would've done without you these past few years. You've been an integral part of my team and you've supported me through some really tough investigations. Thank you – you'll be missed.'

The uniformed sergeant held up his hand to ward off the applause that followed her words, his cheeks flushed.

'Thanks, guv,' he managed after the room quietened. 'It's been an honour working with you, and everyone else here. I'll miss it, that's for sure.'

Barnes turned in his seat to face him. 'You'll get bored within three months, Harry. I know you too well. What're you going to do with your time after your overseas trip?'

Harry shrugged. 'Same as some of the others who get pensioned out early by management every now and again. I'll set up a consultancy and help private security firms, that sort of thing I expect. Diane won't want me cluttering up the house all day.'

'And a hint to all of you – Harry's one of our most knowledgeable officers, so make the most of him while he's here.' Kay winked at him. 'Otherwise I'm sure those post-retirement consultancy fees of his will give DCI Sharp a minor coronary.'

A smattering of laughter filtered through the incident room, and then she flapped the agenda in her hand to straighten the page and turned her attention to the first item. 'Okay, let's move on. First of all, how are you getting on sourcing CCTV and doorbell security footage from neighbouring properties, Debbie?'

The constable took a step forward from where she'd been leaning against one of the tall metal cupboards at the side of the room. 'We've got recordings from two doorbell cameras that belong to the privately owned properties bordering the farm guv, and the manager at the petrol station has emailed a link to theirs for me – I've tasked a couple of junior constables to go through all of those. I'm waiting to hear back from the leasehold agent about any cameras at the abandoned pub. House-to-house enquiries started last night, and should be completed by Friday once we've had a chance to sweep up anybody who wasn't home when we first tried. We've entered keywords into the database so if we get any matches in information, that'll be flagged for us to follow up.'

'Thanks, Debs. Kyle, how did you get on with looking into Justin Mallory's background?'

'Nothing untoward there, guv,' said the newest addition to her team of detectives. 'He went to Brighton University and was awarded an undergraduate degree in business management, then returned to the farm and worked with his dad for a number of years. He and Cassandra met at a farmer's ball in Tunbridge Wells eight years ago – she comes from a farming family south of East Grinstead – and they've gone from strength to strength with the farm since Justin's dad retired two years ago. Cassandra manages a website blog about farming life, and that has an online shop for customers to order merchandise from, and they share videos online about the farming life as well. Two girls – we already know they're currently staying with their grandparents at the moment – and the financial accounts on the Companies House website look healthy as well. I'm currently working through a review of his employees while Gavin's looking at the agency contractors, and I should have an update about those for you in the morning.'

'Good work, thanks Kyle. What's the latest regarding Roland Hammerton?'

'I spoke to Cassandra this morning,' he said, and recounted his conversation. 'She seemed flummoxed about how he managed to hurt himself – apparently he's had lots of experience using the telehandler and he's performed the same task with it a number of times in the past. She showed me the accident log, but it's thin on information. Unless we formally identify him as a suspect, I won't be able to access his GP records or anything to find out if he's raised it with the surgery, either.'

'Okay, in that case – Ian, could you work with Kyle and delve into Roland's background a bit more for me. Friends, work colleagues from past jobs, where he drinks, that sort of thing. I'm after anything that might demonstrate that he's got a violent streak in him, and see if there's any CCTV available around the surgery from neighbouring businesses. I'd like that too, just to see where he's been since Friday.' She waited while the two detectives updated their notes. 'And it goes without saying, the minute you find anything, you let me know.'

'Yes, guv,' they chorused.

Kay saw Laura raise her hand. 'What's up?'

'Just going back to Kyle's background checks into Justin Mallory, guv. I spoke to Gloria late yesterday about the tour visitors, and I'll come back to that when we get to it on the agenda,' said Laura, 'but she did mention that Joseph wasn't too happy about Justin taking over the farm, and she's of the impression that Joseph wanted him to fail.'

'Really?' Kay stopped writing on the whiteboard and turned around. 'Why?'

'According to Gloria, Joseph tried to sell the farm four years ago for housing redevelopment. Apparently, it's worth millions, but Justin persuaded him to hang on to it because of the family history.'

'Interesting. I wonder if—'

A landline phone rang on the desk beside her and Debbie called across from another where she was waving a handset in the air.

'It's Harriet on line two, guv. She says it's urgent.'

FIFTEEN

A silence descended across the incident room while Kay toggled the phone volume higher before murmuring her thanks to Gavin as he brought over a chair for her.

She didn't sit, not yet, and uncapped a fresh marker pen before readying herself beside the whiteboard once more.

The forensic lead's voice carried through the speaker, crisp and professional. 'Good afternoon, Detective Hunter. I thought you and your team would appreciate an early update rather than wait for my initial report in the morning.'

'Thanks, Harriet,' said Kay, unable to keep the relief from her voice. 'And please extend my thanks to your team. They've been working some long hours on this one.'

'Thanks. We've got a way to go yet, but it's appreciated. Are you ready?'

Kay cast her gaze around the assembled officers. Their faces were rapt, pens poised over their notebooks, and Debbie had positioned herself on a seat nearby with her laptop open, ready to notate as much of the conversation as possible so she could update HOLMES2. 'We're ready.'

'Okay, so you're looking for three suspects,' said Harriet. 'At least three. There may have been more, but we only have three clear sets of footprints leading into the hop garden from the direction of the main road. There's a lay-by half a mile from our crime scene where we found traces of fresh engine oil. I'll include the full details in my report, but it's my view that your victim was driven to that lay-by, then dragged from the vehicle. There are scuff marks in the dirt and across the verge consistent with a body being dragged with the toes of his footwear pointing downwards. Whoever did this to him cut a barbed-wire fence separating the neighbouring farm from the road. That field is full of corn waiting to be harvested later in the month, so it would've provided perfect cover. There's a lot of damage to the crop going through the edge of the field to the far corner where they trampled it down to reach a bridlepath that runs between that field and the Mallorys' hop garden.'

The forensic specialist paused to let the investigating team catch up, and Kay eyed the fresh bullet points she'd added to the whiteboard and bit back a rising dread.

There were so many unanswered questions, so many tasks to delegate, and so few officers available.

'After they dragged him across the field, they cut through the fence to access a bridle path that runs alongside the hop garden. They cut through another fence to access the hops,' Harriet continued. 'At this point, it seems your victim was caught by the barbed wire fence as they dragged him through. We found traces of blood, so

I'll send off the samples to the lab, and ask them to copy you in on the results.'

Kay caught Laura's sharp intake of breath, and nodded. 'If it doesn't match that of our victim, that could be our first real breakthrough in this one.'

'Don't worry, I thought as much so I've asked the lab to treat it as urgent, and I plan to follow up that request with a call to them after this. I'm also of the opinion that given there were at least three suspects there was no need for them to use the corn-picking machine to raise the victim's body into position,' said Harriet. 'The angle at which he was found suggests they were able to lift him into place and two people could've held him while a third person tied him to the trellises.'

'That would explain why nobody at the farm heard anything that night,' said Kay.

'Exactly. We've also found a tyre tread mark near the lay-by that may belong to the vehicle that was used to transport him there. Again, I'll let you know as soon as we have the results. I've spoken to Lucas about the weapon used to disembowel the victim. It had a rough edge, like an old knife, and therefore we're both of the opinion that none of the scythes confiscated from the farm were used. Those are razor-sharp so they can easily cut down the bines, and none carried any trace evidence such as blood or bodily fluids.'

'This is all good stuff, thanks,' said Kay, her pen flying across the whiteboard. 'Any other highlights for us?'

'One more,' said Harriet. 'After that struggle next to the fence, someone might've lost a button. It's made from zinc alloy, and it's the sort with a shank fixed to the back that the thread goes through. I'll email you a photo. There's quite an intricate design embossed on the front of it, but do bear in mind that because it's made from zinc alloy, it doesn't rust so it might not be related to this case. The rest of my report will include a map of the route the victim's killers took, and a full breakdown of all the samples we gathered and are testing.'

Kay wandered over to the phone. 'Harriet, that's great, thanks ever so much. Please phone me if you have any other breakthroughs, no matter the time. You have my mobile number.'

'I'll be in touch. Good luck.'

Ending the call, Kay turned to her team. 'Thoughts?'

'If they used a vehicle, they could have travelled from anywhere to that lay-by,' said Kyle, his tone glum. 'There are a lot of villages around there, and abandoned buildings, and it's easy to get to from at least six reasonable-sized towns, including here.'

'Hell of a risk,' Barnes agreed. 'Mind you, I don't think it's busy along that stretch of road late at night. Harriet said there's evidence of three people dragging the victim to the Mallorys' property. Maybe a fourth person stayed with the vehicle as a watchman.'

'That'd make sense,' said Kay. She paced the carpet in front of the whiteboard, the fabric faded in places where she and her predecessors had worn it down. She paused and eyed the map that Laura had pinned to the cork board. 'But where did they come from? Did they hold him hostage somewhere, or snatch him off the street? Harry – anything new about recent missing persons?'

'Nothing that matches our victim, guv,' came the reply.

'And I've extended the search parameters to Sussex as well as asking the Met Police to let me know of any new reports.'

'Okay, thanks. Nadine, Sean – could you see if you can find any reports from the weekend about erratic driving in that area? Extend the search out by ten miles to start with, and increase by five-mile increments if you find nothing to start off with. Also, Tim – I need you to lead a search of possible places nearby that could've been used to hold someone against their will without alerting neighbours. Industrial units, abandoned buildings, that sort of thing. Aaron, could you give him a hand with that, and Debs, I'll need you to assign officers to both of those tasks before you leave today. This is now a priority.'

A collective murmur of agreement met her words.

'Laura, you were telling us about Joseph Mallory before Harriet called, and that he possibly doesn't see eye-to-eye with his son. Can you go and see him tomorrow and find out more about that potential sale four years ago? I'd like you to speak to the land agent who was involved too, see if you can find out who the interested buyers were.'

'Will do, guv,' said Laura.

'What about tour visitors – are there any red flags there?'

'We're still working on it, guv. I'll let you know if we find anything.'

'Thanks.' Kay checked the time on her phone. 'Okay, it's been a long day and I need all of you to be at your best tomorrow so we'll wrap things up in a minute. I want to give you a brief overview of the post mortem findings before you go though. The same rules apply to the full report from Lucas as the photos – if you're not authorised to access it, you won't be able to read it given some of the content, especially if you're part of Debbie's admin team. But I need you to understand what we might be dealing with here.'

A hush fell across the team as she collected her thoughts.

'Enough of you have worked with me in the past to know I don't jump to conclusions, and that I consider every angle when managing an investigation of this nature. You won't find this in the official report, and what I'm about to tell you doesn't leave this room, is that understood?'

'Yes, guv.'

'Understood, guv.'

'Okay.' She paused to take a deep breath, then exhaled. 'During the post mortem, Lucas identified some markings on the victim's skin, knife wounds that weren't as deep as the others, and which were used to create patterns in certain places on the victim's body. He says in some cultures, the positioning of those markings matches *chakras* used in alternative healing methods – on the crown of the head, between the eyes, the throat, the heart, the solar plexus, the pelvic area and the feet.'

'Is he saying this was a ritualistic killing?' said Kyle, disbelief in his voice.

'Maybe, yes,' Kay replied. 'Now, this is a first for me, as I'm sure it is for many of you, but I want you to keep an open mind during your inquiries. I need more evidence to support this as an ongoing basis of our investigation before I can commit resources to it, so what I'm asking you to do is bear it in mind when you're talking to people. Don't tell them about the markings, and keep it out of any emails or other documents that leave this incident room – I don't want this getting leaked to the press – but tell me if you find something that might support the findings. Okay?'

'Will do, guv.'

'No problem, guv.'

'Thank you. That's it for now – finish any open tasks you've got on your desks before you leave today, and I'll see you at eight tomorrow. You've got my number if you need me in the meantime.'

As her officers scrambled back to their desks, she caught Gavin's eye and beckoned to him.

'What is it, guv?'

'Do me a favour,' she said. 'Can you carry out a search in our system and look for any other ritual-like murders in the area, say in a ten-year period? Have a word with Paul Solomon over at Gravesend as well, let him know it's under wraps at the moment, but if he's come across anything similar in his time there, I'd like to know straight away.'

'Do you think Lucas is right?' Gavin said, his face troubled.

'I'm hoping he's wrong,' she replied. 'I'm already worried that whoever did this has murdered before. What scares me is that they'll probably kill again unless we stop them.'

When Laura drove past the Mallorys' hop farm the next morning, the police cordon had been removed from the five-bar gate separating the yard from the road, and there were no forensic vans parked in front of the buildings.

She slowed to see Cassandra Mallory walking back to the house from the direction of the farm office, and there was a man crossing the yard from one of the storage barns, his pace unhurried as he headed over to a four-wheel drive vehicle towing a horse box.

Passing the stone-hewn wall that overlooked the hop garden, Laura risked another glance to see a second tractor working amongst the bines, accompanied by the cherry picker. A lone man stood in its basket, leaning over while he swiped at the hops before the man below placed them in the trailer behind the tractor, their movements methodical.

Then the wall turned to hedgerow, and the view across the Weald was lost.

Laura focused on the road ahead. The turning she was after was only a few hundred metres further along, and sure enough she spotted a faded sign pointing the way to a tiny hamlet three miles away, and took the right-hand fork.

Beech and larch trees crowded the light out here, creating a lush canopy that encouraged ferns and mosses to grow at the side of the road. The leaves only hinted at the golden hues that would follow the harvest and signify the start of the colder months and the verges had been left wild, with thick nettles and grass vying for space. Deep potholes lined the asphalt, and she reckoned within three months the route would be treacherous with ice and snow.

The lane swept around a right-hand bend before ascending a low rise that bordered what Laura estimated to be the far boundary of Mallory's farm. Here and there, she glimpsed rows of hops through the hedgerow, and then she spotted a sign on the right for the two cottages that the Mallorys owned.

She slowed to negotiate a narrow lane with weeds poking out through the middle of the asphalt and as the pool vehicle swayed and lurched along the uneven surface, she gave a sigh of relief that she was using that and not her own car today.

The suspension might not have survived.

Joseph Mallory's cottage was the larger of two that greeted her on the next bend, with a dirt track to the left-hand side of it and a pretty front garden full of late-blooming flowers and shrubs. A wooden fence separated it from the road and the neighbouring property, which appeared empty. There were no cars parked on the gravel expanse in front of it, and Laura saw no movement beyond the windows.

Rather than take the risk of parking on the road, she

braked to a standstill on the dirt track beside Joseph's house and climbed out, slinging her bag over her shoulder.

There was a side door sheltered by a wooden porch facing the track, and as she locked the car it opened to reveal a man in his late sixties who stared at her from under bushy white eyebrows and a mop of matching hair that met his shirt collar.

'That's a private road,' he said, keeping one hand firmly on the door. 'You can't park there.'

Laura held up her warrant card as she pushed through a galvanised steel gate and walked towards him. 'DC Laura Hanway, Kent Police. Joseph Mallory, is it?'

'That's me.'

She nodded, put her ID away and jerked her chin towards the dirt track. 'Expecting any other visitors today?'

'No.'

'Good. I should be all right parked there while we have a chat then, shouldn't I?'

His jaw worked for a moment, and then he gave a slight shrug and stepped to one side. 'Thought you were a journalist or something.'

Laura stepped over the threshold and into a brightly painted kitchen with a laminated oak floor. There was a kettle on the hob, a stack of plates in an open dishwasher that looked freshly cleaned, and a tabby cat that glared at her from its seat on one of four pine chairs that surrounded a matching square table.

'Have you had many reporters bothering you?' she said, standing in the middle of the room while Joseph ushered the cat out of the door before closing it.

'Not yet,' he said, gesturing to the table. 'But it'll only be a matter of time, won't it?'

She didn't have an answer to that, and instead peered at the chairs to see if perhaps one of them was free from cat hairs. It proved to be a fruitless search, so she chose one facing the door and removed her notebook from her bag. 'I would imagine their focus would be on the main farmhouse, wouldn't it?'

'Maybe. Enough of them know where I live these days though.' He pulled out the chair opposite and sat. 'I won't ask you if you want a drink of anything. They do that on the telly, and the answer's always "no".'

Laura bit back a smile. 'That's okay. I was wondering if I might have a chat about your time running the farm.'

'Why?'

'Because I'd like to try and understand why a man was found murdered in one of the fields—'

'It's a hop garden.'

'Sorry, yes, the hop garden.' Unflustered, Laura turned to a new page and cinched her chair closer to the table. 'So, could you tell me how the farm was different while you were running it?'

Joseph leaned back in his seat and tapped his fingers on the table for a moment, then sighed. 'We didn't have visitors, for a start. Not until later. Before that, we just farmed. Prices were good for crops – not just the hops – we had subsidies from the EU to help us out in lean times, and there weren't the same supply issues back then.'

'Whose idea was it to start the guided tours?'

'Gloria's.' The mention of the woman's name elicited a faint smile. 'She always has been one for kicking people up the arse when they need it, and after we lost all the subsidies, I was having to make cutbacks – less part-time staff to help out with seeding and harvesting for instance. I ran a tight operation though, always have.'

Laura saw his back stiffen, and hearing the pride in his voice, chose a different direction for her questioning. 'Why do you think someone was murdered in the hop garden? With all your experience running the place for years, have you ever felt threatened or…'

'Never,' he said vehemently. 'I don't know what Justin's done to deserve that, but it would never have happened on my watch.'

'You think it's payback for something?' Laura asked.

'Has to be.' Joseph shrugged. 'Why else would anyone do that, here of all places? Doesn't make sense. No, I reckon he's pissed someone off proper.'

'Like who?'

'Has he told you about Shane Vincent?'

'No, who's he?'

'One of the labourers. Shane had been with me for years.' Joseph's chin jutted out. 'And Justin didn't even think to speak to me about it before firing him.'

'Does he always consult with you about what goes on at the farm?'

'No,' said Joseph, wagging a finger at her. 'And that's the problem. He's got a lot to learn, but he isn't interested.'

'Why did he fire Shane?'

'He wouldn't say. Said he didn't want to cause trouble, locally like.'

'Did you ask Shane what happened?'

'I tried to. Phoned him the day I found out, but he told

me to piss off and hung up. Then I saw him in the supermarket in Staplehurst and tried to speak to him. He ignored me, pushed his trolley to one side, and walked out. Haven't tried since.'

'Have you got his contact details?'

'Hang on.' Joseph walked over to the worktop near the hob and returned with his mobile phone. Plucking a pair of reading glasses from his shirt breast pocket, he read out the details to her. 'Got his address here too, if you want it.'

'Thanks.'

'I'd be interested to hear what he tells you. I'd like to get to the bottom of what went on. This family's got a reputation to protect, and I can't have my son walking around firing people who've been with us for years. It's not right.'

Laura finished writing and looked across the table at him. 'What would you have told your employees if you'd sold the farm?'

'Eh?'

'You were planning to sell the farm four years ago, weren't you? What would you have told everyone if you'd found a buyer?'

Joseph's eyes narrowed, and she saw a flash of anger before he emitted a tight chuckle. 'But I didn't sell it, did I?'

'Why not?'

'Because Gloria's idea about the tours paid off. She started advertising them on social media, on travel websites, the lot. We used to have to employ two extra part-time staff to cope with the numbers.'

'She didn't mention the extra staff. I thought Justin

and… Trevor conducted the tours,' Laura said, flicking through her notes. 'When do they bring in the extra staff?'

'They don't, not anymore. I used to contract it out to a local lass who was studying viticulture at university and wanted to learn more about the hop trade, and the other was a woman who used to manage a pub who Gloria knew.' Joseph scowled. 'Justin let them go when he took over the place.'

Laura leaned back in her chair. 'It seems to me, listening to you, that you were turning the farm's fortunes around with the tours and with Justin's input into the new hop varieties. Why did you hand over the farm to Justin two years ago?'

To her surprise, the man pushed back his chair, walked around to her side of the table and then stooped and rolled up his trouser leg.

He tapped the titanium prosthetic leg. 'Because I had an accident, and this turned nasty before the surgeon had the sense to take it away. It took me a long time to recover. At one point, I'll admit, I thought I was going to die. And that's when Justin, the little shit, suggested I transfer the farm to him then for a paltry sum rather than subject him to massive inheritance taxes.' He dropped the trouser leg back into place and stalked back to his chair. 'And I stupidly agreed.'

SEVENTEEN

Barnes stretched the car seatbelt away from his waistline for a moment, shuffled in his seat and then released the handbrake as the traffic queue surged forward.

The route southwards from the police station was congested at the best of times, but a bus had broken down on one of the bridges crossing the River Medway, and the whole road system had ground to a standstill two hours ago. According to the traffic officer he saw on the way out to the pool car, a tow truck had been organised but it was another hour away, and by then the schools would be finished for the day.

'Nightmare,' said Kyle beside him.

'No shit.'

'What's wrong with the seatbelt?'

'Nothing.'

'Too small?'

'Cheeky—'

'Must've been all that rich food in Italy last month, sarge. Pasta's the worst.'

'Don't I know it,' Barnes muttered. 'Pia's already planning extra sessions down the gym for us. And it'll mean we'll be eating salad for months. In winter. Who does that?'

'You, apparently.'

Seeing a break in the traffic between a ride-share car and a bus, Barnes accelerated forward and nipped in front of both, reaching the final set of lights. He drummed his fingers on the steering wheel, then surged forward the moment they turned green, relaxing into his seat as they left the urban sprawl behind.

He glanced over at his colleague, who was scrolling his phone screen. 'Found out anything else about Roland Hammerton?'

'Nothing that'll help us,' said Kyle. 'He hasn't posted anything to social media since Thursday—'

'Probably being careful in the circumstances.'

'That's what I was thinking. I've done a couple of online searches for him, but apart from a photo I found in an article about the farm – and he's just standing in the background with the rest of Justin's workers in that one – there's nothing untoward.'

'What about previous jobs?'

'Mostly manual labour, forklift driving, that sort of thing.' Kyle lowered his phone. 'And he's not in our system. Not even for a speeding fine.'

'Okay, so let's see what the owner of the shop in the village has to say about him – that's where he bought his ciggies on Friday, according to him.'

Fifteen minutes later, Barnes pulled the car in behind a dark green SUV outside a convenience store that was a privately-run business rather than one of the many franchises that peppered the surrounding area.

Climbing out of the car, he looked along a curving street that was lined with near-identical buildings comprising a mixture of businesses and shops. Each was rendered a pale colour on the lower floor in between dark exposed beams that criss-crossed their façades. This effect made way for red brick walls on the upper floor under darker clay tiles and, here and there, some property owners had extended up into a roof, adding dormer windows for light.

The village shop sported a bay window each side of its wide-open door and displayed a collection of second-hand books in a crate on one side, and stacked egg boxes in another. An aromatic blend of fresh bread, vegetables and lavender greeted Barnes as he led the way inside.

He was surprised to see how well stocked the shop was. Three aisles of shelving abutted two chest freezers on the right-hand side, the vegetable racks and bread displayed at the end of each facing the door. At the back were two glass-fronted refrigerators filled with milk, beer and soft drinks, beside which a display of greeting cards and stationery lined the remainder of the back wall. A long counter took up the left-hand side of the shop, and a man looked up from his phone as they walked over.

'This looks serious,' he said by way of greeting.

Barnes held up his warrant card. 'DC Ian Barnes, and my colleague DC Kyle Walker. What gave us away?'

He asked the question good-naturedly, realising the sight of two men in business attire might be a rare occurrence in the shop.

'Lucky guess,' said the man. 'How can I help you? I don't believe my staff have reported any thefts or anything.'

'Well, Mr…?'

'Knowles. Warner Knowles.'

'We were hoping you could answer some questions about one of your customers, Roland Hammerton.'

Warner raised an eyebrow. 'Roland?'

'This man,' said Kyle, turning his phone screen.

'Oh. Him.' Warner sneered. 'One of the customers who tends to make us smile a lot – when he leaves.'

'Does he cause trouble?' Barnes asked.

'Tries to. He's rude, more than anything, especially to my wife and my daughter. Whenever he comes in, there's always an issue. Small things, but a nuisance all the same.'

'Has he ever been violent?'

'Angry, yes. But not violent, not to me.'

Barnes looked over his shoulder at the sound of footsteps to see a man in his sixties enter the shop.

He took one look at the two detectives, nodded at Warner, then made a beeline for a rack of newspapers beside the door, taking his time to peruse the vegetables on the way past.

Turning back to the shopkeeper, Barnes lowered his voice. 'Was he in here on Friday, say between three thirty and four thirty?'

Warner's face turned thoughtful. 'He did come here in the afternoon, but I'm not sure about the time. He bought cigarettes and a six-pack of lager, then left. Paid by card. I can check the camera footage if you want an exact time.'

Barnes looked to where the shopkeeper pointed, and

saw a blinking red LED light above a camera on a bracket in the ceiling above an inner door that was closed and marked "private". 'If you wouldn't mind, that'd be great. Have you got any more cameras?'

'One outside, facing along the street so it captures the front door, and one out the back covering the fire exit. That's the only door out there, and separates our storeroom and office from the delivery bay.'

'Aside from Friday's footage, would you be able to let us have a copy of all the footage from Sunday through to Tuesday morning?'

'What's this about?' Warner said, then held up a hand. 'Morning, George. The usual?'

'Yes, please.' The customer sidled next to Kyle, flashed the detectives a wary smile, then turned his attention to the shopkeeper who reached under the counter and pulled out an A4-sized brown envelope and slid it across to George.

'That and the paper, is it?' said Warner.

'Yes.' The man took a ten pound note out of his wallet and almost snatched the change from him. 'Thanks. See you tomorrow.'

He hurried from the shop, his cheeks burning, and Warner gave a chuckle at Barnes's bemused face. 'Don't worry, George is harmless.'

'What was all that about?' said Kyle, bewildered.

The shopkeeper grinned. 'Some of the customers are old-fashioned, preferring magazines to the internet. And some magazines can't be put out on display. Too many kids coming into the shop, for a start. Never mind the vicar and his wife.'

Kyle blushed as realisation hit him. 'Oh.'

Barnes chuckled at his colleague's embarrassment, then grew serious once more. 'How soon can you get that camera footage to us?'

In response, Warner walked around the end of the counter and over to the stationery rack before returning with a thin cardboard pack that he held up. 'If you buy the memory card, I'll copy it all for you now. You'll have to keep an eye on the shop for me while I do it though – I'm on my own here until Mandy gets back from her mother's.'

'Deal,' said Barnes, then gave Kyle a shove. 'Go on then, get behind the counter. I reckon you stand a better chance than me at figuring out how that till works.'

EIGHTEEN

Kay walked out of the café on Maidstone's High Street and squinted in the bright sunlight before walking over to where Barnes waited under the shade of an awning for a shoe shop and handed him one of the takeout cups.

'Thanks, guv.' He held up his phone. 'Kyle's got Sean Gastrell onto the security camera footage from the village shop while he chases up the agent who's selling the pub that's closed to get the old landlord's details. Warner Knowles put a camera up on the outside of the shop to watch over the front door, but it faces the road in the direction of the farm too. With any luck, we'll have a better picture about Roland Hammerton from that footage than we've gleaned so far from social media, and we might catch him driving to the Mallorys' place on Sunday night. You never know.'

'It's worth a shot. Honestly, any breakthrough right now would be something.'

They followed the road as it curved back round to the

river, then used the pedestrian crossing to reach a narrow footpath through the centuries-old cemetery of All Saints Church.

As Kay ran her gaze over the faded inscriptions, she wondered how on earth they were going to identify their victim, and what the hell she was going to tell his family.

'No news on an ID, guv?' Barnes asked.

She smiled, despite her sombre musings. Her detective sergeant had an uncanny knack of reading her thoughts, which was what made them such a good team when the odds were against them. 'Not yet. Lucas phoned while you were out. He's sent off requests for dental records, and a wider DNA search. One of those ancestry research companies might come up with something to help us, or at least give us a point in the right direction.'

'Hope so.'

They turned right at the end of the path and followed an old cobbled carriage route down to the river where a wooden bench seat had been placed beside the stone wall of the Archbishop's Palace. It was mid-morning and quiet, with no passing foot traffic to interrupt them and only the passing ducks for company.

Kay sat with a sigh, and sipped her coffee. 'Lucas emailed me a cleaned-up photo of our victim too, so we'll have this and then go over to the Mallorys' to see if they recognise him now. Cassandra obviously hasn't seen him yet for a start.'

'God knows we could do with a breakthrough, guv.' Barnes walked over to the railings separating the path from the fast-flowing river, and turned to face her. 'It's been, what, five days since Lucas reckons he was killed?'

'And, according to Harriet, there are at least three people walking around free who know something about his death.'

Barnes shook his head. 'Three people who knew what they were doing, by the sounds of it. I mean, they had to have mapped out that route on foot before taking the victim there, right?'

'It'd have been a hell of a risk to just turn up and assume they could get him along that bridlepath and into the hop garden, that's for sure.'

Her colleague froze, his coffee cup halfway to his mouth.

'What is it?' she asked.

'Poachers.' He took a gulp, then wandered over to the bench and sat, his unfocused gaze on the river while he spoke. 'Poachers are always cutting through farmers' fences to drag deer carcasses through. They'd know how to gut someone based on that too, wouldn't they?'

'Bloody hell.' Kay straightened, and took out her phone. 'You're right. Hang on, I'll phone Mark Weston from the Rural Task Force.'

Barnes fell silent while she dialled the uniformed constable's mobile number, and she cursed under her breath when it went to voicemail.

'Mark? It's DI Kay Hunter in Maidstone. We've picked up a homicide investigation that might have some tenuous links to local poachers. I wondered if you could give me a call please when you get this message? Thanks.' She ended the call, then drained her coffee. 'Okay, Ian. Let's go and see what Justin Mallory might be able to tell us about our victim.'

When Barnes drove into the farmyard twenty minutes later, Daniel Ionescu was ambling from the direction of the hop garden towards the larger of the two barns, his scythe over his shoulder.

The Romanian eyed the two detectives with curiosity as they got out of the car, went to raise his hand in greeting, then seemed to think better of it and frowned instead.

'You're back again?' he called.

''Fraid so,' said Kay. She wandered over to him. 'How are you and Alexandru holding up?'

Daniel lowered the scythe, then shrugged. 'I'm okay. Alex… not so much. I don't think he's sleeping. We stay in the same house in the village, and I hear him crying out at night.'

'Does he have someone he can talk to, perhaps a doctor?'

'He won't go.' The man gave a small smile. 'He's a very proud man.'

'I got that impression.' Kay looked around the yard. 'Is Justin around?'

'He and Trevor are in a meeting,' said Daniel, pointing to the farm office. 'I think it's important – both of them looked serious when they went inside.'

Kay frowned as her gaze scanned the vehicles in the yard. 'I can't spot any visitors. Do you know who the meeting is with?'

'It's online. With a customer, I think.'

'Any idea how long they'll be?'

'No, sorry.'

'What about Gloria?'

'She left half an hour ago – a dentist appointment. She'll be back later.'

'Is Cassandra around?'

'Somewhere.' Daniel pivoted, raising a hand to shield his eyes from the sunlight. 'I don't know where though.'

Kay sighed, looked at Barnes, and then at the car. 'Well, it makes no sense driving back to Maidstone now. We might as well have a wander round until Justin's free.'

'I'll let him know you're here if I see him first,' said the Romanian, then continued walking towards the barn, whistling under his breath.

'Do you want to take another look at where our victim was found now that Harriet's lot have packed up and gone, guv?' said Barnes.

'Good idea. At least that'll give us a chance to see the route his killers took back and forth from the bridlepath as well. In fact, let's start there.'

Leaving their jackets in the car, Kay and Barnes followed the track out of the farmyard and through the gate into the hop garden, then turned right and followed a gentle slope down to where a bramble hedge obscured most of the boundary. There was a break in the hedgerow where the barbed wire fence was visible, and it was here that Kay spotted four spiky ends of wire curling upwards.

Beyond that was a narrow dirt path separating the hop garden from the neighbouring field, the tightly packed and parched soil ingrained with horseshoe impressions here and there.

'Want to take a closer look, guv?' Barnes asked. He

reached out and carefully pulled the broken barbed wire aside. 'You should be able to squeeze through here, I reckon.'

'Thanks.' Kay eased her way past the wire, careful not to catch it on her shirt or trousers, then stood at the edge of the bridlepath and looked right, then left. 'That's the way to the lay-by on the main road, and I can see the footprints that Harriet mentioned. They don't go any further than here. There are only hoofprints after this break in the fence.'

Barnes peered over the remainder of the fence to where she was looking. 'I had a look on the map before we came out here. If you go right, instead of following the bridlepath to the road, it comes out next to a manor house about two miles away. They offer horse-riding on their website.'

'Any chance we've got surveillance footage from them?'

'Sean's already checked it, guv. There were no signs of our victim or his attackers around the manor house over the weekend, and the owners reported that they haven't spotted anything untoward. The last group riding lesson they took out was last Wednesday, and they've confirmed it didn't go anywhere near here.'

'Okay, so we can rule out our killers recce'ing the hop farm that way,' said Kay. She peered along the bridlepath to where the fence had been sliced open to the corn field. 'We'll take a look at the lay-by on the way back – let's have another look at the hop garden for now.'

Barnes held back the barbed wire while she made her

way back through it, then jutted his chin towards the crime scene. 'Want to take the route they did?'

'Yes, it'll help us get a feel for any problems they might've had to overcome to do this. Look – you can see where Harriet's lot marked out the route here.'

'We were bloody lucky it didn't rain, guv,' he said, his hands in his pockets while he walked beside her and kept his gaze to the ground. 'We could've lost so much evidence.'

'Wasn't it forecast though? I'm sure Adam said something about expecting a downpour on Sunday night, because he was going to check the fence in the orchard.'

'Must be hard having a partner who's a vet.' Barnes choked out a laugh. 'I take it he's paranoid after last time?'

'Just a bit. Honestly, that sheep is good for keeping down the grass but he's an escape artist all right.'

The sound of a tractor working in one of the fields at the top of the hill carried on the breeze, and somewhere a bumblebee was buzzing back and forth amongst the long grass that feathered the woody base of the crop.

Kay sobered as she reached the first row of bines and cast her gaze along the trellises disappearing up the slope.

Here, the hop cones were thick and abundant, the ground softer due to the natural drainage of the rich soil, and she took a step back at the pungent aroma.

'That's almost overpowering,' she said, craning her neck to look at the top of the bine before continuing on. 'And they seem to encroach on you, don't they?'

'You could get quite claustrophobic amongst these,' Barnes agreed. 'Same with the corn field back there. Have you noticed how they've deadened sound, too?'

Kay paused, then nodded. 'Okay, the wind direction might've changed, but I can't hear that tractor so well now, can you?'

'No – and again, I guess that helps explain why nobody heard him.' Barnes shuddered. 'Either that, or when he screamed it was mistaken for a fox's cry.'

'It doesn't bear thinking about, does it? Lucas didn't say anything about the victim being gagged, so his killers were confident enough not to bother.' Kay paused at a crossroads in the trellises. 'Which way from here?'

'Left, I think. Then a right at that next lot.'

'Or straight on here, then left?'

'Either way will work, but Harriet found the bootprints going left.'

'Okay. We can circle back that way. I want to get a feel for why those bines weren't cut down on Monday, and why our victim wasn't discovered until the next day. Surely twenty-four hours can't make a lot of difference, can it?'

'I think it can,' said Barnes, following in her wake. 'I've been streaming one of those farming documentaries and they're always going on about whether a crop is ready to harvest and whether they'll beat the rain.'

'I take it that's usually set to some dramatic music to heighten the tension?' Kay replied, her cheeks dimpling.

'You'd be correct in that assumption.'

The sound of a different tractor engine reached them near the fringes of the trellis row, and it passed them by, driven by a man in his early fifties with a mop of sandy-coloured hair. He raised a hand in greeting, then continued on his way, the engine stopping a little further down the hop garden.

'That's Howard, the bloke who was working with Alexandru on Tuesday, wasn't it?' said Kay.

'Yeah, don't worry – he checked out. Kyle did a background check on him along with the other staff. Nothing to report.'

'Jesus, Ian. We're nearly forty-eight hours into this one, and we still don't have a motive. Has anyone at headquarters managed to find out anything else about Roland Hammerton?'

'Nothing yet, guv. Andy's lot in digital forensics are still digging, but the bloke isn't very active on social media or anything.'

The trellises formed a gentle curve near the top of the slope, and Kay trudged onwards, her thoughts churning. Somewhere out there, at least three people were guilty of torturing and murdering a man, and yet they had no idea who he was, or why he had been killed – or why he had been killed here, of all places, when it seemed the Mallorys had no enemies to speak of, and a business that was thriving until—

'Guv? Take a look at this.'

She froze, then looked over her shoulder at Barnes who had stopped by the base of the bines at the end of the last trellis they had passed, his gaze intent on the woody stump of a plant that had yellowed and withered. Wandering back to where he stood, she frowned. 'Dead?'

'Yeah, look – all the plants at this end of this row are like it. And the ones behind, but they're not so bad.'

'But all of the others around here are okay, look. What do you think? Have they been attacked by bugs or something?'

'There aren't any bite marks, or any spotting like you'd get on rose leaves.'

Kay turned her attention to the top of the slope where they had been headed. 'Let's ask that Howard chap. It might be nothing, but…'

'To me, they look like they've been poisoned, guv,' said Barnes. 'But I'm no gardening expert.'

'Still, they don't look healthy, do they? Come on.'

She set a brisk pace up the hill, and found the tractor parked a few metres to the right.

Howard was inspecting a row of bines a little further along, and she waved to catch his attention. He seemed reluctant to talk, but ambled over, his gaze wary. 'Yes?'

Kay removed her warrant card. 'Detective Inspector Kay Hunter, and my colleague DS Ian Barnes. I'm leading the investigation into the murder of the man found here on Tuesday. Can you confirm your name please?'

'Howard Masters.'

'How long have you worked here?'

'A few years.'

'And what is it you do?'

'I help manage the harvest, and oversee the planting.' He straightened a little, proud. 'It's because of me we're doing so well with the different varieties. Justin and his dad might've chosen them, but it's me who gets them to this stage.'

'Excellent, then perhaps you can help me. We were just looking around to get a feel for the place, and noticed that there's a couple of rows of bines back there that look as if they've been poisoned at some point. What happened?'

Howard's expression clouded, and he turned away.

'Best you ask the boss or Trevor about that,' he said over his shoulder. 'I can't comment.'

NINETEEN

'Hang on.'

Kay paused at the gate between the hop garden and the farmyard and held up her hand to Barnes, beckoning him over to their car. 'Before we speak to Justin, I want to give Gavin a call without being overheard.'

Her colleague's brow puckered but he followed, then turned his back on her to survey the buildings while she hit the speed dial on her mobile. Glancing up, she saw nobody approaching, and with Barnes keeping a watchful eye, she turned the phone to speaker so he could listen.

'Yes, guv?' said Gavin, his voice harried.

'Everything okay?'

'Yes, just a lot of information coming in at the moment. Nothing to worry about.'

She smiled at that, grateful for his resilience under pressure. 'Remember your theory that our victim was dumped here to ruin the Mallorys' reputation? We might have something to go on in relation to that. Can you follow up with Kyle about who Justin's closest competitors are, and whether any veiled threats might've been made in the past year? I'm thinking social media spats, trade magazine interviews, that sort of thing. You could ask the financial investigation team at headquarters to give you a hand if you need it, too. Amanda Miller's still there, and she'll be interested if you think there's anything like bribery or coercion going on from an organised crime angle, if there is one.'

'I'm already onto it guv – I thought the same thing after speaking with the agency that employs Alexandru and the others yesterday. I just didn't want to bother you with it in case it was a pointless exercise. Kyle's made a start on the research but I hadn't thought of asking Amanda to help. Thanks.'

'No problem. Give me a shout the minute you find anything.'

Kay ended the call, and led Barnes towards the farm office end of the converted stable block. She could hear voices beyond the closed door, and rapped her knuckles against it twice before walking in.

Justin Mallory and another man were facing each other at the desk. She couldn't see the other man's face, but Justin's was a picture of misery, and he looked up at her with baleful eyes as Barnes followed her in.

'Yes?' he said. 'We're rather busy at the moment, as you can see. What do you want?'

Kay raised an eyebrow in response, then pointed at the computer screen which showed a spreadsheet open. 'I take it that your video conference has finished?'

'We're still discussing it,' said Justin. 'Can't this wait?'

Kay ignored him for a moment and turned to the man

in the other chair. 'I don't think we've met before. I'm Detective Inspector Kay Hunter and I'm in charge of the investigation into the murder of the man in the field here. And you are…?'

The man scowled in response. 'Trevor Leavitt. I'm the farm manager here.'

'Excellent.' Kay beamed at both of them. 'Then I've got both of the experts I need. What's going on with the hops on the trellises a few rows behind where the victim was found? They're all yellowing and withered.'

She saw the flicker of a look between the two men, and then Justin waved a dismissive hand at her.

'We're looking into it. It's just an isolated incident, hopefully nothing to worry about.'

'Really? They look like they were perfectly healthy plants for a while there – they're as tall as the ones next to them, after all.'

'They didn't take so well this year. It happens sometimes,' said Trevor.

'They look like they've been poisoned,' Kay said, and watched as Justin's jaw tightened.

'Like I just said, we're looking into it.' He leaned forward as the computer screen went blank and wiggled his mouse until the spreadsheet reappeared. 'And, as you can see, we're still in a meeting at the moment, so if that's all…'

'Actually,' said Barnes, reaching into his pocket and unfolding a single page before handing it over, 'now we've got a cleaner image of the victim we wondered if you could take another look and see if you recognise him.'

Justin shook his head. 'I've never seen him before in my life.'

'Are you sure?' Barnes asked. 'Take another look.'

'I'm sure.'

'What about you?' Barnes handed the photograph to Trevor.

The man shook his head. 'Sorry, no.'

'When we spoke to you on Tuesday, Mr Mallory, I asked you if you were experiencing any trouble here,' said Kay watching Barnes fold up the photograph and stuff it back into his pocket before she looked at the farmer to gauge his expression. 'Would you like to amend your statement?'

'No. There's nothing wrong with the way I run this place.'

'I didn't say there was,' Kay retorted. 'But you've got half a row of rotten bines amongst the new variety you're promoting, which look like they've been poisoned, and then a man was tortured and killed only metres away. Why did you tell your people not to harvest those rows on Monday? Were you expecting to find him?'

Justin's face turned white. 'No, I wasn't. The crops weren't ready to pick, that's why I told them to start on the other rows instead. I've already told you, I've never seen that man before in my life.'

'But you know something,' said Kay. 'Don't you? And you.'

She turned her attention to Trevor, who was attempting a nonchalant posture in the chair beside her that was spoiled by the fact his fingernails were digging into the armrests. 'Are either of you being threatened?'

'No,' Trevor snapped. 'We're just very busy, as Mr Mallory has already explained to you.'

Justin held up a placating hand. 'Look, Detective Hunter. I don't mind answering your questions, but I do have a farm to run here. You can't just come barging in here…'

'Yes, I can.' Kay glared at him. 'And I will, if I deem it necessary to my investigation. Especially if I think other lives may be at risk.'

The farmer's eyebrows shot upwards. 'Other lives? What do you mean?'

'There are currently at least three people walking free who know something about that man's death,' said Kay coldly. 'Three people who knew how to get to your hops from the main road using a footpath and your neighbour's corn crop to avoid being spotted. The same three people managed to crucify their victim amongst your crop and then disembowel him without being disturbed. And if they get away with it, what's stopping them from doing it again?'

Justin's face turned from white to puce. 'Do you think they'll come back?'

'I don't know. Do you?'

He was saved from answering by a brisk knock on the door before Cassandra burst in, out of breath.

'You won't believe what that lying shit has done…' she managed, then clamped a hand over her mouth at the sight of Kay and Barnes. 'Oh, I'm so sorry – I didn't spot your car outside.'

'No problem,' said Kay smoothly. 'Which lying shit were you referring to?'

Cassandra's gaze flicked from her to Justin, then back, her mouth opening and closing. 'Um…'

'Tell them, whatever it is,' said Justin, his voice weary. 'We might as well all hear it, whatever it is. Honestly, this week…'

In response, his wife held a letter and a ripped white envelope aloft. 'This. It's from a solicitor's firm in Maidstone. It just arrived by special delivery, and it says to expect an email from them this morning too.'

'What's going on?' Kay asked.

Cassandra turned to her. 'Bloody Roland Hammerton, that's what's going on. He's only gone and lodged a personal injury claim for that stupid little accident he had on Friday. He wants to sue us for thousands in compensation.'

Gavin ran his thumb over the trickle of condensation running down the cold can of energy drink and contemplated the whiteboard at the end of the room, turning his swivel chair from side to side.

It squeaked at every left turn, but he didn't hear it.

The air conditioning was blowing a minor gale across his neck and sending goosebumps across his forearms, but he didn't feel it.

Instead, he ran his gaze over the crisscrossed notes that covered the whiteboard's surface as the setting sun cast a soft pink glow across it and eyed the photograph of Roland Hammerton pinned in the top right-hand corner opposite that of their victim, clenching his jaw.

'Three days,' he murmured. 'He's cost us three bloody days.'

A rubberised stress ball hit him in the back of the head, jerking him from his thoughts and he turned around to see Laura glaring at him. 'What?'

'Either find some oil for that damn chair or stop

fidgeting, for goodness' sakes,' she said. 'It's driving me up the wall.'

He sighed and then tossed the ball back to her, shuffled the chair closer to his desk and took another sip of the energy drink before pushing the can away in favour of moving his computer mouse. Clicking through the latest updates in their database, he bit back an almost overwhelming sense of disappointment and began reviewing witness statements again.

'I really thought it was Roland too,' said Laura. 'Reading though Ian's notes after he and Kay interviewed him, I got the impression he was hiding something.'

'He was,' said Gavin. 'Just not the something we thought he was hiding.'

'At least we found out where he was on Monday.' Barnes walked over and put his mobile phone and car keys on his desk before leaning against it and running a hand over his close-cropped hair. 'Meeting with the lawyers.'

'That firm has a reputation for dodgy claims too, I've heard,' said Laura. 'They specialise in those no-win, no-fee cases that take forever to get to court, cost the defendant a fortune, and then only end up passing on one or two thousand pounds for their victims after taking their fee.'

Kyle finished the call he was on and called across. 'What are the Mallorys going to do?'

'They're meeting with their solicitor in the morning. Based on our discussions with Roland, we can provide them with evidence that he's been driving around and seems to be moving all right,' said Barnes. He shrugged. 'It might help them prove his is a spurious claim, but we'll see.'

Gavin looked over his shoulder as the door to the incident room swung open with such force that it smacked the plasterwork wall behind it.

Kay stalked towards the whiteboard, removing her jacket as she walked, and threw that and her bag onto a nearby desk before facing the room, her hands on her hips.

'Right, everyone. Briefing. Now.'

'The shit has definitely hit the fan,' Gavin murmured to Laura as they hurried over.

'No kidding,' she replied, then fell silent at a warning glance from the DI.

Kay started the briefing as soon as the last uniformed constable's backside found a chair. 'For those of you who haven't heard, Roland Hammerton is no longer a person of interest in this investigation. It's transpired in the past hour that he's lodging a personal injury claim against the Mallorys for an incident that happened at the farm on Friday that has no bearing on our case. In short, we're three days into a murder inquiry and back to square one. We have no motive, and no suspects. And unless one of you has pulled a minor miracle while I've been at the farm this morning, we still don't know who our victim is, either.'

The assembled officers and detectives remained silent, such that Gavin could only hear a whisper from the air conditioning vents and a soft gurgle from the coffee machine.

'Okay, so let's reset and see where we go from here,' Kay continued. She removed Roland Hammerton's photograph from the board, snapped a photo of the related notes with her phone, then erased them from the whiteboard and uncapped a pen. 'What we did find out while we were at the farm is that somebody has poisoned a section of the hop bines a few rows back from where the victim was found, and Justin and his farm manager are at a loss to explain who or why. Gavin, Kyle – any news about competitors?'

Gavin cleared his throat and rose to his feet before finding somewhere to stand where everybody could see him. 'There are two other hop farms within a six-mile radius of the Mallorys' business but those are long established and haven't had any complaints associated with them. I took the liberty of speaking with the owners of each, and although there's a bit of friendly competition between them, they spoke highly of what Justin's been doing since taking over from his dad and one of them went on to say that he's often loaned equipment back and forth with the Mallorys when one of them's come unstuck.'

He turned to Kay. 'We didn't find anything to suggest one of the other hop farms had anything to do with our investigation, guv – sorry. I've even extended the search to include their usual suppliers, and there's nothing untoward there, either.'

'Dammit.' Kay sighed and recapped the pen.

Gavin turned at movement out the corner of his eye to see Laura's hand raised.

'Guv,' she said, 'when I spoke with Joseph Mallory this morning, he mentioned that since taking over the farm, Justin had fired three long-term members of staff. One bloke seems to have taken it particularly hard, so I wonder whether there might be some sort of grudge there.'

'What do you know about the staff members so far?' Kay asked.

Laura jerked her thumb over her shoulder. 'I've just started looking through their social media at the time and working up profiles for each of them. There were two women who used to help with the hop garden tours too. I can let you know as soon as I find anything.'

'Do, thanks,' said Kay. 'If there is a problem, it makes you wonder why they've left it so long to seek revenge though. I mean, Joseph sold the farm to Justin what, two years ago?'

'Revenge and hatred can fester over time, guv,' said Barnes. 'We've seen it before.'

'True.' The DI turned back to Laura. 'All right, liaise with Gavin to continue those enquiries. Gav, see if you can find out where those people are working now – and whether there's anything in their past that might point to a violent history. Laura, I think you and I should have a word with Cassandra Mallory in the morning to find out what her views are about her father-in-law.'

'Will do, guv. I'll pick you up just before eight.'

Gavin saw Kay glance out the window for a moment, her shoulders sagging before she gave a slight shake of her head and refocused on her team.

'Does anybody have anything to add while we're here?'

Kyle raised his hand. 'Guv, Sean and I have been reviewing the CCTV footage from the village shop where Roland bought cigarettes from. I know he's no longer a suspect, but we realised the outside camera faces the street and the direction of the Mallorys' farm. We ran the footage for Sunday night from seven o'clock onwards, and I think we might've found the vehicle used to transport the victim to that lay-by. It's a long shot, but we're pretty sure it's the only vehicle on that recording that could fit the victim and his three killers inside.'

'Really?' Kay's eyebrows shot upwards as the other officers began talking in excited whispers. 'How sure are you?'

'Put it this way, guv,' said Sean Gastrell, 'we ran the licence plates through the system just before this briefing and that's confirmed the owner of the van that appears in the camera feed reported it stolen on Sunday morning from a plumbing business near Wrotham Heath. He didn't find out until he got back to work on Monday.'

'I was planning to head over there in the morning to interview him,' Kyle added. 'He's out on a job in Sittingbourne at the moment and can't talk to us today.'

Kay's pen was already scratching at the whiteboard. 'Good work, you two. And Kyle, I agree – have a word with the owner in the morning, and also put out a search for the van now. Can you get the vehicle index number from DVLA? I'd imagine the plates have been removed by now.'

'Sean's requested that, so we're just waiting for a response,' said Kyle. 'And I've alerted the traffic lot as well.'

'Good. Okay everybody, it's getting late and I want you all in bright and early tomorrow to refocus on following up statements from neighbours and suppliers for the Mallorys' farm,' said Kay. 'And Gavin, can you escalate working your way through the list of tour visitors to the farm over this summer? Let me know immediately if you find anyone with a previous record, no matter the charge.'

'Will do, guv,' he said.

'Right, well tomorrow's a new day,' said the DI. 'I realise we've had a setback with Roland Hammerton as a suspect but we've still got plenty of leads to work through, and we owe it to our victim to find out who did this to him. We're not going to let him down.'

TWENTY-ONE

Kay sat under an apple tree that was at least forty years old and contemplated the dregs of Sauvignon Blanc at the bottom of her glass.

The stream that separated the orchard from the back garden bubbled its way past her a few metres away, its flow weakened by the lack of rain over the past few weeks but enough to prevent the water becoming stagnant.

A sheep ambled between the apple trees that surrounded her, its gait a little stiff with age but its posture emanating belligerence as it looked up from the grass it was eating and emitted a pitiful bleat.

'You've just had your dinner, Hovis. Keep eating that grass if you're still hungry.'

The sheep turned away with a look of disgust on its face and wandered over to a low timber-framed shed that afforded it both shade and shelter before sniffing at the ground and finding something else to investigate.

A blackbird called from within the hedgerow behind Kay, its sonorous chirping a musical interlude to the rustling of leaves above her while a light breeze passed through the small orchard and feathered the grass at her feet. The sun was setting now, its warmth bathing her toes as she wiggled them on top of the sandals that she had kicked off the moment she sat in the comfortable garden chair, and yet her shoulders were tense and her mind swirled non-stop.

She jerked to attention at the sound of her mobile phone vibrating across the ornate cast iron table beside her, and snatched it up at the sight of the name on the screen. 'Guv?'

'Heard you've got a tricky one,' barked the familiar voice of Detective Chief Inspector Devon Sharp.

Kay put down the empty wineglass and rubbed at tired eyes. 'Are headquarters going to take me off the case?'

'Why on earth would they do that?' Sharp said. 'Given what I've seen of the details in the system, you're doing everything you can with the information you've got. I take it the victim hasn't been reported missing yet?'

'I spoke to Harry Davis before I left the incident room, and he hasn't had anything come through yet. If the victim was single and had no immediate family in the area, it might take a little longer before his friends realise something's wrong. Harry's going to keep on top of it.' She stood up, pacing beside the table and chair set while watching Hovis roam back and forth. 'And Kyle and Sean had the idea to follow up a stolen van that was spotted on CCTV last Sunday night near the hop farm.'

'That's something then,' Sharp said reassuringly. 'When do you want to put out a public appeal for information?'

Kay shuddered. 'Not yet. I don't have the manpower to deal with the crank callers on top of all the leads we're following up. Did you see how many samples Harriet had to send to the lab? My budget for this one's going to be horrendous, I'll warn you now.'

'Your budgets are always horrendous, but you get results so let me worry about that side of things,' said the DCI.

'Thanks, guv. How are things with you? You and Rebecca are off on holiday soon, aren't you?'

'Three weeks and counting,' came the reply. 'And it's as busy as ever here. I've got two inter-agency investigations that are taking up most of my time, and this year's recruitment statistics aren't as good as the chief would like so I'm playing politics as well.'

Kay smiled at the disgust in her mentor's voice. 'Ah well guv, if you ever want to come back to Maidstone, you'd be welcome. Your office is still there.'

'Haven't you moved into that yet?' said Sharp. 'It's been how long?'

'Not that long.' She laughed, then grew sober once more. 'I mean it though. It'd be good to see you.'

'Tell you what, let me get back from holiday and we'll organise something, even if it's just a short visit. It's been a while since I've seen the old crowd. How's Ian getting on?'

'He's well, but it's Gavin I'm more concerned about, guv. He's perfect DS material, but I keep getting pushback from headquarters about having two sergeants on my team. According to them, there's no justification for it.'

'Who said that?' Sharp demanded. 'That's a ridiculous assumption.'

'I know. It was a form response from the staffing team. Unsigned of course, and the admin officer who sent it couldn't offer any answers – she was just the one asked to tell me.'

'Hmm. I'll make some enquiries, see what I can do. I agree with you – it'd be a huge loss to Maidstone if Gavin jumped ship, and cases like this one prove you could use the experience both he and Ian provide.'

'Any help would be appreciated, thanks. Laura and Kyle are doing a great job, but Gavin's as good as Barnes and I'd miss him if he weren't here.'

'Understood.' There was noise in the background, and then Sharp returned. 'Got to go. One more meeting, and then I'm heading off.'

'Thanks for calling, guv. Enjoy your holiday if I don't speak to you before then.'

'Look after yourself, Kay.'

He ended the call and she stood for a moment, staring at the screen while a pang of loss stabbed at her heart. She loved her job, loved the responsibilities that came with it, but at times like these, she missed her old mentor and friend, and his acute observations during an investigation of such magnitude.

'Penny for your thoughts?'

She spun around at the sound of Adam's voice to see him crossing the little bridge over the stream and heading towards her, a glass and the wine bottle in one hand. 'You're home.'

He enveloped her in a one-armed hug and kissed her

before holding up the bottle. 'Top up? I'm officially off duty until Saturday morning.'

'Yay. I'd almost forgotten what you looked like.'

Adam grinned. 'Coming from the woman who's already gone to work by the time I've been getting in in the mornings. I take it you've got a difficult one.'

'Yes, I was just talking to Sharp about it.' Kay held up her glass while he poured. 'Just a splash, thanks – I've already had a small one, and I want to be out the door early tomorrow.'

'Can you talk about it?' he asked, sitting opposite her and toeing off his old tennis shoes that he used for gardening.

'There's not much to talk about at the moment, to be honest. We thought we had a suspect, but it turns out he's just trying to sue his employers for a personal injury claim and has nothing to do with our victim. Kyle has a lead he's following up in the morning, but Laura and I have to go back to the farm. After that…'

Adam reached across and squeezed her hand, saying nothing.

She sighed. 'Anyway, enough about me. How's your week been?'

'Better, now that I'm here,' he said with a smile. 'Scott was back in this morning – he and the missus had a great time in Tallinn and he's given me the details for the guesthouse where they stayed, so if you fancy a short break to Estonia later in the year—'

'Yes,' said Kay, then grinned. 'A break anywhere sounds good at the moment. Was it busy without him?'

'Very, so thank goodness Claire could cover for him –

I've been speaking to her about becoming a full-time member of staff as well.'

'Really?'

'The surgery's doing well for itself, and it's getting to the point where both Scott and I are booked days in advance, sometimes weeks for routine surgeries,' he explained. 'I think I'm ready for the investment.'

Kay clinked her glass against his. 'That's so exciting. Congratulations.'

'Thanks.' Adam took a sip of wine before continuing. 'Of course, it'll mean we'll have more time together in between your shifts too, and I can maybe take on one or two extra speaking engagements next year.'

Settling into her chair, Kay looked around at the orchard as the sun's rays turned burnt orange above the neighbouring rooftops, and then eyed her phone screen as another three email alerts appeared.

She sighed. 'If we're planning on spending more time together, then I definitely need two detective sergeants. I've just got to hope that headquarters agrees.'

TWENTY-TWO

The next morning, Kay stood at the end of her driveway and held up her hand in greeting as Laura's pool car appeared at the top of the lane and headed towards her.

There was a freshness to the morning, with a distinct drop in temperature from the past week and a half, and an autumnal chill to the air that warranted a jacket for the first time in days. It was noticeably darker when the alarm went off too, and as she had crept around the bedroom after her shower whilst trying not to disturb a slumbering Adam, she eyed the shorts she had been wearing the night before and wondered if it was the last time she would see them until the following year.

Laura lowered the window as she eased the car to a standstill. 'Morning, guv. Traffic's not too bad at the moment.'

'Makes a change.' Kay slung her bag into the passenger footwell after retrieving her mobile phone and got in. 'Does Cassandra know we're coming over?'

'No,' said Laura, shooting her a sideways glance

before returning her attention to the road. 'Is that okay? I figured this way, she wouldn't have time to discuss anything with Justin before we turn up, or wonder what we were going to ask her.'

'Good idea.' Kay adjusted her seatbelt and watched as the urban sprawl of Maidstone gave way to lush greenery, the hedgerows and trees now fringed with rich golds as the summer was left behind. 'I'd like you to lead this one. You've already spoken to Joseph, so you'll be able to better gauge what his relationship is like with his daughter-in-law.'

'I agree. I want to find out more about the farmhand he said Justin fired – the bloke who won't talk to either of them now, and I'll also mention the two women that used to run the tours with him in case there's anything untoward there.'

'That's a good start. Do you have names for those people?'

'Joseph told me, yes. I've managed to track all three of them down, and Gavin's going to phone them this morning to arrange interviews with them as soon as we can. Hopefully that'll be today.'

'Great, thanks.' Kay spotted the turning for the village leading to the farm ahead of them, and checked her emails while Laura navigated the narrow winding lane.

There were still no lab test results from Harriet's forensic search, and she hated having to ask the busy specialist when they would be received, but her conversation with Sharp last night and the thought of the victim's family having no idea what had happened to him galvanised her into action, and she typed a quick apologetic text to Harriet requesting an update.

She finished typing as Laura turned into the farm yard, and saw that Justin's four-wheel drive was missing along with both tractors. 'Looks like it's business as usual here.'

'That's Cassandra's car over there, so at least she's around this morning,' said Laura. She pointed to a second car. 'And Gloria's here early.'

'I'd imagine she's doing her best to salvage what she can from the tours,' Kay mused. 'Okay, well let's go and see what Cassandra has to say, shall we?'

Laura led the way over to the farmhouse, rang the bell, and stared at her feet while she waited for the door to open. Kay said nothing, letting the younger detective have a quiet moment of reflection for any last-minute questions she was contemplating and instead looked up at the window above at the twitch of a curtain.

Moments later, footsteps on the hallway's tiled floor reached her, and the door swept open.

'Sorry, I thought you were another reporter,' said Cassandra, her face stricken as her gaze darted beyond them to the lane. 'Come in, before anybody sees you.'

Kay glanced over her shoulder before going inside, but failed to see any strange vehicles. 'I can't see anyone.'

'Trevor gave the last one an earful before sending him on his way.' Cassandra closed the door. 'He can be quite… persuasive when he needs to be. Gloria keeps telling us to keep the gate locked but if we do that, it's a pain in the backside for any deliveries and the tractor drivers when they're all under pressure to get the harvest in.'

Laura listened to Cassandra and said nothing while they followed her into the living room.

The woman indicated the armchairs next to the empty hearth, then fussed over tidying the coffee table of magazines before sitting on the sofa opposite the two detectives.

'I appreciate that it must be very difficult for you,' Laura began. 'I do have some more questions for you though. Would that be all right?'

Cassandra sighed as she sank back into the cushions. 'I suppose so. I mean, of course – some poor man's been killed, and you're trying to find out who did it. What do you need to know?'

'I'd like to learn more about Shane Vincent, the labourer who used to work here. Why did he leave?'

'Shane Vincent? But that was two years ago, just after Joseph retired. What's that got to do with—'

'If you could just answer the question please.'

'He and Justin had a disagreement. To be honest, it was always going to happen the moment Joseph retired.' She smiled sadly. 'And it doesn't help with him still living here, even if he is over in the cottage.'

'Could you elaborate? What was the disagreement about?'

'Justin suspected Shane was siphoning off fuel for himself, and confronted him. He denied it at first, but then Trevor saw him drinking in the local pub with someone who was known to have been involved with machinery thefts from farms, and Justin didn't have a choice. He terminated Shane's contract the next day – and that's why all our machinery has been kept under lock and key in the sheds at night since. Shane's the type of person who'd retaliate.'

'What did Joseph have to say about it?'

'He hit the roof,' Cassandra said. 'He and Shane go back years – he felt that we were overreacting. Justin couldn't make him see that if fuel was being siphoned off it was likely we were haemorrhaging in other areas as well.'

'Did you report Shane to our Rural Crimes team?'

'Like I said, it was only a strong suspicion. Too hard to prove, but we knew.'

'Has he caused you any trouble since firing him?'

'No. Justin made it clear that if he did, we'd get the police involved.' Cassandra grimaced. 'It did make it bloody difficult for a while though, what with him living locally as well. Our name was mud for a while in the village, until other people got the measure of him and calmed down. It's only this latest harvest that I've been happy enough to leave that gate open during the day, and that's only because we installed those security cameras at the beginning of the year.'

'Was there any particular reason for that?'

Cassandra shrugged. 'A sad fact of farming is that thefts are all too commonplace. It made sense to invest in them, and it keeps the insurers happy – although the premiums keep going up anyway.'

'And the two women who used to conduct the hop garden tours alongside Justin and Trevor? Why did you end their contracts?'

'Because we were taking less bookings than normal for a little while. We couldn't afford to keep them. Justin's focus was taken with re-establishing areas of the land that Joseph had neglected for too long, and so he and Trevor opted to run all the tours themselves. I think from next year we'll need to get some extra help in though, even if it's just for one or two days a week.' Cassandra paused. 'That's if we've still got a viable business next year, after what's happened.'

'Does Justin get on with his father?' Laura asked.

Kay saw the other woman stiffen before answering.

'He gets on with him. If they weren't family, I don't think he'd have much to do with him though.'

'Why?'

'Justin said from the start that he wanted to return the farm to its original roots, reduce our reliance on arable crops and increase hop production. It's how his grandfather farmed the land. Joseph was different – he worked against the soil around here, not with it. He plied so much fertiliser into the two fields at the southern end of the property, it's taken until now to get them into a state where the hops will grow as well as the ones you see just through the gate. And all because he wanted to produce grains that just aren't suitable for growing around here.'

Laura frowned. 'Surely Joseph would've wanted to do what his own father was doing before him if the farm was so successful all those years ago.'

'You'd think so, wouldn't you?' Cassandra gave a slight shake of her head. 'But Joseph always has to be right – and he's often contrarian with his views too, which doesn't help. He'll deny it, of course. But then when he found out how much the land might be worth, he lost interest in farming altogether. He was running the place into the ground just to prove his point that it was time to move on. Thank God Justin persuaded him otherwise.'

'Has Joseph ever been violent towards anyone here, past or present?'

'Not that I've seen, no, and nobody's ever reported anything like that. He can be cruel with his words, but I don't think he's ever been physically violent.'

Laura glanced at Kay, who gave a slight shake of her head and reached into her bag.

'Thanks for your time, Cassandra,' she said. 'One last thing – this is a photograph of the man who was found in your field. It was taken once he'd been cleaned up before the post mortem earlier this week. May I show it to you in case you recognise him?'

'Yes, okay.' The woman took the photograph from Kay with a shaking hand, peered at the image, then gave it back. 'I've never seen him before, but as you can see, I spend most of my days in the office here in the house where we manage the financial side of the farm. If he was sneaking around in the yard or something, I wouldn't have seen him. Did Justin know who he was?'

'Sadly not,' said Kay, putting the photograph away and rising to her feet. 'He remains a mystery at the moment.'

'Thanks for your time, Mrs Mallory,' said Laura. 'We'll see ourselves out.'

Standing in the yard a few moments later, Kay watched as Howard steered a laden trailer through the gate and turned his tractor towards the drying facility. He nodded by way of greeting as he passed, and then her gaze caught movement in the window of the farm's reception office in the converted stable block opposite.

'Let's have a quick word with Gloria while we're here, in case she's heard anything new,' she said, already setting off. 'I get the impression she's the eyes and ears of this place.'

Laura smiled, dropping the car keys back into her bag and falling into step beside her. 'You wouldn't be wrong there, guv.'

TWENTY-THREE

After leaving the incident room and weaving his way through the usual heavy traffic out of Maidstone and onto the M20 motorway, Kyle settled in for the short drive to Wrotham Heath behind a Belgian-licensed articulated truck and turned up the radio.

Tapping his fingers along to a ten-year-old rock hit that had taken the charts by storm at the time, he hummed the chorus under his breath, then stopped as his mobile phone trilled from its position in the dashboard cradle. He recognised the number and toggled the answer button on the steering wheel.

'Tell me you've found it,' he said.

'Morning to you, too,' replied a female voice. 'And yes, we have.'

Kyle beat the wheel with his fist. 'Awesome work, Nadine.'

'Don't thank me,' said the young constable. 'I got a phone call from traffic division just now – they got a report of a burnt-out vehicle matching our description down a lane outside Kemsing that's notorious for fly-tipping. By the time the fire brigade got there, the flames had taken hold and they were more concerned about the surrounding vegetation because it's been so dry lately.'

'Oh no,' Kyle groaned. He eased off the accelerator, his initial excitement waning. 'How much is left of the van?'

'Not a lot,' said Nadine, her voice grim. 'I called Harriet anyway and she's sending Patrick and another two SOCOs over there now to take a look for us. Oh, and the licence plates were removed before it was torched, so it was only identifiable by the VIN on the chassis. At least you can let the owner know so he can tell his insurers.'

'Yeah, there's that.'

'Sorry to be the bearer of bad news.'

'No problem – we knew this was going to be a long shot. I'll see you when I get back.'

'Okay.'

Kyle ended the call, then angled the car off to the left and down the slip road signposted for Wrotham. He found Rex Trimble's plumbing supplies business along a narrow road that had once been coated with asphalt but now had a cracked crème brûlée-like surface.

He winced as the car's suspension found another deep pothole, the vehicle rocking from side to side before lurching forward once more.

The road was a dead end that widened to accommodate three dilapidated industrial units and a fourth that had been reinforced with steel shutters across its singular window and warehouse-like entrance. The doors to the warehouse were open and two pale blue panel vans were parked outside, the paintwork of each liveried with the name of the business. Beside those was a smaller van bearing the insignia of a local security camera specialist.

The specialist himself was up a ladder, fixing a new camera above the shuttered window. He glanced down as Kyle emerged from his car.

'You the police?'

'Is Rex around?'

'In the office, at the back of the warehouse.'

'Thanks.'

Kyle ignored the man's inquisitive gaze that followed him through the open door, and blinked to adjust his eyesight to the gloomy interior.

There was strip lighting in the ceiling but its inadequate luminosity cast shadows into the corners and sent dust motes spiralling in the air. The space itself was filled with stainless-steel interlocking shelving that ran in long rows between the door and the back of the unit, resembling one of the large DIY warehouses on the fringes of Maidstone, and just as organised.

As he passed PVC piping, toilet U-bends, gleaming taps, ceramic cisterns and sinks, he wondered why Rex Trimble had only now thought to install security cameras after having his van stolen.

He followed the sound of raised voices and found the plumbing supplies owner in a box-like room at the back of the warehouse talking to a second man who was wearing a polo shirt with the company name embossed across the left breast pocket.

Trimble had his back to Kyle but the other man held up

his hand to silence him at the sight of the detective, and Trimble glanced over his shoulder.

'Help you?'

'Detective Constable Kyle Walker, Kent Police. I was wondering if I could have a word, Mr Trimble?'

'Of course. Wayne, I'll leave that with you, but like I said – make sure we don't end up paying for the ones that were broken this time, all right?'

'No problem, Rex. Leave it with me.'

The polo shirt-wearing man gave Kyle a curt nod as he passed, then disappeared into the warehouse.

'Problem?' Kyle asked.

'One of our suppliers changed courier company last week, and they're hopeless,' said Rex, running a hand over thinning pale brown hair that was flecked at the edges with silver. He beckoned Kyle over to a desk that was rapidly disappearing under delivery dockets and invoices and pulled over a metal and plastic chair from the corner, pointing to it before he sank into a matching one in front of a computer screen. 'And Wayne didn't check last week's delivery until after the courier had driven off so now I'll have a hard time proving the goods were damaged on arrival, and not since they've been here in the warehouse.'

'I'll try not to take up too much of your time, then.'

'No, no.' Trimble patted his hand in the air. 'Sit. I appreciate you coming out here. I take it this is about my van. Have you caught the bastards who stole it?'

'Sorry to be the bearer of bad news, but I was on the way over when I received a call to say the van's been found abandoned and burnt out.'

'Shit.' Rex sighed and shook his head, then frowned. 'You said you were on the way over here when you heard about that. What are you here for then?'

Kyle reached for his notebook. 'I have some questions in relation to another active investigation we believe your van might've been involved in.'

'Oh? Like what?'

'First of all, when did you discover that the van was missing?'

'Monday morning when I turned up here. I've got eight vehicles in the fleet – you saw two out there, the other five now are doing deliveries. The drivers take them home and I usually do the same, but we're having our driveway relaid at the moment and there's only room for the missus's car on the street so I left my van here and she picked me up when I finished on Saturday afternoon.'

'I saw the camera being fitted outside. I don't suppose you have any others?'

'Only in here,' Trimble replied, wagging a finger to indicate the warehouse. 'That's where all the money is, after all. Usually, anyway. Obviously after this, I'm taking more precautions. The insurers are taking the piss with the excess, and now that someone knows this place is here, I'm a target, aren't I?'

Kyle didn't correct the man. He knew too well from his days in uniform that repeat burglaries on properties were common, especially those in out of the way or remote locations.

'Did they take anything else?'

'Just the van, but that's put our delivery schedule under

pressure this week, and I've got no idea when the insurers are going to tell me to get a replacement.' Trimble's lower lip puckered. 'At least it's been found, I suppose. They might process the claim faster now.'

'What time did you leave here on Saturday?'

'Just before four. We offer deliveries up to noon but then I usually spend an hour or so sorting out paperwork, any last-minute orders for Monday morning, that sort of thing. I phoned Julie at three to say I was ready and could she pick me up – she was at the gym, the one in Sevenoaks, so I s'pose it was about ten to four by the time she got here.'

'Did you see anybody acting suspiciously, hanging around here or by the entrance to the main road?'

Trimble shook his head. 'There's nobody else here – those units out there have been empty for nearly a year now. I guess that's half the problem. If it was busier, it might've put off the bastards who stole my van. And I didn't spot anybody at the end of the lane. To be honest, I was too busy checking messages on my phone while Julie was driving, and we were in a bit of a rush because she'd bought tickets to see a band at Leeds Castle that night.'

Kyle nodded, updating his notes. 'I saw the posters for the concert. Any good?'

'Yeah, brilliant.' Trimble's face clouded. 'Just a shame it was spoiled finding out the van had been nicked when I got back here on Monday.'

Reaching into his pocket, Kyle took out a still image from the village shop's CCTV footage where Sean had frozen it to capture the van driving past. 'Can you confirm this is your van, Mr Trimble?'

The man leaned forward and took the photograph, his brow furrowing. 'Yeah, it is. Where'd you get this?'

'A village convenience shop a few miles from Mallory's hop farm. Do you know it?'

'I drink beer, I don't worry about where it comes from,' Trimble said, and handed back the photograph. 'What was it doing there?'

'That's the subject of our enquiries at the moment,' Kyle replied. 'But you're sure it's your van?'

'Yes, that's mine all right.'

Kyle looked around at the filing cabinets and dust-covered shelves bowing with the weight of the equipment manuals lining them, and then back to Trimble. 'Have you had any other trouble here in the past?'

'No, never. That's why this has been a bit of a shock to be honest.' The man leaned back in his chair, his face weary. 'We've been lucky until now, I suppose. And maybe I've been guilty of being naïve thinking this place was tucked out of the way enough to be safe. I mean, the shutters came with the building when I first leased it ten years ago, but having to put up cameras now… I'm going to be paranoid for a while yet, that's for sure.'

'Can you recall seeing anybody in the past month or so who might've been recce'ing the place, or hanging around the other units here?'

'No, nothing like that.' Trimble frowned. 'And they don't usually send out a detective for a stolen vehicle, do they? What's going on?'

'I wish I knew,' said Kyle, then pushed his chair back. 'Thanks for your time, Mr Trimble. We'll be in touch if we have any further questions.'

'No problem. Do me a favour? Tell your lot to hurry up and send that paperwork through to my insurers.' Trimble waved his hand over the documents strewn across the desk. 'I need to get a new van and sort out these orders before my customers go somewhere else.'

TWENTY-FOUR

The door to the farm office swung open before Kay and Laura had a chance to knock, and Gloria Barkham stood on the threshold, her expression one of curiosity.

'Any news?'

'Not yet, Mrs Barkham,' said Kay. She withdrew her ID. 'I'm Detective Inspector Kay Hunter. You've already spoken with my colleague, DC Hanway. I wondered if I could ask you some further questions?'

'Of course.' Gloria ushered them inside.

Kay looked at the display showing the Mallorys' farm through the years, the attention to detail in the mock English pub at the back of the room, and the gleaming beer pumps along the bar, and bit back a sigh at the thought of the repercussions for all involved if she didn't find out who murdered their victim.

The Mallorys had done well for themselves, working long hours and at the mercy of both the weather and bureaucracy, and were now faced with financial ruin unless she and her team managed to get a breakthrough soon.

And then there was the victim's family, who were currently unaware that their son, husband, father perhaps, now lay in the Darent Valley Hospital.

Kay gave a slight shake of her head at a polite cough from Gloria, who shot a brief smile at Laura, then sat behind her desk and rested a hand on a series of brochures that were fanned out across it. 'I was just proofreading our new marketing campaign for next year's crop. Justin's keen to have these ready for the hop festival to showcase what we're doing here to some of the trending small breweries.'

Kay cast her gaze across the shiny flyers with photographs showing the lush bucolic scenery around the Mallorys' farm. 'I realise you've already spoken to DC Hanway, but we've now got a photograph of the man who was found dead here, and I wondered if you'd take a look in case you recognise him?'

Gloria paled. 'I don't know... will it give me nightmares? I don't sleep well as it is at the moment.'

'It was taken before the post mortem, but there's no blood or anything,' said Kay. 'He could be sleeping.'

Gloria still looked unsure, so Laura leaned forward.

'Gloria, we need to try and find out who he is. He's got a family out there somewhere, friends who are going to be wondering where he is.'

The woman closed her eyes, and then nodded before looking at Kay. 'All right, show me.'

'Thank you.' She handed over the photograph, and then watched as Gloria's brow puckered. 'What is it?'

'He was here. In the summer.'

Kay's heartbeat skipped. 'Are you sure?'

'I think so. He looks familiar. Hang on.' Gloria dropped the photograph on top of the brochures then hurried over to a dark green metal filing cabinet in the corner and started riffling through hanging files.

She slammed the top drawer shut, then started on the next, muttering under her breath before snatching up a file near the back and bringing it over. 'These are the health and safety declarations we get every tour visitor to complete for our insurers, in case they're injured. It basically states that they understand that this is a working farm, and that they're to comply with our instructions at all times, no messing about, etcetera.' She gestured at the bar area behind them. 'It's why we're so careful about how much alcohol we serve here too, even if most of the tourists turn up in a minibus with a designated driver.'

Kay inched her chair forward and watched as Gloria sifted through the records. 'And what are those documents, in amongst the declarations?'

'The list of visitors for each tour,' she said, holding a stapled set of pages. 'After each group of guests signs their health and safety declaration, I collate them and add the final list from our booking system to the top so I've got everything in one place. It just makes it more efficient if I ever have to go back and follow up with something, like lost property, permissions to use photographs of guests for marketing images, things like that.'

'I don't suppose I could convince you to come and work for us, could I?' said Kay with a slight smile. 'My exhibits officer would love you.'

'Oh, well. I just do the best I can.' Gloria's cheeks coloured, and then her eyebrows shot upwards and she pulled a set of pages from the folder. 'Here it is. I remember this one because he was with some friends of his, and Trevor had to ask them twice to tone down their language. I think they'd had a few drinks before they got here, and they were a bit loud. He said they were making the other visitors uncomfortable.'

'Do you have a name?' Kay resisted the urge to reach across and snatch the pages from the woman.

'Hang on.' Gloria flicked through the pages until she found the one she sought. 'Here you are. I remember him, because he was nicer than the others. He came and apologised to Trevor and me just before they left. I think he was embarrassed by the others' behaviour. He's Dean. Dean Spencer.'

Kay took the pages from her and looked at the signature that adorned the bottom line of the health and safety declaration. She smiled, recognising the awkward slant of someone who wrote with their left hand, just like Adam whenever he signed a formal document. 'I don't suppose you've got the address for him, do you?'

'Not for him, because he only had to sign the health and safety declaration,' said Gloria. 'But I do have someone else's contact details. It was his friend who booked the tour, you see.'

She reached over and pointed to the front page and waited for Kay to turn to it. 'That's him.'

For the first time since Tuesday, Kay felt a surge of adrenaline at the thought that she finally had the breakthrough she and the team had so desperately sought. 'May I take a copy of this?'

'Of course you can. Give me a minute.'

Kay watched as Gloria walked over to a small printing and copier machine. The motor whirred to life while Laura updated her notes.

'That was lucky,' said the younger detective. 'His name wasn't on the list she gave me on Wednesday.'

'Very,' Kay replied. 'Now we just need our luck to last a little longer while we find out who the bloody hell killed him.'

TWENTY-FIVE

Gavin climbed out of the pool car and eyed the row of terraced houses along a run-down street on the fringes of Staplehurst.

The houses were of a similar design with slate-tiled roofs, two upper windows and a front door and living room window below. In front of each house was a small garden area that most residents had either turned to gravel or concrete. The one belonging to Shane Vincent was tidy, like the neighbouring property, with potted plants in terracotta tubs dotted around the gravel area.

Gavin turned his attention from the house to his mobile phone and reread the text from Kay that had appeared a few moments ago. Her conversation with Cassandra changed his interview strategy, but he still had questions for the man who Justin Mallory had fired two years ago.

He locked the car and with a renewed determination made his way across the road to number fourteen.

Small square concrete slabs led the way between the

pavement and the front doorstep, and Gavin stepped around a small pile of cat shit before ringing the doorbell.

A woman answered after a few moments and peered up at him, her sandy blonde hair tucked into a topknot and her cheeks flushed. She used the cuff of her denim shirt to wipe away her fringe from her eyes and sighed. 'Whatever it is you're selling, we're not interested. Can't you read?'

Gavin glanced at the sticker above the letterbox that wished numerous ills upon any unwanted guests, then held out his identity card. 'Detective Constable Gavin Piper, Kent Police. Is Shane in?'

The woman frowned. 'What's this about?'

'Is he here?'

She shrugged, then stepped aside to let him through. 'He's out in the garden. You'll need to go through the kitchen to get to it. It'll save you walking to the end of the street and then down the alley.'

'Thanks.' He wiped his feet on the coir mat, waited while she shut the door with a resounding thud, and then followed her along a short hallway and into a tiny kitchen that had been extended at the rear with a conservatory. 'And you are…?'

The woman paused and looked over her shoulder. 'I'm Louise, his wife. The door through to the garden's open. You'll find him either in the shed, or down the back somewhere.'

With that, she walked out of the kitchen and he heard another door slam at the end of the hallway. Turning his attention back to the garden, he spotted movement beside a wooden arbour.

A man in his late forties had his back to the

conservatory and was busy pruning a spindly grapevine that covered the trelliswork, his brown hair tied back in a ponytail while he worked. He wore a light blue T-shirt speckled with dirt and grass stains over faded jeans, while a pair of sturdy but battered walking boots protected his feet.

Gavin cleared his throat as he approached. 'Mr Vincent?'

The man jumped in surprise and turned around, one hand clutching tendrils of small branches while a pair of wicked-looking secateurs were grasped in the other. 'Who the hell are you? Who let you in?'

'Your wife answered the door,' said Gavin, then held up his warrant card and introduced himself once more.

The man's eyes narrowed. 'What do you want?'

'I'd like to ask you some questions about Mallory's hop farm, in particular, your relationship with Joseph and Justin Mallory.'

'There *is* no relationship.'

'Is there somewhere we can talk?'

'I've got nothing to say about them.'

'I'm in the middle of a murder investigation, Mr Vincent, and I've got no time for this bullshit.' Gavin glared at him. 'We can talk here, or down the station, which means I'll have to phone for a patrol car and then wait while they escort you to it in front of your neighbours. Your choice.'

'All right, all right. No need to get your knickers in a twist.' Vincent stalked over to a growing pile of branches, leaves and other detritus, then crossed to a wooden picnic table near the arbour and put down the secateurs. He folded his arms and leaned against the table. 'What do you want to know?'

'Why did Justin Mallory end your contract at the farm?'

'We didn't see eye to eye, and he thought it was best I leave.'

'Eye to eye about what?'

'He accused me of stealing fuel.' Vincent snorted.

'Did you?'

'No, I bloody didn't.' The man stuck out his chin. 'I told him where he could stick his job.'

'Was that before or after he gave you your marching orders?'

'What does it matter?'

'Just answer the question, Shane. My offer of a slightly uncomfortable room back at the station is still open.'

Vincent sneered. 'He didn't believe me, no matter what I said. He just wanted me out of the way because he was trying to save money.'

'Why would he do that? The farm was doing well after he took over from his father, wasn't it?'

Vincent crossed his arms. 'It was, which is why I asked him for a pay rise. I hadn't had one for over a year, and I reckoned once his idea about growing lesser-known varieties took off he'd be raking it in. But he said he couldn't afford it, and maybe if I asked him in a few months' time he might be able to consider it. Then about a week later, I got accused of stealing fuel. I looked it up online. It's called a constructive dismissal, so I didn't stand a chance. Justin gave me a week's pay and told me to foxtrot oscar.'

'I heard you ignored Joseph a few weeks after you left the farm, when he saw you at the supermarket. Why do that if you and he were so close while you worked for him?'

'I was embarrassed. Thanks to bloody Justin Mallory, everyone around here thought I'd been stealing from them. I couldn't get any work for a few months. I didn't want anything to do with any of them anymore.'

Gavin frowned. 'It seems extreme for Justin to fire you just because you asked for a pay rise. Are you sure that's all it was about?'

'Yes.'

'Where were you on Sunday?'

'What?'

'Sunday. Where were you between the hours of four in the afternoon and seven o'clock the next morning?'

Vincent's eyes narrowed. 'What's this about?'

'Where were you?'

'I was visiting my dad at his nursing home in Sittingbourne until about five on Sunday, and then I called in to my sister and her husband's place on the way home for a barbecue. I had a day off on Monday, so I stayed over and had a few beers with them.'

'I'll need their details.' He ignored the sigh that preceded Vincent's answer, wrote down the sister's address and then looked up from his notebook. 'Where are you working now?'

'I'm contracting with a tree surgeon based near Aylesbury. Bit of a hike some days, but the money's good.' Vincent glanced sideways at a noise from the conservatory and Gavin turned to see Louise standing at the door. 'What?'

'I'm going out. I won't be back for a few hours.'

'Whatever.' He turned back to Gavin. 'And before you ask, we're getting a divorce.'

'None of my business, Mr Vincent,' Gavin replied, and tucked away his notebook. 'I'll see myself out.'

TWENTY-SIX

Laura took one look at the picturesque whitewashed cottage that nestled between a large willow and a wizened apple tree, and bit back a sigh.

Fifteen minutes ago, Lucas Anderson had confirmed that the body in his morgue was that of Dean Spencer, the young man's photograph matched with those on his social media profiles. A formal identification would be required, but for now Laura and Kay were able to let Dean's family know before they learned of his brutal murder via the media.

There was a tidy privet hedge separating the house from the lane and a large garden in front of it that boasted a lawn that had the sort of ramrod-straight tramlines she would normally associate with a tennis club, which was bordered by various shrubs and saplings. The sweet aroma of freshly cut grass filled the air, and she could hear the whirr of the mower somewhere around the back of the property.

The cottage had an aged thatched roof through which a

brick chimney poked out at one end. A satellite dish fixed to one side of that was the only concession to modernity, otherwise she felt that she had stepped back in time. There was even a Victorian-style cast iron lamp post beside a pond to the left of the gravel path. She approached the front door, which had two vertical frosted glass panels set into the solid oak.

Kay's footsteps crunched behind her, their pace slowing as they drew nearer.

'I hate being the one who has to tell them,' Laura murmured over her shoulder. 'It breaks my heart every time.'

'Same here, but they need to know. Imagine what the alternative would be – there are plenty of others who have loved ones on our missing persons list and have no idea what's happened to them.' The DI rang the doorbell, then straightened her jacket and squared her shoulders. 'Here goes.'

The door opened, and a woman in her mid-sixties peered out, her expression one of confusion. 'Yes?'

'Margaret Spencer? I'm Detective Inspector Kay Hunter, and this is DC Laura Hanway. Is your husband in?'

'What's this about?'

'May we come in? Then I'll explain.'

Laura heard the sound of the lawnmower cut out, and a few moments later a male voice rumbled through the house. 'Mags? Was that somebody at the door?'

'It's the police,' the woman called. 'They want a word.'

She ushered them inside, and Laura found herself in a reception room that was painted in a pale yellow that accentuated the exposed beams crisscrossing the walls. A series of watercolours were hanging from picture hooks on the far wall, and a pair of comfortable-looking armchairs had been placed beside the window. Margaret hurried past those and led them into a kitchen at the back of the property where a man with closely-cropped silver hair balanced against the back door frame, toeing off a pair of old trainers.

He looked up as they entered, and Laura saw the confusion in his eyes.

'What's going on?' he asked.

Kay looked around the room and gestured to a walnut-hewn round table with four chairs beside a bookshelf laden with cookery books and an Aga oven. 'Shall we sit down?'

Laura saw the couple share a worried glance, but they did as the DI suggested and each took a seat beside the bookshelf.

'Margaret, Rowan, I'm very sorry but I'm going to have to ask you some questions to begin with,' said Kay. She pulled out a chair and sat in front of them while Laura remained standing and tried not to let the imminent grief pinch at her heart.

'Okay,' said the woman. 'But call me Maggie. Everybody else does.'

'Thank you. Please could you tell me, when did you last speak with Dean, your son?'

'Why? What's happened?' Rowan's eyes widened as Maggie's hand shot out to clutch his. 'What's going on?'

'Could you tell me when you last spoke with him?' Kay said. 'It's really important.'

'On Friday evening, just before he was about to go into

a meeting,' said Maggie, her face pale. 'He's coming here for lunch next Sunday.'

Laura saw a flicker of pain in Kay's eyes, and then the DI took a deep breath and clasped her hands together on the table.

'I'm very sorry to have to tell you this, Maggie and Rowan, but we have cause to believe that Dean is the victim in a homicide investigation I'm leading—'

'No…' Maggie wailed, and turned to Rowan, her face stricken. A wail wracked her body, while tears streaked her husband's cheeks.

Laura bit her lip and looked at her feet while the couple's grieving filled the kitchen. She blinked and looked out the window at the sunlight bathing the lush grass as an orange and black butterfly fluttered amongst purple-flowering shrubs, then turned back at the sound of a loud sniff.

'We will need a formal identification from you,' Kay said softly, 'but we've been able to confirm from social media photographs that our victim is Dean, and we are doing everything we can to find the person or persons responsible.'

'How did… How did it happen?' Rowan asked.

'That's the focus of my investigation,' said Kay. 'And I give you my word that I'm going to find out who did this.'

The man nodded in response and hugged his wife closer. 'Where was he found?'

'At a farm, in a field,' Kay said. 'I'll be able to give you more details in time, but may I ask you some more questions? I'd like to get to know Dean, and what he might have been doing over the past few weeks.'

Maggie straightened, and wiped her fingers across her eyes before looking at Kay. 'You ask whatever you need. Anything.'

'Thank you. Where does Dean work?'

'At home,' said Rowan. 'He's been working remotely as a freelance graphic designer since leaving university. He's got clients all around the world.'

'It's why it was quite late when we spoke on Friday,' Maggie added. 'He had a meeting with a customer in Vancouver, and they're eight hours or so behind us.'

'May I ask what you spoke about?'

'Oh…' Fresh tears ran down Maggie's face. 'He wanted to ask if we were free next Sunday so he could come over for lunch. It's been ages since we've seen him and he's not great at keeping in touch – he gets so busy with work, and I suppose he has his own friends to see in his free time.'

'He can't… couldn't resist one of Maggie's Sunday roasts though,' said Rowan, wrapping his hand around his wife's and squeezing. 'Never could.'

'How did he sound to you?' Kay asked.

'Busy,' said Maggie. 'I think his mind was already on the Canadian meeting. He did say he was hoping to go out for a drink with some friends on Saturday – I think there was a football match on the TV they were going to watch in town at one of the pubs they like.'

'I don't suppose he told you which pub, did he?'

'No, sorry.' She crumpled then, leaning against Rowan while her body shook and she wailed.

Laura swallowed, trying to separate her emotions from the professional need for answers, and wondered how Kay managed to look so stoic while she gave the couple a moment. When she did speak, her voice was calming.

'Maggie, Rowan – may I trouble you to ask you for a recent photograph of Dean?' she said. 'And would you be able to let me have a note of his address? I'd like to see where he lived.'

Rowan nodded. 'Wait here. I'll be right back.'

'Thank you. Maggie, can I get you anything?' Kay reached into her bag and passed a packet of tissues across to the other woman. 'Would you like me to make you a cup of sweet tea?'

'No, thank you.' Maggie plucked a tissue from the packet and blew her nose. 'Oh my God. Why us? Why Dean?'

'I'm going to find out, I promise,' said Kay.

Laura glanced over her shoulder as Rowan returned, his mobile phone and a set of keys in his hands.

'Do you want me to send you some photos?' he asked Kay as he sat beside his wife once more.

'That would be perfect, thank you.' Kay read out her mobile number, then confirmed safe receipt of the images. 'What are the keys for?'

Rowan handed them over and recited an address. 'Dean's flat in Maidstone.'

'I'll get these back to you as soon as we've finished having a look around,' said Kay, 'and thank you for trusting me with them. Is there anything at the flat that you'd like me to bring back here?'

'His teddy bear,' said Maggie, her voice shaking. 'It's in the living room, on a bookshelf next to some photos from a backpacking trip he did a few years ago. He's had it since he was a baby.'

'I'll do that personally,' said Kay, then slid a business card across the table. 'I'll arrange for one of our family liaison officers to call in later today – they'll keep you up to date about how the investigation is progressing, and they'll be your main point of contact, but if you want to talk to me about anything, my direct numbers are on that card. You can call me anytime.'

'Thank you,' said Rowan.

'Is there anybody we can call who can come over and be with you?'

'My sister,' he said. 'She lives nearby, and she and Dean are… were… very close.'

Kay wrote down the number, then pushed back her chair. 'Again, I'm so very sorry for your loss. Thank you for giving me Dean's keys. I'll bring them back as soon as I can.'

'Take as long as you need to,' said Maggie and looked at Laura, then Kay. 'Just make sure you catch the monster who killed my baby.'

TWENTY-SEVEN

By the time Kay sat at her desk and began working her way through her emails, the sun was a low orb on the horizon casting gold and ochre hues over wisps of cloud that hinted at rain.

The smell of burnt coffee beans filled the incident room, mixing with the scent of someone's freshly applied deodorant and Gavin's current can of energy drink at the desk across from hers.

After delivering such devastating news to Dean Spencer's parents, she and Laura had returned to an incident room charged with a renewed sense of determination. Every one of her officers was now focused on finding out why the young man had been singled out for such brutal torture, and how he and his killers had crossed paths.

Kay rested her chin in her hand and scrolled through the various reports from the HOLMES2 database, running her gaze over the results of the house-to-house enquiries and the requests for security camera footage but to date, nobody had seen a man fitting Dean's description anywhere near the hop farm over the weekend. She glanced up as her desk phone trilled, and reached out to answer it before it went to voicemail.

'Hunter.'

'Kay, it's Harriet. I'm about to sign off on Patrick's report about the burnt-out van that was located outside Kemsing, but wanted to warn you – it's inconclusive whether it can be placed at that lay-by near the Mallorys' place.'

'Shit.' Kay rubbed at tired eyes. 'I don't suppose there's anything that can point us in the direction of who stole it?'

'Whoever did this used an accelerant such as petrol to douse the insides before setting it alight, and that's the problem – the subsequent fire completely destroyed the tyres. All that was left were the steel belts that support the outer tread and the wheel rims. The rubber's all burnt off or stuck to the track where it was located. We certainly can't tell if it was used to transport Dean or his killers. However, we did find a knife with a serrated blade under the passenger seat. It's been badly damaged in the fire though, so I'm unable to find any trace samples on it for DNA testing.'

'So all I've got now is CCTV footage showing the van travelling in the direction of the hop farm,' Kay said. 'And that's not going to stand up to scrutiny in a court.'

'I'm afraid not,' said Harriet. 'Look, I've got to head off, but I'll email this to you before I go so you can share it with your team. Let me know if you've got any further questions.'

'Thanks, Harriet.'

After ending the call, Kay refreshed her screen until the report appeared, then flagged it for Debbie to add to the database.

'Bugger,' she murmured, then pushed back her chair and beckoned to the four detectives who eyed her with interest. 'Let's have a talk about tasks for tomorrow.'

She led the way over to the whiteboard, calling over to Debbie as she passed, and waited while the five team members hurried over to join her.

'I don't want to distract the others from what they're working on,' she explained, 'and given that these tasks only involve you, we should be able to keep this short. First of all, the report is in about the van and unfortunately it's in such bad condition after the fire, Harriet and Patrick are unable to link it to the tread marks found near the farm. The knife they also found is badly damaged too, so we're back to square one. Laura, please can you and Kyle continue looking into Dean's friends on social media and draw up a list of people we can start interviewing in the morning? Given that it's a weekend, with any luck we should be able to speak to most of them before Monday and get some traction on this investigation at last.'

'No problem.' Laura turned to Kyle. 'If I do the social media accounts, do you want to take a look at his graphic design business and see if there's anything from that angle?'

'Sounds good,' said the newest member of the detective team. 'I'll ask Aaron to speak with Dean's parents to find out if he used an accountant or regular solicitor for his business too. I take it Aaron's going to be FLO on this one?'

'He is,' Kay confirmed. 'He's on his way over there now, so give him a couple of hours with Maggie and Rowan before you call him.'

'Will do.'

'While they're doing that, I'll put in a request with his mobile phone provider to get his call records,' said Barnes, checking his watch. 'If I do that within the next half hour, I should be able to catch somebody before they leave for the weekend.'

'Best do that now,' said Kay. 'I'll let you know if there's anything else.'

'On it.'

She watched while her colleague hurried back to his desk, then glanced at Debbie. 'Is there anything I've overlooked that you need us to do from an admin point of view? I might not be back here after going to the flat, and I'll be out early tomorrow morning as soon as Laura and Kyle tell us who we need to interview.'

'Just some overtime approvals that I've left in your tray,' said the uniformed constable. She lowered her voice. 'And I've organised a card and collection for Harry's retirement. His party's next Saturday night remember, so don't forget to put it in your diaries. I will personally hunt you all down if you forget.'

Kay smiled, and raised her hands in surrender. 'Perish the thought – and thanks, Debs.'

'Do you need me to do anything, guv?' Gavin said.

'Yes, I'd like you to come with me to Dean's flat. I'm

heading over there in about twenty minutes. I'm not expecting trouble, but just in case…'

'No problem, guv,' said Gavin. 'Better safe than sorry, especially given the nature of this one.'

'Exactly. Okay, thanks everyone. You've got my number if you need me this evening, but otherwise I'll see you here at eight tomorrow and we'll divvy out Dean's friends' interviews between us.'

She caught up with Barnes as he walked back to his desk. 'Ian, could I have a word?'

'Sure.' He paused next to the photocopier and raised an eyebrow. 'What's up?'

'Could you give Lucas a call and ask him to get in touch with Aaron to organise a formal identification? The sooner the better. I mean, we've confirmed Dean's ID with the public posts on his social media but it'll still need to be done. If he's unable to accompany the Spencers, could you go?'

'No problem, guv.' His eyes grew concerned. 'How did it go this afternoon?'

She sighed. 'Pretty awful, like they always are.'

'Did you do your usual thing and promise them you'd catch Dean's killer?'

'Yeah.'

'Guv, one day we're going to have a case that we don't solve, you know that, don't you?' he said, his brow furrowed. 'It's the law of averages.'

'I know, Ian.' Kay patted his arm and turned towards her desk, calling over her shoulder. 'But I mean it when I say it. We will find these bastards.'

TWENTY-EIGHT

Kay saw Gavin's sporty hatchback turn into the public car park and swept her handbag off the passenger seat before climbing out of the pool car and waiting while he manoeuvred into a spare bay next to hers.

The brick-clad apartment block where Dean Spencer had lived was along a short alleyway from the car park. The back windows of six of the flats overlooked the car park. Frosting was applied to half a dozen of those windows and most had blinds rolled up at the top too, so Kay assumed these were bathrooms. The remaining windows had blinds drawn and on some of the sills she could see plants in pots or crystals dangling from latches catching the last of the sun's afternoon rays.

A small park was on the other side of the cars, with a footpath that wound alongside the river and spat out pedestrians and cyclists near Maidstone's town centre.

Kay pulled a set of keys from her bag as Gavin got out of his car. 'What time are you meeting Leanne?'

'Not until seven, and that's only if she doesn't make it

home first,' he said. 'And I didn't book the restaurant until eight so we've got plenty of time if we need it.'

'Thanks.' She fell into step beside him and headed for the alley. 'At least you're on the right side of town to get home.'

'True.' He threw her a sideways glance. 'Expecting trouble?'

'I hope not. But I wanted to ask you what your thoughts were about the Mallorys without clouding everybody else's judgement. You said Shane Vincent reckons he was constructively dismissed, right?'

'Yes. He completely refuted the story about stealing fuel, and reckons they concocted that so they could get rid of him without him being able to build an unfair dismissal claim against them.'

'And now we have Roland Hammerton pulling a personal injury stunt to do something similar.' Kay paused at the communal door to the apartment block.

There were numbered doorbells for each of the twelve apartments but no single one for a building manager. Sifting through the keys that Rowan Spencer had given her, she found one that fitted the front door and opened it for Gavin.

'Flat number four,' she said, and followed him up the stairs. 'So, my question is – do you think the Mallorys warrant further investigation? Have you had a chance to speak to the two women that used to work there?'

'On my list for tomorrow, guv,' he said over his shoulder. 'I'm planning to take Laura along with me once she's finished interviewing Dean's friends with Kyle.'

'Great idea, thanks.'

'Do you think the Mallorys are up to something, and anybody who gets too close to finding out what finds themself jobless, or…'

'I don't know. Maybe. I mean, Hammerton doesn't fit into that pattern, but something doesn't feel right, does it?' She caught up with him and lowered her voice. 'And at the moment, we have no idea why Dean Spencer was killed on their property.'

Gavin paused on the second landing and opened the fire door through to the next two apartments for her. 'I'll bear it in mind tomorrow, guv, but yeah – I agree there's something not right there. I'll keep it to myself for now, and I'll catch you in the office or phone you to keep you up to date if you like.'

'Thanks.' She winked. 'Knew I could count on you. Right, do you need some gloves before we do this?'

'Got some here, guv.' He delved into his jacket pocket and extracted a pair of nitrile gloves.

'Good.' Kay pulled out a pair of her own from her bag, then found the key to number four and unlocked the door.

It opened into a short passageway with a scruffy mountain bike leaning against the wall and a jumbled heap of various sports trainers and work-like shoes behind the door. The hallway had three doors leading off of it, one for a bathroom, one for a master bedroom and the other for a smaller box-like spare bedroom that Dean had turned into an office. Walking past them, Kay found herself in an open plan living room and kitchen, with the kitchen window overlooking the car park and river as she had suspected.

'All right, do you want to take the master bedroom and

bathroom and I'll start here?' she said. 'We can do the office last.'

'Sounds good. Yell if you find anything, guv.'

Gavin wandered off as she put her bag on the kitchen counter and then walked towards a bookcase next to a large television in the corner.

She found the teddy bear Maggie Spencer was keen to have and put it next to her bag before turning back to the photographs that filled the spaces between various books about art, architecture and business management.

Recognising one or two faces from Dean's social media, she cast her eyes over the rest then turned her attention to the two drawers set into the base of the bookcase.

The first revealed some old board games, the cardboard covers frayed with age and use. She sifted through those until she found a fireproof document wallet and pulled that out.

Unzipping it, she discovered it contained a Will, Dean's birth certificate and his graduation certificate, together with a list of passwords for various banking and share dealing sites. Flicking through the legal document, she raised an eyebrow at the details, jotted down the beneficiaries' names and addresses in her notebook, and then straightened and put the wallet next to the teddy bear.

'Anything yet, guv?' Gavin called.

'A Will, but nothing untoward in here. You?'

'I've finished in the bedroom – I'll make a start on the bathroom.'

'Okay, thanks.'

Kay moved to the middle of the room and eyed the

sofa. Three cushions had been scattered across it, all bearing various travel motifs, but it didn't look like anyone had sat on it recently. Walking over to the kitchen area, she opened the refrigerator, and then recoiled at the stench of sour milk. There was a dried bowl of cold roast potatoes on one shelf and half a dozen cans of lager in the salad drawer. The freezer section contained a lasagne, an ice cube tray and nothing else.

She slammed shut the door and checked the oven and microwave next, then moved on to the cupboards.

Nothing.

'I'm done in there,' she said as she passed the bathroom. 'I'll make a start on the office.'

'I'll be there in a sec.' Gavin turned from a cupboard with a mirrored door above the sink. 'There's not much in here, just stuff for headaches and indigestion, and some condoms.'

'Okay. Nothing in the cistern?'

'Clean as a whistle, guv.'

'Thanks.'

Dean's office was uncluttered, organised, and designed so he could work as efficiently as possible. Kay whistled under her breath at the sight of the artwork hanging on the walls, noticing his signature in each corner, then spotted the 3D printer in the corner and some of the artist's latest designs displayed on a shelf beside it.

'He was talented, that's for sure,' she said as Gavin appeared. 'And busy, if that file over there full of invoices is anything to go by.'

Her colleague moved across to the desk and sifted through the documents in a two-tier tray. 'He's got contracts here from all over the world. Some big corporate names too.'

'I found his Will in the other room. He's left a lot of money to friends and charity.'

'How old was he?'

'Twenty-six.'

'Jeez, I've got a few years on him, and I haven't even got a Will.' Gavin dropped the documents back into the tray and turned to her. 'Do you think he was afraid for his life?'

Kay shook her head. 'I don't think so. Well, not when he made the Will – it's dated two years ago, and there are investment passwords with it too. I think maybe Dean worked hard, invested wisely, and was doing all right for himself.'

'Maybe somebody didn't like that then.'

'Maybe.' She glanced around the room once more, then moved to the window and looked down at the street below. An old man was walking a scruffy terrier further along, but apart from that it was quiet, the afternoon school runs and commuter rush over. 'What the hell are we missing, Gav? Why on earth was Dean killed? I can't see anything here that suggests he was up to anything dodgy, can you?'

'No, guv,' said Gavin. 'But then, I can't see anything that suggests he spent much time here at all, do you?'

'I agree.' She turned to face him. 'So where did he go when he wasn't here?'

<h1 style="text-align:center">TWENTY-NINE</h1>

Kyle finished scrolling through Dean's social media profile as Laura slowed the car to a standstill outside a row of two-bedroom townhouses in the centre of Maidstone and peered through the window at the corrugated steel wall of a large industrial warehouse that towered over the cul-de-sac's eight properties.

'Blimey,' he said. 'They squeezed these in, didn't they?'

'And charged a premium for them,' said Laura. 'I remember when they came on the market. I'd have needed a chief inspector's salary to even get a toe in the door here back then. God knows what they go for now.'

'There isn't even anywhere to park. We're in a deliveries-only spot, by the way.'

'I know.' Laura reached over and popped open the central console, then pulled out a well-worn piece of paper with a single word scribbled on it. She held it up and grinned before placing it on the dashboard. 'Reckon they'll leave us alone once they know we're the police though.'

'Or slash the tyres,' said Kyle, and opened his door. 'Come on, then.'

He led the way over to number seven, which was tucked into the furthest corner from the entrance to the dead-end street and under the shadow of the warehouse. Dark green moss filled the cracks within the concrete path that led to the front door and clung to the undersides of the white uPVC guttering and drainpipes. He could see a light on in the living room beyond slatted opaque privacy blinds.

'I guess these don't even get any sunlight,' he said under his breath.

'Yeah – the industrial site was developed the year after these were sold,' Laura replied. 'So I'm glad I didn't buy one in the end.'

She fell silent and waited while he looked for a bell and failed, then rapped his knuckles against the glass panel set into the door.

A man in his late twenties opened it, his brown hair sticking up in tufts. He blinked, then his eyes widened at the sight of Kyle's warrant card. 'Police?'

'Are you Dominic Bridger?'

'Er, yes.'

'Can we come in?'

'Er, why?'

'We've got some questions about your friend, Dean Spencer,' said Kyle. 'When was the last time you saw him?'

'Er, last week. I think. Yeah. Saturday before last.'

'Have you spoken with him since?'

'I texted him last Friday, coz we were going to go and have a beer and watch the footy.'

'What about this week?'

Dominic looked at Laura, then back to Kyle, a frown forming. 'What's going on?'

'If we could come in please, and then we'll explain.'

The man sighed, then turned away. 'Come on then. Don't judge me though – I ain't had time to clean yet. I usually do that Sunday.'

Kyle gave Laura a warning look, then stepped over the threshold ahead of her, his gaze darting left and right as he took in a narrow hallway leading to a kitchen at the rear of the building and a doorway through to a living room on the right. He glanced over his shoulder. 'All clear.'

She gave him a slight nod, then closed the door behind her and followed.

When Kyle walked into the living room his first impression was that a tornado had hit the place. Empty pizza boxes and fried chicken buckets were on one end of a two-seater sofa and covered half the coffee table, on which eight empty cans of lager were scrunched up.

A large television screen took up most of the wall space opposite the window, and a first-person shooter game was frozen in time, the scenery one of a post-apocalyptic nightmare while a score in the top left corner suggested that the man was a seasoned player.

He saw the logo in the bottom of the screen, and frowned. 'Is that the new—'

'Yeah.' Dominic grinned as he leaned across the sofa and opened the window, letting in a wisp of a breeze. 'Got it yesterday. 'Scuse the smell in here. I've been up all night playing it.'

Kyle saw Laura turn away and cover her nose for a moment until fresh air began circulating, and then focused on Dean's friend.

'You said you saw Dean last Friday, Dominic,' he said. 'Did he seem okay when you caught up?'

The man dropped into an ergonomic gaming chair and spun it lazily from side to side. 'Yeah I s'pose. We just met at that pub on the corner down the road and had a few pints while the game was on.'

'What did you talk about?'

'I don't know. The usual bollocks.' Dominic frowned and stopped the chair, planting his feet on the laminated fake wooden floorboards and stared at the two detectives. 'Look, what's going on? Is Dean all right?'

'We're sorry to have to tell you this,' said Laura, 'but Dean was found dead on Tuesday morning.'

'Dead?' Dominic blurted, his eyes widening. 'How? He only had three or four pints on Friday... he was absolutely fine when we left the pub. What happened?'

'That's what we're trying to find out,' Kyle said. He moved to the sofa, pushed aside some of the takeaway cartons, and offered the seat to Laura before perching on the armrest beside her. 'And we're hoping you can help us.'

Dominic's mouth opened and closed, and then he swallowed. 'How did he die?'

'We can't share those details at the moment,' Laura said. 'Were you aware of any problems Dean might've been having?'

'Like what?'

'Was he was worried about anything?'

'He didn't say anything to me, no.' Dominic swallowed, then leaned his elbows on his knees and closed his eyes. 'I feel sick.'

'Would you like me to get you a glass of water?'

'Yes, please – there's a filter in the fridge door.'

Kyle waited until Laura walked out to the kitchen, then turned back to Dean's friend. 'Was anything troubling him when you saw each other on Friday?'

'No.' Dominic blinked, then sat back in his chair and gazed out the window, his eyes unfocused for a moment. 'I can't believe this is happening.'

Laura returned with the water and handed it over to the man, who took a tentative sip before placing the glass next to an array of used beer and soft drink cans beside his computer keyboard. 'How long had you known Dean?'

'A few years. We met at university. He was already doing freelance design work back then, and it just took off for him after we left.'

'Dean's body was discovered at a hop farm that you'd visited with him and Liam Peyton earlier in the summer. Any idea why that might've been?'

Dominic frowned, then shook his head. 'No, not at all. Dean organised that trip at the last minute. We were meant to be going over to Orpington for a music festival but it got cancelled a few weeks before and we were all at a loose end. It was a good laugh, actually. When he first suggested it, I thought it was a bit lame.'

'We heard it got rowdy,' Laura said.

'Yeah, it did. That was my fault, actually. At least Dean

had the sense to apologise though. Why, do you think someone there killed him?'

'It's still an active investigation, and we're unable to say at the moment.'

'Where were you on Sunday night between ten o'clock and four in the morning?' said Kyle.

'Here. Gaming.'

'Can anyone vouch for you?'

'No, I was here on my own. Sometimes I log in and challenge other players, but Sundays I like to chill out. I'm often taking client calls early on a Monday, especially if they're overseas in Australia or Asia.'

'What do you do?' Laura asked.

By way of answer, Dominic jerked his thumb at the computer. 'I run a few websites doing drop-shipping, agency services for restaurant bookings, that sort of thing.'

'Business doing well?' said Kyle.

'Yeah, actually it's not too bad.' The man managed a smile. 'At least it gives me time to do what I love.'

'The gaming?'

'That, and travelling whenever I want.' He shuddered. 'I don't know if I could work in an office, not with all those people, and the politics and all that. I did some contract work while I was building up my business, and it was bloody awful.'

Kyle handed over one of his business cards. 'Again, we're sorry for your loss. Would you call me if you think of anything that might help us? Even the smallest detail can be useful.'

'Sure.' He took the card, then followed them to the

front door. He called out as they were walking towards the car. 'Detective Walker?'

Kyle stopped, then turned. 'Yes?'

'I wasn't kidding – get that game,' said Dominic, his face earnest. 'Wait until you see what they've done with stage three.'

'So what do we know so far about Liam Peyton?' said Kay, plucking her jacket from the back seat of the pool car and falling into step beside Barnes.

The house they were heading towards was a semi-detached brick home with a wide front garden and a paved driveway to the right-hand side of it. One of thirty houses that fringed a winding avenue in the eastern suburbs of Maidstone, it was set back from the road with various shrubs providing a screen to afford the residents some privacy from their neighbours and passing vehicles.

Barnes had parked a few doors along behind a building contractor's van, and pocketed the car keys before speaking.

'He lives at home with his parents, and according to his social media it's a temporary measure while he's waiting for his house purchase to go through,' he said, toggling his mobile phone to silent mode. 'We couldn't glean from our searches where that house is going to be, but I get the impression he's moving away from the area.

Some of his other posts show him hiking in the Lake District, so maybe he's heading that way.'

'Any other interests?'

'Gaming, drinking, live music, the usual,' Barnes replied. 'Same as most twenty-somethings.'

'How's yours getting on?'

'Emma's fine,' he said, a warmth radiating within him at the thought of his only daughter. 'She's coming over at the end of the month to stay with us for a weekend, which means I won't get a word in edgeways – she and Pia get on really well.'

'That's good.'

Barnes reached down to unlatch the gate that blocked the Peyton's driveway and eyed the three cars parked nose-to-tail, spotting the silver hatchback that belonged to Liam behind an older SUV. 'He's in, at least. Let's just hope he's up.'

His colleague chuckled, then rang the doorbell, her expression turning from mirth to one of neutrality as the door swung open.

A woman in her late fifties peered out. 'Is Charlotte all right?'

'Your daughter's fine,' Kay assured her without missing a beat. 'Sorry to bother you – I'm Detective Inspector Kay Hunter, and this is my colleague, DC Ian Barnes. We were hoping to have a word with Liam.'

The woman held her hand to her chest. 'Oh, thank goodness. I imagined the worst then. What's this about?'

'Just some routine questions about a matter we're investigating.'

'Is something wrong?'

'Like I said, it's just some routine questions about a matter we're investigating.'

'Oh. All right then, come on in and I'll go and find him for you.'

Barnes followed Peyton's mother and Kay into a wide living room with two large three-seater sofas arranged in an L-shape that faced a television. There were family photographs printed onto canvas lining the walls showing Liam and his sister at various life stages, the cutest ones being when they were toddlers.

He wandered over to peer at one of the pair of them at their university graduation, and raised an eyebrow. 'Twins.'

'She's older than me by two minutes,' said a voice behind him.

He turned to see Liam standing in the doorway, his face pensive. 'And I'll bet she lets you know it at every opportunity, too.'

'You're not wrong.' Liam dragged a hand through shoulder-length sun-streaked hair, then eased an elastic from his wrist and tied it back in a low ponytail. He wore a creased blue T-shirt with a familiar sports logo over black jeans, and looked like he had just woken up. 'Mum said you needed to speak with me. What about?'

'Dean Spencer,' said Barnes. 'Do you want to have a seat?'

'I don't like the sound of this,' said Liam, lowering himself onto the nearest sofa and looking up with widened eyes. 'What's going on?'

'I'm sorry.' Kay moved closer, her voice pained. 'But we have to tell you that Dean was attacked and killed six days ago. We've notified his parents, and we're trying to find out who did this to him.'

'Fucking hell.' Liam leaned back in his seat and covered his face with his hands for a moment. 'Shit.'

'Do you want me to get your mum?' said Barnes.

'No, it's okay.' The young man dropped his hands to his lap, his face miserable. 'Charlotte's off travelling in Vietnam at the moment, and mum's worried sick about her even though she messages every other day to tell us what she's up to. News like this will just make her worse.'

'Just tell us if you change your mind.'

'What happened?'

'We're trying to piece that together at the moment,' said Barnes. 'When was the last time you saw Dean?'

'Wednesday, last week. We play five-a-side footy at that club in Tovil. I can't stand going to the gym, and Dean is… was… pretty good so it was just our regular thing.' He broke off, his gaze travelling to the photographs on the wall. 'I wondered where he was this week.'

'You didn't call him?'

'I tried – it went straight to voicemail, so I just assumed he was too busy with work and I'd catch up with him tomorrow at the pub. There's a game on TV we were planning to watch together. Shit.'

'You visited a hop farm with him and Dominic Bridger over the summer,' said Barnes. 'Were there any issues?'

Liam frowned. 'The hop farm? Why is that important?'

'It's where he was found. We're trying to work out why. We heard things got a bit out of hand on the farm tour.'

'Bloody Dominic, that's what happened.' Liam shook

his head, a sad smile crossing his features. 'Dean told him not to drink shots at the pub where the minivan picked us up from before the tour, but he wouldn't listen. Dom was just gobby, that's all, but obviously it didn't go down well. Dean apologised to the bloke who was leading the tour though, and the woman who did the paperwork at the beginning. Do you think somebody there killed him?'

'We've got several lines of enquiry open at the moment.'

'Liam, this is a standard question we have to ask,' Kay said. 'Where were you on Sunday afternoon through to four the next morning?'

'I was here, just chilling out and catching up on some films I'd downloaded,' he replied. 'I nipped out at about seven to go down to the shops for some lager because we'd run out, but otherwise that was it.'

'Can anyone vouch for you at that time?' said Barnes.

Liam frowned. 'Why would… oh. Yeah, Mum was here – she was on a video call with Charlotte at some point, and then she had some friends around in the evening for a meal and drinks – it's their regular thing since they all took early retirement, sort of a revolt against the old days of having to work late night shifts.'

'What did your mum used to do?'

'She was a nurse, specialising in cardio recovery,' said Liam, a hint of pride in his voice. 'She loved it.'

'And your dad?'

'He's a financial advisor. Still working. Probably always will, even if it's just a few hours a week.'

Barnes looked at Kay, raised his eyebrow and saw her

give a slight shake of her head in response. He turned back to Liam and handed over a card.

'Again, we're sorry to be the bearers of such terrible news. If you think of anything, anything at all, give me a call on that number. My mobile's on there as well.'

'Okay.' Liam took the card and turned it between his fingers. 'Do you know how Dean died?'

'Yes,' said Barnes, then sighed. 'But we won't be sharing the details. That wouldn't be fair on you.'

Liam's gaze dropped to the card. 'I hope you find him, the one who killed him.'

'Oh, we will,' said Kay, leading the way to the door. 'Mark my words, we will.'

THIRTY-ONE

Gavin checked his watch, then turned his attention to the late-Victorian pub that nestled between a thriving charity shop and a derelict homeware store.

This end of town was avoided by tourists, forgotten by locals and frequented by many who preferred to keep their distance from the more affluent centre unless visiting out of necessity.

The pub was lacking in both character and appeal. A bright blue tarpaulin covered one end of the slate-tiled roof where scaffolding clutched to the side of the building and a faded sign announced it was undergoing repairs. Paint was peeling from window sills that had once been white and were now a dirty shade of grey, and the glass panes were smeared, with a crack in the lower corner of one that appeared to have been caused by a stone being thrown at it.

Standing in the shade of a butcher shop's awning on the opposite side of the street, the stench of raw meat and an underlying tone of detergent and bleach assaulted Gavin's senses while he bided his time and waited.

It was almost twelve o'clock, and he planned to speak to Kathryn Garnet before the lunchtime session began in earnest. The pub's doors remained resolutely closed until two minutes before the hour, and then he spotted movement and the outer door swung inwards.

Moments later, a woman in her late forties dragged a sandwich board outside and chained it to a lamp post. Gavin squinted against the noon sunlight and saw that it advertised a range of sandwiches and baguettes for lunch, the chalk marker pen streaked in places where the board had been moved back and forth each time.

He waited until a double-decker bus passed, then jogged across the street and pushed open the inner door to the pub.

It was gloomy inside, and he paused on the threshold to take in the tired-looking decor. The parquet flooring looked clean enough, but when he walked towards the bar, he felt his shoes stick to the surface and grimaced, remembering some of the nightclubs he used to frequent in his late teens and early twenties.

The bar smelled of stale lager and ale and the faint splash of lemon-scented cleaning products did nothing to disguise it, while dust clung to the beer taps. Somewhere in the building, he could hear the crash and clatter of pots and pans and assumed the kitchen was behind the back wall of the bar. A wooden swing door with a round window in it was off to the left, and the lights were on so he waited and watched to see who would appear.

The woman who had dragged out the sandwich board

pushed through the door a minute or so later, her hands laden with cutlery wrapped in red napkins and humming under her breath. She visibly jumped when she turned to the bar.

'Oh my God, you gave me a fright,' she said, then gave a light chuckle before placing the cutlery into a plastic tray on top of the bar. 'I didn't hear the front door go.'

'Sorry,' said Gavin, and held out his warrant card. 'Are you Kathryn Garnet?'

'I am, but I don't know about anybody reporting a problem to the police.' She frowned. 'Reg would've told me if something kicked off – he's always worried about our safety, bless him.'

'It's not about this place,' said Gavin. 'I was wondering if I could have a word with you about Justin and Cassandra Mallory.'

Kathryn's gaze darted to the front door, then back. 'Um, I don't know – we could get customers at any time.'

Gavin looked around the bar, taking in the dim lighting and bare walls, the worn chairs next to tables that bore scrapes and scratches like battle scars, then turned back to Kathryn. 'It doesn't look like it's going to get busy just yet. And this won't take a moment.'

Her shoulders sagged. 'All right. What do you want to know?'

'Why did you leave? I heard you were a tour guide there until two years ago.'

'I didn't want to leave. Joseph might've been a grumpy old bastard sometimes, but we muddled along and I enjoyed showing people around. I love anything to do with local history, so when Gloria told me they were looking for someone, I applied straight away.'

'Have you known Gloria for some time?'

'We were at school together but lost touch for a few years until she spotted me as a mutual friend on social media and sent me a request. We try to meet up at least once a month for coffee these days. What's this about, anyway?'

'Gloria hasn't told you?'

Kathryn gave a rueful smile. 'She might be a good friend, but she's also loyal, so no – she hasn't told me.'

Checking over his shoulder and seeing that the pub remained empty, Gavin lowered his voice anyway so it didn't reach whoever was working in the kitchen. 'The body of a young man was found in the Mallorys' hop garden. We're trying to find out why.'

'Jesus.' Kathryn covered her mouth. 'That's horrible. Do you know who he is?'

'His family have been notified, yes. I need to ask you, where were you on Sunday between six in the evening and four the next morning?'

'Here,' said Kathryn without hesitation. 'I worked the last shift, closed the doors at ten and it probably took me an hour to clear up afterwards. Then I went to bed. Sam runs the kitchen, and he and I have the flat upstairs. Perk of the job.'

Gavin heard the twinge of sarcasm in her voice and wondered what state the flat was in if the downstairs bar area was anything to go by. 'Why did Justin Mallory let you go?'

She shrugged. 'I got the impression he wanted to do

things differently, and in order to do so he wanted anyone associated with the way his father did things out of the way.'

'But Gloria stayed.'

'Gloria's indispensable. They couldn't run the place without her. Besides, the tours were her idea – and she does all the arrangements and insurances. I don't think Justin or Cass would have the time.'

'How did you feel, being made redundant like that?'

'Gutted,' said Kathryn. 'Like I said, I loved that job. Obviously it was busier in the summer months, but in the winters we were still busy helping Gloria with the other marketing bits and pieces and we still held private functions, especially at Christmas.'

'Last question for now,' said Gavin. 'Have you spoken to the Mallorys since you left?'

'No need to. They got rid of me with only a week's notice and didn't even let me have time off during that to look for new work. As far as I was concerned, it was good riddance.'

THIRTY-TWO

Laura saw Gavin's car drive under the security barrier into the police station's car park and stepped out from under the shade of the building as he circled the other vehicles and drew to a standstill beside her.

'Good timing,' she said, climbing in and fastening her seatbelt. 'Kyle and I only got back here five minutes ago.'

'How'd you get on?' Her colleague pulled into the traffic on Palace Avenue and drummed his fingers on the steering wheel while a single-decker bus in front of them discharged a stream of passengers onto the pavement at the bottom of Gabriels Hill. 'Kyle do okay?'

'He's fine, no problems there.' Laura turned the dashboard vents towards her and flapped her blouse collar until the cool air reached her neck. 'But Dominic Bridger wasn't able to shed any light on who might want to kill Dean. I'm hoping Kay and Ian had better luck with Liam. What about you?'

She listened as Gavin told her about his conversation with Kathryn Garnet, then sighed. 'It's got to be something to do with the Mallorys, hasn't it? I mean, Dean's body's there for, what, a day and a half before anyone notices him, and then there's the poisoned bines that Kay found.'

'Except we can't find a motive. Even Kathryn seemed quite stoical these days about Justin firing her when he took over the farm.'

'What about Joseph?' she tried. 'He seemed bitter.'

'Yeah, but he didn't lift Dean up into those bines on his own, did he? And why poison the plants?' Gavin shook his head. 'He might not run the farm anymore, but if the business fails, he'll be out on his arse too because the cottages will get sold alongside it, won't they?'

Laura sighed. 'True. Shit. We're getting nowhere, aren't we?'

'It certainly feels like it today.' Gavin changed gear and accelerated as he left the confines of the town's roads.

Hanging onto the strap above the passenger door, Laura tried not to dig her feet into the footwell at each bend, and instead tried to trust her colleague's natural driving instinct. She failed and gave an outward gasp as he floored the car around a tight right-hand curve. 'Gav, it's not a racetrack you know.'

'I know, but these are some of the best roads in the county.' He shot her a grin before easing off the throttle and settled into a more leisurely pace. 'That better?'

'Thank you.'

'Talk about driving Miss Daisy.'

'Very funny.' She unwound her fingers from the door strap and delved into her bag for her notebook. 'Okay, so Mia Gates was the one who studied viticulture while she was working part-time for Joseph Mallory. I traced her to a local vineyard, and the website says she's in charge of marketing these days. They've won quite a few awards, and it's been a family business for over twenty years. I checked the company's details online and everything seems fine there. Mia isn't working today, which is why we're speaking to her at home.'

'Given that you've done the background checks, why don't you lead this interview with Mia? She might respond better to you asking the questions anyway.'

'True, okay.' Laura looked up from her notes as the car slowed and saw the sign for Bethersden. 'The turning for her road is the second one up here on the right.'

Gavin pulled up outside a modern semi-detached house with a slate roof and red-tiled upper storey matching those of the other properties in the estate on the fringes of the village.

The lower part of the house had been rendered in a pale cream and there were four large half barrels arranged under the living room window containing bright evergreen shrubs.

A tidy gravel area was next to a driveway with parking for two cars and as they eased to a standstill, Laura spotted a woman in her late twenties at the door, waiting.

'Thanks for being on time,' Mia Gates said as they walked over. 'I've got to take my dog to the vet's at three.'

'I hope he's okay,' said Laura after making the introductions.

'Hugo's fine, thanks.' Mia stood to one side and ushered them through to the kitchen where a white West Highland terrier was curled up on a dog bed with a plastic protective cone fixed to his collar and a bandage around one of his back legs. 'He caught himself on some barbed wire while we were out on a walk the other week and it needed some stitches. Thank goodness they're coming out today, because he's been driving me up the wall with that cone.'

Gavin bent down and held out his hand to the dog, who gave it a curious sniff, then wagged its tail. 'He looks like he's going all right.'

'Yeah, just as well given that he's just cost me six hundred quid,' said Mia. 'Good job I love him. Right, um… do you want to sit over here? Sorry about the mess.'

She crossed to a battered oak table with four chairs around it that took up the corner of the kitchen and pushed some wine magazines and an A4-sized diary to one side.

Taking a seat beside Gavin, Laura waited until Mia was settled, then pointed at the magazines. 'I spotted the vineyard you work at in a feature in one of those online – was that all your work?'

'Yes.' Mia huffed her fringe from her eyes. 'It's non-stop though, trying to get publicity like that. There are so many vineyards in the UK now, especially here in the south east. There's a lot of competition.'

'What about competition with other growers, such as hop farmers?'

'It's a completely different business,' said Mia, her brow furrowing. 'And you're obviously here to talk about the Mallorys, so what do you want to know?'

'We'd like to learn more about your relationship with them, particularly Justin,' Laura said. 'And I'd like to understand why he fired you when he took over the farm from Joseph.'

'Because he could.' Mia shrugged. 'I was only there while I was completing my studies anyway, but I was enjoying the work.'

'Did the news come as a surprise?'

'I suppose so.' The other woman looked thoughtful for a moment, her gaze drifting to the magazines. 'I mean, we had tours booked through the remainder of the year and I thought Kathryn and I did a good job representing the farm. I loved the contrast from talking about wine all the time for my master's degree, and I got on well with everyone else there.'

'What about Joseph?'

Mia managed a small smile. 'He was all right. He had his moments, but then I suppose he was under a lot of stress running the place, especially as it was losing money until Gloria suggested the tours.'

'Were you aware that he was planning to sell the land to a housing developer?'

The other woman's eyebrows shot upwards. 'No — really?'

Laura remained silent, watching as her words sank in.

Eventually, Mia sighed. 'Well, I guess after the accident he must've felt that he couldn't cope.'

'But why sell it, instead of transferring the title to Justin?'

'I don't think he and Justin saw eye to eye about the way the farm should be run,' Mia admitted. 'And he did have a spiteful streak in him from time to time.'

'When was the last time you saw the Mallorys?'

'I haven't seen Justin or Cassandra since the day I left two years ago, but I bumped into Joseph a few months ago. I was filling up my car at that garage on the A20 between Ashford and Charing, and he was paying at the till when I walked in. He asked what I was up to, and that was it really.'

'Have you spoken to him since?'

'No, why would I?'

'One last question,' said Laura. 'Where were you on Sunday night?'

Mia frowned, and sat back in her chair, eyeing the two detectives. 'What's this about?'

'Could you just answer the question please?'

'I was playing squash at the local club. I hurt my wrist over the summer so I'm only just getting back into my playing. There were four of us there just having a knockabout.'

'We'll need their details please.'

'Okay, hang on.' Mia walked over to the counter and returned with her mobile phone. After reading out the contact details for her three squash partners, she slid it to one side. 'Are the Mallorys all right?'

'Why do you ask?'

'It's just that with all these questions, I'm wondering if something bad has happened.'

Laura gave a tight smile, then rose to her feet and signalled to Gavin that the interview was over. 'I'm afraid we can't comment. Shall we see ourselves out?'

Once outside, Gavin waited until they were approaching the car before he spoke. 'I get the impression Mia's not our suspect.'

'Me too,' said Laura, and sighed. 'And she was just at the Mallorys to get some different experience – it's obviously worked for her too, seeing the success she's having at the vineyard.'

'Hang on.' Gavin was staring at his mobile phone. 'I've had three missed calls from Kay.'

Laura fished out her phone from her bag while he phoned the incident room to discover that she too had received a series of missed calls and voicemails while they'd been speaking to Mia. Then she heard Gavin's voice turning to one of concern and waited, her heart thudding. When he finished the call, his jaw was clenched. 'What's wrong?'

'Jonathan Aspley at the *Kentish Times* has somehow found out about our victim's injuries,' he spat. 'The story's broken, and Kay's gone into damage control to try to protect Dean's parents. We need to get back to the station – now.'

THIRTY-THREE

Kay paced the carpet beside the whiteboard, her jaw set while she thumbed another text message to DI Devon Sharp and wondered which of the investigative team had betrayed her.

The incident room was subdued with only a skeleton staff remaining after the rostered officers had gone, and those left were keeping a wide berth while she gave orders and liaised with headquarters. Debbie ventured across to her with a steaming mug of coffee that she gratefully received, and gave Kay a reassuring look.

'We've been through worse, guv,' she said, her voice lowered so the other staff wouldn't hear. 'And the leak might not have come from within the team. We've had to outsource a lot of the lab testing to contractors for this one, and any one of those might've said something they shouldn't have.'

'Hmm. We'll see.' Kay put the mug on a desk beside the whiteboard and contemplated the notes covering its surface. 'Right now, I want to contain this before it goes national. It's been a slow news cycle this weekend, and I'd like to make sure we're not the ones to break that. Debbie, could you update the roster for tomorrow in case we need some more bums on seats to answer phones? If I can't slow this down, we're going to be bombarded with calls from reporters, and I don't want them clogging up the lines in case someone's trying to get through with urgent information for us.'

'Will do, guv.'

'And thanks for the coffee.'

'No problem.'

Kay turned to her detective sergeant. 'Ian, can you take a look at the task lists for tomorrow and see who's available if we need to send over a patrol to the Mallorys' farm to ward off any journalists? That's a narrow lane along there and I don't want them causing any accidents.'

'Okay. What about Dean's parents?'

'I'm going to give Aaron a call now. I've got an idea.' She dialled the uniformed constable's mobile number and he answered on the second ring. 'Have you heard?'

'Harry gave me a heads-up fifteen minutes ago, guv. What do you need me to do?'

Some of the tension left Kay's shoulders as she listened to Aaron's calm voice, and she realised that Debbie was right – none of her team would let her down by contacting the press. They cared too much about the family involved.

'Have any reporters turned up there yet?'

'Aspley was here an hour ago.'

'What happened?'

'He seemed surprised when I opened the door instead

of Maggie or Rowan, then asked if he could speak to them. I told him he couldn't, and that all media enquiries were being managed by HQ. He said he knew Dean had been tortured before he'd been killed, and that we have no suspects.'

'Did you ask him who his source was?'

'He declined to answer that question, guv.'

'Did the Spencers hear any of this?'

'No, I spoke to him on the doorstep. There haven't been any other attempts to speak with them, nobody else has turned up and I've been taking any calls that come through to their phones just in case, at their request.'

'Thanks, Aaron, that's great. I don't think it's going to stay like that for much longer though. Can you ask them if they've got friends or a relative they can stay with until we can work this out?'

'Hang on.'

She heard muffled voices in the background, and a few minutes later Aaron returned.

'Guv, Maggie says they can go and stay with her brother. He lives outside Ashford, so close enough for me to stay as liaison officer, and far enough away from here to put some distance between them and Aspley.'

'Okay.' Kay eyed the sunset hues casting a glow across the town beyond the windows. 'I'm not taking any chances with them being followed by reporters, Aaron. I need them to move tonight. Can you organise it?'

'No problem, guv. Oh, hold on – Maggie would like a word.'

'Detective Hunter?' Dean's mother sounded anxious.

'I'm here. I'm so sorry for the intrusion. That reporter should never have tried to approach you like that.'

'It's not your fault. Aaron's just explained that you want us to go to my brother's house tonight.'

'It's probably for the best.'

'I understand, it's just that… I forgot to ask you the other day. There are some photos in Dean's flat that I'd hate to lose. I wondered if you would fetch them for me?'

Kay checked her watch. 'Leave it with me, Maggie. I won't be able to get over there tonight, but I'll pick them up tomorrow. Could you ask Aaron to text me with the details of the ones you want?'

'I will, thank you. Here he is.'

'Okay, guv. I'll be going,' said Aaron. 'I'll have a word with a couple of the traffic lot to see if they're passing by here tonight and ask them to help us get Maggie and Rowan over to Ashford in case anyone's watching the place. I think using their car or a taxi might be too risky.'

'I agree, and thanks. Send over that list of photos and I'll catch up with you in the morning.' As Kay ended the call, she saw another familiar name appear on the screen as the phone started to vibrate. 'Guv?'

'It was the bloody lab,' Sharp barked by way of greeting. 'One of their freelance contractors.'

'Great, just great. Was there a bribe involved?'

'No – just loose lips after too many glasses of wine out with her girlfriends last night. She won't be working anywhere locally again, that's for sure. Harriet's livid.'

'I'll bet she is.'

'In the meantime, Kay, I have to warn you – the chief super's starting to ask why we haven't got anyone in custody yet. Expect a request next week for a review if your team don't get a breakthrough soon.'

'Shit.' Kay turned at the sound of the incident room door opening and Gavin and Laura walked in. Then she saw Kyle standing beside his desk, a phone in each hand while he coordinated between the laboratory and the team's legal advisor to draft a joint press release. 'We're doing our best, guv.'

'I know,' said Sharp, his tone not unkind. 'But it might not be enough this time.'

THIRTY-FOUR

The lane was dark, lit only by an occasional streetlight on a bend in the narrow road as it wound its way through the older streets of Bearsted, away from the pub on the village green.

Kay buried her chin in the collar of her fleece as she followed Adam and his latest patient, a brown Labrador called Poppy who was recovering from a hip operation. Their pace was slow but steady and she savoured the quietness that was only broken now and then by a passing car. She cast her gaze over the houses they passed, some with chinks of light appearing through the drawn curtains where she could see flashes of colour as television screens lit up the rooms beyond.

It wasn't yet cold enough to see her breath in front of her face, but a freshness was in the air now with the promise of colder weather to follow, and one or two of the larger houses' chimneys belched woodsmoke into the night sky, the sweet aroma reminding Kay of weekends spent at her grandparents' as a child.

'You're quiet back there,' said Adam over his shoulder. 'You okay?'

'Not really,' she admitted. 'Still in shock I guess about the leak. It's rare that it happens, but when it does… I do wish these people stopped and thought about the families they affect instead of just thinking of a way to have a go at us. It's bloody selfish, and the hours we've lost managing this crisis instead of looking for his killers…'

The lane widened as it curved towards the main road and she moved to walk alongside him, then sighed. 'Enough about me – how's Poppy doing?'

'Really well, actually.' Adam looked down at the dog, who paused to sniff at a privet hedge. 'Not bad for an old girl.'

'How are her owners?'

'Calmer since Poppy's out of the recovery room and on the mend. One of the staff members at their sheltered housing accommodation helped them set up a video link to her kennel so they could see her after her operation and I'll text them after our walk with a little video I just took to show them how well she's walking now.' He smiled as Poppy decided to leave the hedge alone and wandered ahead, her lead going taut as her nose lifted in the air. 'Given her age, I'm really pleased – and I can already tell it's given her a new lease of life.'

'Thank goodness the insurers agreed to pay for it,' said Kay. 'How long is she going to be staying with us?'

'A week or so I reckon. Her owners have enough on their plates with health issues at the moment so her recovery is one less thing they have to worry about. I'm going to drive over to see them with her tomorrow though,'

Adam said. 'Nothing like pats and hugs to keep the three of them healthy.'

Kay reached out and squeezed his hand. 'And that's why I love you so much.'

He looked down at her and grinned. 'And there was me thinking it was my lasagne-making skills.'

'That too.' She groaned as her mobile phone rang and Poppy looked back at her with a reproachful glare. Seeing the name on the screen she let Adam go on ahead before answering. 'Harriet.'

'First of all, let me say that I can't apologise enough, Kay. I've worked with that laboratory for years, and never had a leak like this. Jonathan Aspley should know better too. I thought he had more integrity than this.'

'Me too, and it's not your fault, Harriet. Thanks, though. Unfortunately the way things are being siphoned out to third parties these days, we can't control what people do with the information we give them, even if we do have strategies in place for chain of custody requirements when it comes to evidence.'

'Even so…' Harriet broke off and sighed. 'I'm afraid I've got some more bad news for you – I thought you'd want to hear it from me now rather than read it in an email when you get into work tomorrow.'

Kay froze to the spot and watched as Adam and Poppy strolled towards the junction and waited on the corner for her. 'What is it?'

'The blood sample we took on the barbed wire fence between the corn field and the Mallorys' hops isn't a match for Dean's.'

'So maybe it's from one of his killers.'

'Maybe, but we've run it through the system and there's nothing coming up.'

'So whoever killed him hasn't been arrested before now.'

'Exactly. Like I said, sorry to be the bearer of more bad news but at least it's one more thing you can cross off your list.'

'Thanks for taking the time to phone. Are you on your way home now?'

'Just as soon as I send this over to you. I'll speak to you on Monday if I've got any further updates to share.'

'Thanks. 'Night.'

Ending the call, Kay hurried to catch up with Adam and the dog, falling into step beside them as they turned back towards Bearsted.

'Bad news?' Adam asked, reaching for her hand once more.

'Frustrating news,' Kay said, her gaze lowered to the ground while she walked. 'And I'm really on the ropes with this investigation now.'

THIRTY-FIVE

Gavin stared at the plasterwork ceiling while a pale light started to eke its way through a crack in the bedroom curtain as morning approached.

A light breeze carried through the open window and he heard a blackbird chirp, closely followed by an answering call further along the street. Beyond the end of the road he could hear the occasional purr of an engine from an early delivery van heading into the town centre, but that was all.

He sighed, then reached out to the bedside table and tapped his phone screen to read the time. 'Shit.'

It was another four hours until he was due at the incident room and he knew he could use the sleep, but worry nibbled at his thoughts and disturbed his dreams.

No investigation managed by Kay had ever been subjected to a review, and he knew that was because she and her tight-knit team of detectives worked tirelessly to ensure they missed nothing.

Except this time, they had.

Gavin turned to the empty space beside him in the bed

and smiled. Leanne would be home soon from her shift with Kent Fire Services Search and Rescue, and given her workload he knew she probably hadn't eaten for much of the night. Their shifts were the reason that they often didn't see each other for days sometimes, so he threw back the sheet and headed for the shower, keen to spend some time with her before she succumbed to sleep.

He heard her key in the front door as he was towelling his hair dry and wandered to the top of the stairs. 'Morning, love. Everything okay?'

'Ugh. It was a slow night, thank goodness, but my God that makes for a long shift,' Leanne called, then appeared at the bottom of the stairs and smiled at him. 'Well, hello.'

'I was thinking of doing a fry-up for us both before I head off. Hungry?'

'Starving.'

'Give me five.'

'I'll put the coffee on.'

The smell of freshly roasted beans greeted Gavin when he walked into the kitchen a few minutes later, and Leanne was pulling a box of eggs and some bacon and sausages from the refrigerator.

'Here, sit down,' he said, taking them from her. 'You've been up all night.'

She kissed him, then sank into one of the chairs at a small table set for two. 'And you're up early.'

'I couldn't sleep,' he said, as he started frying the sausages. 'Someone leaked our investigation to the press, we don't have any suspects, and headquarters are threatening to send in another DI to oversee us.'

'Shit, sorry to hear that.'

Gavin busied himself preparing the food while his girlfriend caught up with her social media, then carried two loaded plates over to the table and grinned. 'Tuck in.'

Leanne took a sip of coffee, then launched herself at the sausages. 'This was such a good idea, thanks. So, what are you going to do next?'

'What do you mean?'

'You haven't slept, and you've got that determined look in your eyes that I've seen before. What are you thinking?'

He chuckled as he mopped bacon into a split egg yolk. 'I was thinking that we've probably got two, maybe three days before the chief super can assign a DI to audit the investigation. She won't do anything today, so I've got a head start.'

'And nothing to lose.'

'Exactly.' He waved a forkful of sausage at her while he spoke. 'So I'm going back to the beginning. Starting with the farm where our victim was found and then work my way forward.'

'How many statements are you going to have to read all over again?' Leanne said, her eyes wide.

Gavin smiled. 'I'm not going to read the statements. I'm going to speak to people.'

———

Trevor Leavitt lived in the end cottage of a terraced row of grey-bricked houses three miles from the farm and frowned when he opened his front door and saw Gavin on the step.

'What do you want?' the farm manager growled. 'It's bloody five thirty and a Sunday morning. There's got to be rules about this.'

'There are, but we're investigating a murder.' Gavin held up his warrant card. 'I don't believe we've met.'

'I'm due at the Mallorys' in an hour.'

'I realised that, which is why I'm here early. I'll keep it brief. You spoke with my inspector, Kay Hunter last week.'

'Yeah, and I've already given one of your plods my statement as well. Young girl in uniform. Blonde.' Trevor scowled. 'So, what do you want now?'

'May I come in?'

'I'm having breakfast.'

'You can talk and eat, can't you?'

'Fuck sakes.' Trevor turned away and headed down the hallway, disappearing from sight. 'Close the door behind you so you don't let the flies in. They were muck-spreading the field over the way yesterday.'

Gavin walked in and after closing the door passed a row of coats and jackets on a hook above a jumbled pile of shoes and work boots. A narrow staircase was on his right, and somewhere upstairs he heard a child giggle. He followed Trevor into a gloomy kitchen that overlooked an untidy garden backing onto a freshly ploughed field. The door to the garden was firmly shut, as was the window above the sink, and he paused beside an oven with a grease-flecked hob while Trevor leaned against the sink and shovelled the remains of a bowl of cereal into his mouth.

'So, what did you want?' the man asked. 'And keep

your voice down – if you wake up the kids, I'll never hear the end of it from the missus.'

'Have you had the results back yet from the lab about the bines that were poisoned?'

Trevor swallowed, then placed the bowl in the sink and ran water into it. 'No. I was going to chase them up on Friday but we're four days behind schedule on the harvest and that took priority. Mind you, it might not be poisoning – could just be aphids or something.'

Gavin waited until the man turned to face him once more. 'How long have you worked in the industry, Mr Leavitt?'

'About fifteen years.'

'And what did you do in the army before that?'

Trevor raised an eyebrow. 'How...?'

'Justin told us.'

'Not that it's any of your business, but I was involved in reconnaissance missions overseas.' Trevor crossed his arms over his chest. 'And that's all I'm prepared to tell you. Official Secrets Act, and all that.'

'Not a problem. Who reported the poisoning?'

'It's not necessarily... never mind. I did. I walk the trellises two or three times a week, so does Justin. When I saw what had happened, I went back to the farmhouse, got my soil testing kit and took some samples. They were sent to the lab the same day.'

'Which lab?' Gavin asked, then wrote down the details the other man provided. 'In your fifteen years in the hop industry, have you ever seen bines in that state before?'

'Once or twice.'

'And what caused that damage in those instances?'

'I don't know.' Trevor shrugged. 'I was new to the industry back then, and working for someone else. Could've been insects, or poor soil. Agriculture isn't an exact science, Detective Piper.'

Gavin pulled a copy of Dean Spencer's photograph from his pocket and turned it to show the other man. 'Do you recognise him?'

'No, I told the copper who interviewed me on Tuesday I didn't, and the same to your boss when she showed me that photo on Thursday,' said Trevor. 'And I've got no idea why he was killed at the farm either.'

'Gloria's informed us that Dean was part of a group of four men who visited the farm for one of the hop garden tours over the summer. A tour that you showed around, Mr Leavitt.'

'I show lots of people around. Did she also tell you how many visitors we've had to the farm over this summer? I can't remember everyone.'

'Apparently he and his friends were memorable because they turned up drunk,' said Gavin. 'In fact, Gloria said they were so disruptive that Dean felt the need to apologise for their behaviour once the tour finished.'

Trevor held up his hands. 'We get all sorts. Like I said, I don't remember him.'

'Where were you last Sunday, Mr Leavitt, between six in the evening and four the next morning?'

'Pardon?'

'Answer the question, please.'

'I was out, with the wife and kids. We took them swimming and then went for pizza afterwards. Got back around seven, and stayed in for the rest of the evening.'

'And will your wife provide an alibi for you?'

Trevor frowned. 'Of course she will.'

'Is she here?'

'She's a nurse. She's been at work since midnight, and won't be back for a few hours.'

'Do you have any issues with Justin and Cassandra Mallory?'

'Like what?'

'Anything at all. Any problems working for them I should be aware of?'

'No.'

'What do you think about Roland Hammerton's personal injury claim?'

'I think he's reaching.' Trevor smirked. 'The man won't win that one, and he's shot himself in the foot. He'll never get agricultural work around here again with that sort of reputation.'

'What about Joseph Mallory?'

'What about him?'

'I understand he has a reputation for being difficult when he was running the farm. Did you have any problems working with him?'

'Not that I can remember, no.'

Gavin snapped his notebook shut, and handed over a business card. 'Ask your wife to call me when she gets in, please, Mr Leavitt. And do bear in mind that I'll be corroborating your statements with the leisure centre and the pizza restaurant.'

'Whatever,' Trevor sneered. 'I'll show you out.'

Gavin walked ahead of the other man, and glanced over the framed photographs on the hallway wall as he passed. There was a selection of images showing the two children as they grew up, two of Trevor's army days, one of him in uniform at a ceremony and another dressed in full camouflage posing beside a colleague in a jungle somewhere, and then one of him and his wife on an anniversary date.

As he got to the front door, his gaze fell upon the jackets hanging from the coat hooks and he frowned, pausing a moment before reaching for the latch.

'Thanks for your time, Mr Leavitt,' he said. 'Don't forget to have your wife call me.'

'I'm telling you the truth, detective,' said Trevor, lowering his voice. 'And she'll back me up.'

Gavin said nothing, and instead hurried back to his car, his heart thumping.

Trevor Leavitt was lying, and he had just seen a way to prove it.

THIRTY-SIX

Kay held a pile of manila folders under her arm and carried a takeout coffee mug in her hand as she strode across the police station car park towards the back door.

There was a freshness to the air, the forecasters predicting rain for the coming week, and she shivered as a gust of wind caught her hair and lifted her jacket.

A uniformed constable was finishing his cigarette when Kay drew near, then stubbed it out and swiped his security pass across the lock before holding open the door for her. 'Morning, guv.'

'Thanks. I was wondering how I was going to do that while I'm carrying all this stuff.'

'Any news yet, guv?' the young officer asked, his eyes hopeful.

'Not yet.' Kay forced a smile. 'But I'm not known for giving up.'

'We're counting on it, guv. Have a good day.'

'You have a safe shift – and thanks again.'

She left him to make his way through to the custody

suite while she climbed the stairs to the incident room, and spotted a familiar figure at the top of the stairs as she rounded the first landing. 'Kyle, hold the door for me, will you?'

The detective constable frowned as she reached him. 'Did you take that lot home with you last night, guv?'

'It was the only way I was going to get this month's reports done on time.'

'What time did you leave?' he asked, following her through the door and along the corridor.

'Half eight.'

'And I'll bet that's only because Adam phoned you to say he was dishing up dinner.'

She grinned. 'He made lasagne. I couldn't say no, could I?'

Kyle rolled his eyes in response. 'If any of us worked as hard as you, guv, you'd have words.'

'I know, but Dean is ultimately my responsibility. A few days working long hours won't hurt me.'

He didn't look convinced, but had the decency to remain silent as they entered the incident room.

Kay placed the folders on Debbie's desk for the exhibits officer to process when she started her shift, then turned to cross to the detectives' desks.

'Guv.'

'Woah.' She jumped back as she walked straight into Gavin, slopping tepid coffee over her hand. 'You made me jump.'

'Sorry.' His eyes widened. 'Was that hot?'

'Not very. It's okay.' Kay frowned. 'When did you get here?'

'About an hour or so ago.'

She looked at her watch. 'It's only just gone half past seven.'

'I couldn't sleep.' He saw her expression, and raised his hands as he walked back to his chair and sat. 'It's okay. I had an idea, that's all, and I figured I might as well make a start to see if I was onto something, and then I found out about Trevor, and I was going to speak with a few of the other farm hands to see what they knew, but I figured I'd come in here first so I could bring you up to date first.'

Kay eyed the can of energy drink on his desk and raised an eyebrow. 'Had a few of those, have you?'

'What? No, it's just that… well, yes, I've had two. And a couple of coffees. But I went and spoke to Trevor Leavitt this morning. At home, before he left for the farm.'

'Bloody hell. What time was that?'

'Um, five thirty, but it's okay because Leanne had just come in from work and I knew I had to get to Trevor before he left for work because I didn't want to speak to him around Justin Mallory or the others.'

'Right…'

'And I got there just as he was having his breakfast.'

'Okay.' Kay folded her arms across her chest and leaned against Laura's desk. 'So, what prompted this visit?'

'So, first of all, I went there because I was reading through Ian's notes about when you were speaking to Trevor and Justin on Thursday and it seemed to me they were both dodging your questions about the hops you found that looked like they'd been poisoned. They said…'

he said, before consulting his notes, '…that they were "looking into it".'

'And because Cassandra interrupted us and told us about Roland Hammerton's personal injury claim, we didn't get the chance to follow up,' said Kay. 'All right. So you went and spoke to Trevor. What's got you all excited? Apart from the sugar overload, that is.'

'Remember the button Harriet's team found in the hop garden where Dean was killed? There's a jacket hanging on a coat rack in Trevor's hallway with exactly the same buttons.' Gavin grinned. 'And one of them is missing.'

Kay's heart lurched. 'Really?'

'I couldn't take a closer look without him seeing me, but the buttons have such a distinctive design. The jacket's old, sort of like a three-quarter length parka jacket, and dark blue – perfect for wearing at night if you don't want to be seen.'

'Bloody hell, Gav.' Kay glanced over her shoulder to see Kyle emerging from the small kitchenette off the side of the incident room. 'Hey, Kyle – he's only gone and found our breakthrough.'

The younger detective hurried over. 'Who?'

'Trevor Leavitt,' said Gavin. He spun in his chair to face his computer screen, moved his energy drink can out of the way and wiggled his mouse to wake it up before stabbing his forefinger at the open windows. 'Hope it's okay guv, but I knew time'd be of the essence for you so I emailed DCI Sharp and asked him if he had any old army contacts who could help us find out exactly what Leavitt used to do when he was enlisted. Trevor told me he worked in reconnaissance but wouldn't say anything else, and cited the Official Secrets Act.'

Kay's shoulders relaxed a little as the detective constable spoke, hearing the same enthusiasm in him that had driven her all these years, and content to let him bask in his success. 'What about previous? Anything?'

'No, Leavitt's clean, guv. And I've just spoken to his wife who supports his claim that they were out with their kids until seven last Sunday, and she said they were all at home for the rest of that night. She said he left for work at six as usual the next morning.' Gavin turned back to face her. 'I'm going to request CCTV images from the leisure centre where they say they went swimming on Sunday afternoon, and the pizza restaurant they took their kids to as well. Leavitt said he had no recollection about Dean when he visited the farm with his mates on that hop tour Gloria told you about, and said he couldn't remember the incident, but I'd definitely recommend we bring him in based on the jacket and get that tested straight away, to see if there's any trace of Dean's blood on it.'

Kyle chuckled, then winked at Kay, who bit back a smile.

'Tell you what, Gav,' she said, picking up the now empty energy drink can and dropping it into the nearest bin. 'Let's get some food inside you first to soak up some of that, and *then* we'll bring in Trevor for questioning. At the moment, the recording equipment isn't going to be able to keep up with you, the rate you're talking.'

THIRTY-SEVEN

Ian Barnes walked into the incident room at seven fifty-five to find Gavin at his desk shovelling a bacon and egg sandwich into his mouth and an open bottle of water standing next to his keyboard.

There was another greasy wrapper screwed up into a ball beside that, and the smell filled the room, making his stomach rumble despite – or perhaps because of – the bowl of granola and fruit he had eaten half an hour ago.

Sitting at his desk opposite the detective constable he raised an eyebrow. 'Leg day at the gym, was it?'

'No,' said Kay, walking over with a stack of briefing agendas in her hand and handing him one. 'Someone's sky-high on caffeine and luck after finding us the breakthrough we've been after.'

Barnes looked over at Gavin. 'Really? Who?'

'Trevor Leavitt,' he said, then licked his fingers, wiped them on a napkin and tossed the rubbish into the bin under his desk before explaining what he had been up to in the early hours.

When he was finished, Barnes saw Kay watching the younger detective with a slight smile. 'He's come a long way, guv, hasn't he? At this rate, we'll have to let him out on his own more often.'

She laughed while Gavin swore good-naturedly under his breath, and then turned serious. 'Okay, I think the caffeine's subsided enough. Do you think Trevor had any idea you'd spotted the jacket?'

'No, I don't,' Gavin replied. 'His focus was on getting ready for work and making sure his kids didn't wake up before his wife got home from the hospital where she's based, and I was careful not to react in front of him. I've been putting some thought into interview strategies while I've been eating as well. I think we ought to get a patrol to pick him up and bring him in, and seize the jacket at the same time to go into evidence.'

'You don't want to be the one to arrest him?' Barnes said, surprised.

Gavin shook his head. 'I want to be the one to interview him. I don't want to give him a chance to try to explain anything to me before that, even if he does understand his rights.'

Barnes nodded. 'Makes sense.'

'Speaking of which, Ian,' said Kay, 'as much as I want to be here, I need you to do the interview with Gav. Sharp phoned just before you got here and I've been asked to go over to Gravesend. I can't get out of it – they're holding a press conference at ten to talk about Dean's murder and we'll need some time to go through the plan for that with the media relations team. What else did you have on this morning?'

'I haven't had Dean's phone records back yet – they should be here by the morning according to his mobile plan provider, so I was going to start reviewing Laura's notes about Joseph Mallory to see if he's got a history of violence or anything.' He looked at Gavin. 'But it makes sense to wait and see what Leavitt's got to say for himself first. If Harriet's theory is right, that it took three people to get Dean strung up on those bines, then maybe Leavitt will give up those names rather than take full responsibility himself.'

'Fingers crossed,' Gavin said, and checked the time on his phone. 'I'm waiting for the leisure centre to open in a minute to request their CCTV footage, but I'm still trying to track down a number for the manager of the pizza restaurant. I'd rather not wait until they open at twelve to speak to someone.'

'Waiting for the CCTV footage shouldn't delay your interview with Trevor,' Kay advised. 'You can hold him without charge for up to thirty-six hours if Sharp approves the extra time, and I don't see him having a problem doing that if you need it. If we need longer than that, we'll need a magistrate to approve it. Ian, why don't you phone the leisure centre while Gav's organising the arrest and the restaurant footage?'

'No problem,' said Barnes, and winked. 'And if Leavitt has to sit in a cell for a couple of hours while we do that, it'll give him time to contemplate his future won't it?'

Ten minutes later, Kay had left for her meeting at headquarters and Barnes was sitting at his desk, his phone to his ear while he listened to the leisure centre's automated answering service and worked his way through the different options to reach the reception desk.

A woman answered after the third attempt, her voice bright and friendly. 'This is Wendy. How may I help you?'

'This is Detective Sergeant Ian Barnes with Kent Police,' he said. 'I'd like to talk with someone please about obtaining your CCTV camera footage. Who's the best person to speak to?'

'Oh.' He heard Wendy's nails tapping at a keyboard, and then: 'That would be our duty manager, Harvey Melton. He's checking the chlorine levels in the pool at the moment though. Would you like to leave a message?'

'Yes please,' said Barnes, standing and picking up his car keys. 'Let him know I'll be there in twenty minutes.'

———

Barnes waited at the barrier leading into the leisure centre's car park, drummed his fingers on the steering wheel while a green light beside the gate started flashing, and eyed the camera on the gate post as the bar lifted. He found a parking space near the leisure centre's front entrance and walked towards the double glass doors. Inside he found himself in a reception area that offered a shop selling a selection of sportswear and a self-service coffee machine.

There was a man and a woman behind a white glossy reception desk, both wearing polo shirts in the leisure group's signature colour and the logo for the centre embroidered in gold thread above the left breast pocket. The woman eyed his suit and gave him a wary smile.

'Detective Barnes? I'm Wendy, we spoke on the phone.' She gestured to the man in his late twenties beside her. 'This is Harvey, the manager here.'

The man thrust out his hand, jutting out a chin covered in a pale brown beard that had been trimmed short. His body resembled an ungainly inverted triangle with wide shoulders and a trim waist, and Barnes wondered for the nth time why some men preferred bench presses rather than overall strength training.

'Hope this isn't too much of an inconvenience,' he said.

'Not at all,' Harvey replied. He gestured to the interior glass window overlooking the pool and then up a flight of stairs to the gym. 'As you can see, it's quiet at the moment. What can I help you with?'

'A few things, and in confidence if you could.' Barnes turned to Wendy. 'Can you confirm if you've got a membership under the name of Trevor Leavitt in your system?'

She turned to the screen and after a few mouse clicks, shook her head. 'No one by that name, sorry.'

'What about card transactions? Do you keep a note of those?'

'Only the last four figures.'

'Could you run off a list of transactions for last Sunday, between noon and closing time please?'

'Sure, no problem.'

'Thanks.' He turned back to Harvey. 'Am I right in thinking you use an automatic number plate recognition system in your car park?'

'Yes – in fact you'll need one of these to get out,' said

the manager, handing him a paper voucher with a code on it from a basket on the desk, and pointing to a tablet display beside it. 'You enter your registration number into that, and if you're a member you don't pay for parking. If you're not a member, it'll tell you how much you need to pay, depending on how long you've been here. You're holding a guest pass, so you don't pay. We record everything on our system.'

'Could you run a check to see if this car registration was here last Sunday?' Barnes read out Trevor Leavitt's licence plate, and waited while Wendy stood aside so Harvey could use the computer.

After a few minutes, the manager shook his head. 'Sorry, nothing here matching that. If we were busy though, he might've parked out on the road. That sometimes happens.'

'We weren't busy last Sunday,' said Wendy. 'I was here, and there were plenty of parking spaces available. But if he walked or cycled here, we wouldn't have a record of him anyway.'

'Okay, what about your security cameras?' Barnes suggested, pointing to one above the reception desk and another that faced the front doors. 'Could I have copies of that footage please?'

'No problem,' said Harvey. He took the memory stick Barnes handed over. 'What's this about anyway?'

Barnes waited until the manager finished copying the file, then tucked the USB into his shirt pocket and gave the man one of his business cards. 'A murder investigation. We may need to speak with you both formally as witnesses, so could you let me have your full contact details please?'

THIRTY-EIGHT

Kyle Walker palmed through the documents spread out across his desk, his notebook open beside him and a new page already half filled with a bullet point list that was growing exponentially.

Bright sunshine pooled across the carpet beside him, the beams escaping through the cracks in the blinds he had pulled down to shield his computer screen, and behind him two uniformed constables were watching a television screen fixed to the wall that was tuned in to the media conference that was about to start at headquarters, their muttered commentary none too polite about Aspley and his cohorts at the *Kentish Times*.

Upon entering the incident room forty minutes ago, he had been cornered by Gavin with the news that Trevor Leavitt was being brought in for formal questioning, and tasked with reviewing all the witness statements from the farm's owners and workers.

'What am I looking for?' he asked.

'Anything that links Leavitt to Dean Spencer, apart

from the jacket button,' came the reply. 'We know Dean was on one of the hop farm tours that Trevor managed but we don't have a motive. I'm open to suggestions.'

Kyle cricked his neck and turned his attention to his computer screen. On it, he had Leavitt and Dean's social media pages displayed side by side while he had alternated between the two, scrolling through the years to see if the two men appeared together at any other time.

So far, it had proven to be a frustrating search with no results to show for the time spent.

'Why the hell did you kill him?' Kyle muttered. He looked up from his computer screen as Barnes walked back into the incident room, and raised a hand in greeting. 'Sarge, Gavin's just gone downstairs to meet Leavitt's solicitor. He's asked me to sit in on the interview in the observation suite, in case you need anything. This is the interview strategy we've drawn up.'

'Okay, good.' Barnes dropped his car keys on the desk and took the manila folder Kyle held out, casting his gaze over the contents. 'What's your feeling about this?'

Kyle pointed to the witness statements. 'I can't find anything to connect the two men except for the hop farm tour. Gloria told Laura that Dean was there with three friends, who she said had already been drinking before they turned up, but he took the time to apologise for their behaviour when the tour was over. There's nothing in here to indicate there was a problem between him and Trevor at the time, and I can't find a connection between them prior to that on social media, so until the day of the hop farm tour, I don't think they'd met.'

He paused as Gavin appeared at the door and headed towards them. 'Everything okay?'

'We're ready downstairs. Ian, are you okay to make a start in five minutes?'

'Sounds good.'

'Sorry, I've not found anything to help you,' said Kyle.

'Don't worry, we'll get to that in the interview.' Gavin looked at Kyle and gave a wolfish smile. 'Keep an eye on Leavitt's reactions and let me know if there's anything you think we should ask him. It's three against one, so let's go and get some answers.'

———

Kyle sat facing a computer monitor and listened while Barnes and Gavin paused outside the observation suite and discussed their final thoughts about their interview strategy.

On the screen he watched Trevor Leavitt and a man in a dark suit conversing, their heads bowed together while the solicitor's face remained grim. There was no sound yet – that would remain switched off until the formal interview began to give the two men some privacy and adhere to legal requirements, but it seemed like an animated conversation.

Leavitt was wearing blue jeans and a white polo shirt with a retailer's branded logo on the left-hand side, his tanned arms sporting a tattoo on his right bicep and a chunky sports watch on his left wrist. His hands were spread as he spoke, and he shook his head from time to time as he listened to the legal adviser.

Kyle glanced over his shoulder. 'What's the solicitor's name?'

'Bernard Crossley,' said Gavin, handing two evidence bags to Barnes before opening the manila folder he had collated all his notes in and arranging the photographs he had chosen so they were at the front. 'He's a local criminal law specialist who's been in that seat a few times over the years.'

'He doesn't look happy about it either,' said Barnes.

'Good,' Gavin replied, then called to Kyle. 'Are you all set in here?'

'Ready to go,' he said. 'I'll switch on the sound once you're in the room. Are you expecting any trouble from Leavitt?'

'I think we'll be all right.'

'Okay then, good luck.'

Seconds later, Gavin and Barnes appeared on screen, and Kyle toggled the volume controls until he heard their chairs scrape across the floor as they sat opposite Leavitt and his solicitor.

Gavin began the recording equipment before reciting the formal caution and seeking introductions from the two men, then clasped his hands on top of the manila folder with his notes in and looked at Trevor Leavitt.

'Mr Leavitt, when I spoke to you earlier today, you maintained that you had nothing to do with the murder of Dean Spencer. Is there anything in that statement you'd like to change or retract at this time?'

'No.' Leavitt's reply was emphatic, and Kyle saw Barnes look up from his notebook and give the man a sharp look.

'Tell us about the farm tours,' said Gavin. 'Whose idea was it for you to do those?'

'Mine. Justin's the best one to do them, obviously, but he's too busy with the business side of things to do tours on his own.'

'I thought you were the farm manager – what keeps Justin busy?'

'I manage the day-to-day running of the farm, he still has to deal with all the bureaucracy that comes with it, as well as the financial side of things. Cassandra's good, she does all the bookkeeping and wages, things like that, but Justin's the one with overall control of the budget and paying suppliers.'

'Do you enjoy doing the tours?'

'Yes, for the most part. Sometimes they're hard work.'

'Like when visitors are drunk?'

Trevor clamped his mouth shut, and his solicitor leaned forward. 'Is there a point to this question, detective?'

'I'd like to understand how your client feels about high jinks behaviour,' said Gavin. 'Particularly given that alcohol is sold and consumed on the premises.'

'They're okay, mostly,' said Trevor after Bernard Crossley gave him a slight nod. 'One or two need to be told to calm down and we've only ever escorted one person off the premises in the time we've been doing them. You speak to any of the vineyards in the Weald and they'll tell you the same thing.'

'Was Dean Spencer drunk when you showed him and his friends around the farm?'

'I don't remember. I don't remember *him*, to be honest.' Trevor leaned back in his seat. 'In the summer, we run two tours a day as well as some corporate and private evening functions. What with ensuring we're going to be ready for harvesting, I can't be expected to recall some random bloke.'

'The leisure centre you said you went to with your family late Sunday afternoon doesn't have a record of your being there,' said Barnes. 'Care to explain why?'

Trevor's face turned stony. 'Not everybody who goes there can afford a membership.'

'Your vehicle wasn't recorded entering or leaving the car park.'

'They charge too much if you're not a member. We parked around the corner.'

'Next to a main road, with two young kids and all the stuff you'd have to carry for them?' said Barnes.

'They use their own backpacks for their swimming kit and towels,' said Trevor, a note of pride in his voice. 'They like being independent. You should see them when we go camping. There's no stopping them.'

'How did you pay for your session?' Gavin asked.

'Cash.'

'Unusual these days.'

'We sold some old furniture online. Ask my wife. The buyers gave us cash, which we don't normally use so we're just using it for days out to get rid of it.'

Kyle saw Barnes reach down for the bulkier of the evidence bags he had placed by his feet and put it on the table.

'For the purposes of the recording, DS Barnes is showing Mr Leavitt a dark-coloured jacket that was found at his home,' said Gavin. 'Do you recognise this?'

Trevor crossed his arms over his chest. 'Yes.'

'Who does it belong to?'

'Me.'

'How long have you had it?'

'Donkey's years. Bought it in a camping store in Tunbridge Wells. I don't remember the name of it – I don't think it's there anymore.'

'Ever wear it to work?'

'No. Why would I?'

Barnes then put the second bag on the table. 'You appear to be missing a button from your jacket, Mr Leavitt. Would you care to tell us what this was doing in the corner of the hop field where Dean Spencer's body was found?'

Kyle watched as Leavitt's whole demeanour altered. His body sagged in the chair, and his expression changed from one of belligerence to fear.

'I'd like to talk to my solicitor in private,' he managed.

'As you wish.' Gavin noted the time for the recording, then picked up the two evidence bags and the manila folder and followed Barnes from the room.

Kyle swung around in his seat and hurried out to the corridor as they shut the interview room door shut, and grinned as he exchanged a fist bump with Gavin.

'We've got him,' Kyle said. 'We've bloody got him.'

'Maybe,' Barnes replied. 'But there were at least two more people in that field with him and Dean, and we still don't know why. We've got a way to go yet before we celebrate.'

'Guv, we're here.'

Kay jolted upright and looked through the windscreen to see Dean Spencer's apartment building, then blushed as she glanced at Laura who was opening her door. 'Jesus, how long was I asleep for?'

The detective constable shot her a reassuring smile. 'Only five minutes. You looked exhausted after the press conference though. Don't worry – I'm not planning on telling the others. Adam's been on call this past week too hasn't he?'

'Yeah.' Kay rubbed at tired eyes, then flipped down the vanity mirror to check her make-up before emitting a sigh. 'And you're right – the vultures were on form today.'

She climbed out and followed Laura over to the communal entrance, then led the way up the stairs. 'And thanks for offering to drive.'

'No problem, guv. I figured if you had to go there, I may as well drop in to see if Andy Grey had had any success with all the security footage we've been sending over to him.'

'And has he?'

Laura grimaced. 'No, unfortunately. He and his team tried to enlarge the footage that we got from Warner Knowles of the van going past his shop that Friday, but it pixellated before he could make out any faces.'

'Dammit.'

'We still might get something yet, guv, especially with Trevor Leavitt in custody. Once we get his phone records we'll be able to see who else is involved, won't we?'

'I bloody hope so. I could've done without having to go to headquarters today of all days.' Kay reached into her bag and checked her phone for messages. 'Still nothing from Gavin or Ian, either.'

Laura paused on the landing. 'Is Gavin going to leave us?'

'Not if I can help it.' Kay frowned. 'Why, what have you heard?'

'Nothing. It's just that you asked him to interview Trevor Leavitt. I thought you would've asked him and Ian to hang fire until you got back from the press conference so you could do that.'

Kay exhaled with relief. 'I thought I was going to hear some bad news then – it's bad enough that Harry's been persuaded to take early retirement without somebody poaching detectives from me. The thing is, with the exception of Kyle who just needs more experience, you're all capable of interviewing suspects. Yes, I really want to be there but you're never going to learn if I'm constantly doing all the interesting stuff, are you?'

Laura smiled. 'And that's why I love working on this team, guv.'

'Good. And if you hear any rumours about anybody leaving, you tell me, okay? Headquarters would love the chance to get their hands on any of you.' She reached into her bag for the keys to Dean's flat and handed Laura a pair of protective gloves. 'Put these on, just in case. Harriet's team have searched the place and confirmed there's no sign of a struggle, but we might need to come back through to look for more evidence depending on how Gavin and Ian get on with interviewing Trevor.'

'Right, thanks.'

Kay led the way into the flat, and paused in the short hallway. It already seemed like the place had been forgotten, and a feeling of melancholy hung in the air as she looked around. A rotten smell was still emanating from the refrigerator, and when she followed Laura into the kitchen she saw that a stack of plates and empty coffee mugs remained in the sink.

'I guess those will just stay there until his mum and dad arrange for someone to clean up,' said Laura, wrinkling her nose.

'They'll have to,' Kay admitted. 'Harriet's taken prints off everything but there's no sign of anybody else using those, just Dean. We don't need anything in there for evidence purposes at the moment.'

'Okay.'

Kay looked down at her phone as it trilled with a new text message from DCI Sharp, then groaned as she read it. 'Oh no.'

'What's wrong, guv?'

'Apparently Susan Greensmith has been approached by Jonathan Aspley at the *Kentish Times*. He's asked for an exclusive interview about the case and she wants me to do it.'

'Really?' Laura's eyes widened. 'What on earth for? The last thing we want is a journalist involved, especially him after what he's done.'

'I'd already told her that after the press conference,' Kay sighed, scanning the message. 'According to Sharp, she reckons it'd be good to show what it's like being a female detective to help with her winter recruitment campaign targeting next year's university graduates. Like I've got bloody time to do that.'

'Can't she ask one of the others?'

'I can try to persuade her.'

'Tell her about that cocaine investigation that East Division are running out of Medway,' Laura said with a grin. 'Apparently it's worth millions.'

'I might just do that, good idea. Right, let me find those photos that Maggie and Rowan want, and we'll head back.'

She walked through to the living area and made her way over to the shelves, checking the images against the list on her phone.

Favourites of Dean's parents included a photograph of him with them at a family wedding, several of the young man's various travels around the world, and one of his graduation ceremony, both parents beaming with pride. Then there were one or two of him from his school athletics days, with Dean as a six-year-old winning an egg and spoon race particularly poignant.

'I hate it when I see a life this full destroyed,' said Laura, taking each framed photograph that Kay handed to her and placing it in a hessian tote bag. 'He seemed like he was having such a good time.'

'He did, didn't he?'

Kay picked up another photograph from Dean's backpacking days. This time, it appeared that he had travelled with Liam and Dominic to Thailand, the three of them grinning while they posed beside a rickety rope bridge over a tumbling waterfall, their foreheads slicked with sweat from what appeared to be a steep climb given the mountainous views behind them.

'It must be so hard for his friends, too,' she said.

Laura looked over. 'I got the impression that Liam's trying to lose himself in computer games when we spoke to him – I don't think he's got anybody to talk to about Dean.'

'God, what a mess.' Kay handed over the photograph and checked the list. 'Okay, that's the last one. I'll drop them off to the Spencers on the way home from work tomorrow – by the time I leave the incident room tonight, it'll be too late. Let's go.'

Her phone rang while they were walking towards the car, and as soon as she saw Gavin's number she switched it to speakerphone while Laura started the engine. 'Gav, how're you getting on?'

'How far away are you, guv?'

'On our way back now. Why?'

'Trevor Leavitt has asked to speak with his solicitor in private, which is what they're doing at the moment. We're waiting for CCTV footage from the council that covers the street outside the leisure centre to see if we can corroborate Leavitt's insistence that he parked there instead of the car park last Sunday.'

'What did his wife have to say for herself?'

'She's given him an alibi, guv, but I reckon she's only doing that to protect the kids.'

'Could well be.'

'In the circumstances, guv, we want to wait until tomorrow to continue the interview, so we're going to keep him in custody overnight. We'll still be well within the twenty-four-hour period before we have to ask for a time extension when we start in the morning.'

'Do you think Leavitt's a flight risk then?' asked Kay.

'Yes, I do, guv. And given that there are at least two more people out there who are as guilty as him, and what we know they could do to him if they find out he's talking to us, I wouldn't blame him, would you?'

FORTY

Gavin chose to walk to the police station the next morning, and at a later time than the previous day.

Sleep had been a stranger to him, and despite his best intentions, he had started the day with a strong coffee after his shower and now clasped a takeout cup from a favourite café he passed on the way.

It was over a week now since Dean Spencer had been brutally murdered, and Gavin walked with a sense of determination, hoping that if he reached the police station before Kay arrived, he would be the one she chose to continue interviewing Trevor Leavitt.

The man's solicitor had left late yesterday afternoon, too late to continue with the interview, and so Leavitt had spent a night in the cells under the watchful gaze of PS Ellis Hughes.

Gavin reached the pedestrian crossing beside the bridge over the River Medway and eyed the swirling current as it travelled towards Allington Lock, wondering if this would be the investigation that brought him a promotion.

He shook his head to clear the thought.

An innocent man had died in terrible circumstances, and his own career didn't matter right now. What mattered was making sure all the evidence was brought together in such a way that Leavitt – and whoever was with him that night – was put away for a long time.

The pedestrian crossing lights turned to green and an electronic zap sound jerked him from his thoughts. Hurrying over the dual-lane road, he entered the police station a few minutes later and jogged up the stairs.

When he entered the incident room, Kay was already sitting at her desk, but Kyle and Laura were nowhere to be seen. Barnes was over at the whiteboard, updating the notes, and gave Gavin a nod before returning to his work.

'Morning, guv,' said Gavin, sliding his backpack under his desk and throwing his empty takeaway cup into the bin. 'I thought I'd nip downstairs and see how Leavitt got on last night.'

'Already done, don't worry,' said Kay. 'Hughes caught me downstairs when I got in this morning. He said Leavitt's been a quiet guest, and there've been no issues. His solicitor's available from nine o'clock, so do you want to tell me where you're up to?'

'Sure.' Gavin sat and pointed at her computer screen that displayed the transcript from the previous afternoon's interview. 'After I spoke to you, I reread this, and decided to call Justin Mallory to get a statement from him on the record. He was shocked, but confirmed he hasn't had any issues with Leavitt in the past. He wasn't able to shed any light on what he did while he was in the army, either – any time he brought it up in conversation, Leavitt changed the subject or said he couldn't talk about it. I did some digging around on various regimental websites though and found out that he's got a couple of distinctions for operations behind enemy lines, but that's all they say. DCI Sharp didn't find out anything either.'

'If he's decorated though, I'm pretty sure he would've seen combat in those ops,' said Kay. 'So he might've killed before.'

'But even if he can, I can't work out why,' said Gavin. 'Dean and his mates turning up drunk on a hop farm tour just doesn't seem enough, especially as Dean apologised to Trevor and Gloria afterwards.'

'Did you get any idea what he wanted to talk to his solicitor about?'

'No,' Gavin sighed. 'And when they'd finished, Bernard Crossley said he needed to make some phone calls and do some research before he could advise his client further, so he agreed that Trevor would spend the night with us.'

Kay frowned. 'Well, that's not the action of an innocent man, is it?'

'That's what I thought,' said Gavin, nodding. 'It sounds to me like he's preparing to give up the other two blokes who were involved, but wants to find out what that might mean for him.'

'A long time behind bars,' said Barnes, walking over and sitting at his desk. 'It's gone half eight, Gav. Are you ready to restart the interview when Crossley gets here?'

Gavin spun around to look at Kay. 'You want me to do it?'

'Of course.' She smiled. 'The best thing we can do right now is to ensure continuity. You and Barnes are across all the evidence and facts, and you found the jacket, so go for it. I'll join Kyle in the observation suite.'

'Two seconds, Ian. Let me check my emails first.' Gavin shot to his desk and started gathering up his notes, wiggling his mouse to wake it up and checking his emails for any updates. 'So, there's nothing about the CCTV from the leisure centre yet, but I've got a note here from the manager of the pizza restaurant Leavitt and his wife say they went to.'

'What does it say?' Kay asked.

'Apparently there's no reservation under that name.' Gavin sighed. 'That doesn't mean anything though, does it? They might've just turned up.'

'And paid cash, like they did with the swimming session,' Barnes said, then leaned over and slapped Gavin on the shoulder. 'We've still got that button though, and the CCTV images might turn up while we're talking to Leavitt.'

Gavin looked over his shoulder as the incident room door swung open and Kyle and Laura walked in, their hands full with takeout coffees for the team, and smiled. 'You must've read my mind.'

'I doubt it,' Laura said, grinning as she handed him one of the cups. 'That's decaf.'

Trevor Leavitt looked decidedly worse for wear after a night in the police station cells.

Gavin sat beside Barnes and eyed the man across the table in interview room three and noticed that his hair was dishevelled as if he'd run his hand over it several times. His white polo shirt was creased in places, although thankfully when Hughes had handed over the custody suite management to Harry Davis earlier that morning the two officers had arranged for complimentary soap and deodorant before allowing Leavitt a short shower before his breakfast.

Bernard Crossley sat beside his client, his legal notebook open on the same page he had finished writing yesterday and his pen poised, his gaze downcast while he listened to Barnes run through the formalities to restart the interview.

That done, Gavin opened the manila folder under his arm and slid a photograph across the table to Leavitt.

Both he and his solicitor recoiled at the image of Dean Spencer as he had been found amongst the hop bines, with Crossley looking away first and clearing his throat.

'Tell me why you did this,' said Gavin, tapping the image with his forefinger.

'I didn't.' Leavitt's voice was strangled, and he closed his eyes. 'It wasn't me.'

'At the moment, Trevor, you've given us two alibis for your movements last Sunday that can't be verified and you haven't explained why this button from your jacket was in the same field where Dean was found.' Gavin snatched the photograph back and glared at him. 'Presently, you're the only suspect in his death, and I don't believe for one minute that you're telling us the truth.'

Leavitt exhaled and glanced at his solicitor, who gave an encouraging nod before the man turned back to face the two detectives. 'I didn't have anything to do with that man's death. The reason you found the button from my jacket in the field was because I went there late one night a few weeks ago and poisoned the hop bines that other detective saw.'

Gavin blinked. 'What?'

'I parked away from the farm and walked back to it along the bridlepath that cuts between the Mallorys' place and another landowner. The fence is broken about halfway, so I ducked through that to get into the hop garden.'

'Why did you poison them?' Barnes asked while Gavin sifted through his notes to find out where Harriet's team had discovered the button.

'Because I was paid to,' said Leavitt, jutting out his chin.

'By whom?'

'Somebody who wants to work with the same brewery that Justin managed to negotiate his deal with. They're growing the same experimental variety in Suffolk, but Justin got in first.'

Gavin scanned Harriet's notes and saw that she had found the button exactly where Leavitt had described, and managed to bite back his disappointment. 'You say you were bribed to cause criminal damage to the Mallorys' crops – why do that, when you'll be affected by the deal falling through if all of those hops die?'

Leavitt shrugged. 'Same reason Roland's faking an

injury to get compensation I expect. Justin and Cassandra are as tight as a duck's arse and won't pay us a reasonable wage. We haven't had a pay rise in three years, and we're getting less than anybody else around here. So when the other lot said they'd give me ten grand to make sure the harvest failed this year, I couldn't say no.'

'Yes, you could have,' said Gavin, gathering up his notes and the evidence bags before glaring at Leavitt. 'In the meantime, we'll be charging you with criminal damage to property. You do not have to say anything, but it may harm your defence if you do not mention now something you later rely on in court. Anything you do say may be given in evidence. Interview terminated...'

That done, Gavin ended the recording and followed Barnes from the room, a sickness in the pit of his stomach.

The older detective gave him a reassuring smile as they closed the door, and then Kay and Kyle emerged from the observation suite, the DI's expression one of frustration.

She gave Gavin a slight shake of her head and pointed upstairs. 'Save it. We'll talk in a minute.'

His shoulders sagged as he trailed behind the others to the incident room and then he trudged over to his desk and threw the manila folder onto it before slumping into his chair. He spent a few moments checking his emails, then looked up as Kay finished speaking with Barnes and walked towards him.

'Dammit. I really thought I was onto something there. Sorry, guv.'

'Don't apologise,' said Kay, her voice stern as she sat at her computer. 'We all thought that button could be key evidence in Dean's murder. Instead, you've successfully proven that two crimes were committed at the Mallorys' farm – the crop poisoning being one, and Dean's murder.'

'Yeah, but we still don't know who's responsible for that,' said Gavin. He ran a hand over his spiky hair then pointed at his screen. 'And Paul Solomon's just come back to me too – there's no recent history of ritualistic-like murders in the area. So we're back to square one, and headquarters aren't going to be happy, are they?'

Kay had no answer for that, and he let out a sigh as he turned his attention to his computer screen, a desperation seizing him.

'Shit,' he murmured. 'What the hell do we do next?'

FORTY-ONE

Kay eyed the landline phone in the middle of the conference table and snarled at it while a monotone beep emanated from the speaker.

The chief superintendent had ended the call after a request to send all of the investigation files to headquarters, insisting that an audit be started immediately given the media interest in the case, and Kay had had no option but to acquiesce.

Sharp, also in the same room as the chief super on the other end of the line, had sensibly remained silent, having delivered the news to her by text only minutes before the formal meeting request was made half an hour ago.

'Bollocks,' she murmured, then slammed the heel of her hand into the phone console to end the beep, before leaning forward and resting her head on her arms, closing her eyes for a moment. 'Shit.'

Despite acknowledging Gavin's success at closing out the poisoning angle of the enquiry, Susan Greensmith's tone had been curt when turning her attention to Dean's murder, sharing her disappointment that Kay and her team had no viable leads to follow, and reminding her for the nth time that the entire police force would be held accountable by the media should his killers remain free.

'Ugh,' Kay groaned, and raised her head as her mobile phone trilled. Sharp's name was on the screen. 'Yes, guv?'

'I couldn't do anything, Kay. Sorry.'

'It's okay. She's got a fair point.'

'Even so… What are you planning on doing the rest of the day while your team pull their files together?'

'Dean Spencer's phone records came in this morning while we were interviewing Trevor Leavitt, so Ian's going through those now. Gavin got the council's CCTV images through and we've confirmed that Trevor and his family did go to the leisure centre on Sunday, and they also provided footage of a car park close to the pizza restaurant later on that night – Leavitt's definitely not our man for Dean's murder.' Kay swivelled out of her chair and strode over to the window, watching as a steady stream of workers made their way out of offices and towards the town centre for their lunch breaks. 'I'm going to drop off some of Dean's personal effects to his parents that I picked up from his flat yesterday, and when I get back from doing that I'll put together my summary report for the auditors. Do you want me to send you a copy before I submit it?'

'Please,' said Sharp. 'A second pair of eyes wouldn't do any harm, after all.'

'Thanks, guv.'

'And don't sound so despondent,' he admonished. 'This is perfectly normal, and you never know – the audit might win you some more manpower to assist with your investigation.'

'If it isn't transferred to Gravesend instead,' said Kay. She let the window blind snap back into place. 'I'd best go, guv. I imagine I'm going to have to give the pep talk of my life when I do the briefing later today.'

'Good luck.'

Kay ended the call and stared at the phone for a moment. 'I'm going to bloody need it, Devon.'

She sighed and made her way out of the conference room and down the stairs to the next floor, the sound of voices and telephones reaching her before she reached the incident room.

Gavin was at his desk, a burger in one hand and a pen in the other as he completed all the evidence checklists expected by the Crown Prosecution Service to process the charges against Trevor Leavitt, and Kyle and Laura were standing with Debbie while they sifted through all the evidence that had been collated to date.

Barnes looked up from Dean's mobile phone records when Kay reached under her desk for the tote bag containing the photographs from the young man's flat and raised an eyebrow.

'You look done in, guv,' he said in a low voice. 'Don't let the bastards get you down.'

She shot him a grateful smile. 'Thanks, and no – I won't. How're you getting on?'

He spread his hand over the statements. 'I've got calls to and from Liam and Dominic's numbers, plus his mum and dad's. Some of the numbers correspond to clients Andy Grey identified from Dean's computer. There's a few overseas numbers he was speaking to weekly – probably clients but I'll verify that after I've worked through the rest. I've got another here that he dialled or received calls from on a regular basis – I'm waiting to hear from the mobile provider to find out who that belongs to. Could be another friend, or a client. And then there's this other lot that he phoned less regularly. I'm just going through those now.'

'Okay, thanks.' Kay held up the tote bag. 'I'm going to drop this off to Maggie and Rowan, so call me if you need anything urgent.'

'Will do. Catch you later.'

Fifteen minutes later, Kay was on the A20 heading out of town and through the outskirts of Bearsted, opting to avoid the busy motorway. The pool car handled well, and by the time she passed the golf course next to Leeds Castle, she was tapping her fingers on the steering wheel and humming along to the radio under her breath.

The turning for Maggie Spencer's brother's house on the fringes of Ashford soon appeared and Kay turned into a housing estate that was a rabbit-warren of cul-de-sacs off the main thoroughfare, all with names of birds that might once have lived in the fields the buildings now occupied.

She found the house at the end of one such dead end, and parked beside Rowan's hatchback car on a paved driveway outside a tidy detached house with a red-tiled roof and a shallow portico over the front door.

Aaron Stewart opened the door as she got out the car, and waved her inside.

'Thanks,' she said. 'Any trouble?'

'No sign of any reporters, guv, and the neighbours

keep to themselves around here so I think we'll be good for now,' said the constable. 'Maggie and Rowan are in the living room if you want to go through. I was just putting the kettle on for them. Want a coffee?'

Kay nodded. 'Do you know what? I will. Thanks.'

'Coming right up.'

He disappeared along a wide hallway into a kitchen that caught the afternoon light, and Kay turned her attention to the closed door to her left. Squaring her shoulders, she knocked briefly before entering, and found the Spencers sitting together on a large sofa beside a coffee table strewn with photographs.

'Detective Hunter,' said Rowan, standing and waving her to an armchair opposite them. 'Did you find the pictures Maggie was after?'

'I did,' said Kay, handing him the tote before she cast her gaze over the assembled collection already on the table. 'Looks like Dean was quite the traveller.'

'He loved it,' said Maggie, her eyes red-rimmed. She sniffed, then delved her hand into the bag. 'Especially the big trips like this one.'

'We didn't think he was going to come back from Thailand,' said Rowan, looking over her shoulder with a sad smile. 'He had such a good time.'

Kay leaned forward and peered at the photograph. 'That's Liam and Dominic in the picture with him, isn't it?'

'Yes, that's right. They always went to far-flung places together – had done since before university.' Rowan sniffed. 'I don't know if the boys will go without him in future though. Dean was always the one coming up with the ideas and sorting out the flights, that sort of thing. Some of the places like this were off the beaten track but he loved it. The less tourists, the better. That's what he used to tell us.'

Kay frowned. 'So who took the photograph? It's not a selfie.'

'That would've been Isaac,' said Rowan. He palmed through the photographs on the coffee table. 'Hang on, I've got a photo of him here somewhere. Ah, here you go. Dean's known him since they started secondary school together when they were eleven.'

Maggie wrinkled her nose as Kay took the photograph that Rowan held out. 'He went off the rails after school though. I'd heard he got into drugs, and Dean said he was a nightmare sometimes in Bangkok. He was really worried they'd get into trouble with the police there because of Isaac.'

'Where is Isaac these days?'

'I think he's got a job over at Sittingbourne, working for a consultancy.'

'Dean mentioned he helps out his dad from time to time as well, just to earn some extra money,' Rowan added. 'I think he got into trouble a few years ago, owing money to people—'

'Probably for the drugs,' Maggie said.

Kay looked at the photograph again, and ran her thumb over Isaac's face, an idea forming. 'What's his surname?'

'Trimble,' said Rowan. 'His dad owns a plumbing business over near Sevenoaks.'

FORTY-TWO

Kay pushed open the door to the incident room, almost knocked over a junior constable who was about to leave with an armful of files and apologised to him, then hurried across to Gavin's desk.

'Where's everyone else?' she said, holding up the framed photograph of Dean Spencer and his backpacking friends. 'We've just been given that breakthrough in Dean's murder we needed.'

The detective constable's mouth opened in shock before he recovered. 'Barnes is downstairs overseeing Leavitt's release from custody pending his court hearing, and Kyle and Laura are out getting something to eat.'

'Call them. Get them both back here now – and ask them to pick up a coffee for me on the way, would you?'

He grinned. 'Yes, guv.'

Heart still thumping from Rowan Spencer's revelation, Kay hit the speed dial for Barnes's number on her phone. He answered within two rings. 'How soon can you get back up here?'

'Almost finished, guv. Another five minutes, and—'

'Make it two, Ian. We've got our murder suspect.'

Ending the call, she walked over to the printer and copying machine and carefully lifted Dean's photograph from its frame. After making a number of copies, she put the original on her desk and pinned one of the copies to the whiteboard, then took the rest over to Debbie who was already prepping an agenda.

'I heard,' said the uniformed constable. 'And I'm guessing you're going to be calling an immediate briefing, would that be right, guv?'

'Yes, and can you include these with the agenda? It'll help with the context – and if anybody else is out at lunch, recall them now please.'

'Onto it already, guv.'

'One more thing – I need you to allocate four officers to accompany Kyle, Laura and Gavin when they go and arrest Liam Peyton and Dominic Bridger. I want to interview the pair of them here as soon as the briefing's over.'

'Will do.'

'Thanks, Debbie.'

Kay walked back to the whiteboard and took a moment to calm her churning thoughts as she cast her gaze over the contents, listening while the uniformed constable rounded up the rest of the investigation team and handed out agendas as, one by one, they joined her at the front of the room, their faces expectant. Turning to face them after a few moments, she gave a reassuring smile while Gavin leaned against a desk to the left of the whiteboard, his jaw set. 'We'll just wait for a few stragglers before I begin, but I want to take a moment to thank each and every one of you for your efforts to date. I know we've been struggling to make headway with this one, but rest assured, I'm aware of how many hours you're putting in to finding Dean's killer and I appreciate it. We've already made one arrest in the process of eliminating suspects, and I'm hopeful that by the end of today, there will be more.'

She looked across the seated officers as the incident room door opened and Barnes, Kyle and Laura walked in. They hurried towards her, and Kyle handed her a steaming takeout cup.

'Thanks,' she said and lifted the lid before taking a tentative sip. 'That's better. Right, let's begin. We know that Dean Spencer, Dominic Bridger and Liam Peyton visited the Mallorys' hop farm over the summer for a tour, and that by the time they left there had been some drunken antics, such that Dean apologised for the others' behaviour. Fast forward three months, and Dean's found dead in the same place, after being strung up and stabbed several times before being disembowelled. However, Harriet has said all along that it would've taken three people to lift him and tie the ropes that were used. We know that a van was used to transport him, and that van was stolen from a plumbing supplies company owned by Rex Trimble over at Wrotham.'

She took another sip before placing the cup on the desk beside Gavin and giving him a warning glare, then turned back to the rest of the team. 'The photograph in your briefing pack was taken in Thailand a few years ago when Dean and his friends were on a backpacking trip. Dean's parents confirmed to me less than an hour ago that Isaac Trimble took that picture.'

A murmur passed through her officers, and she heard Kyle swear under his breath.

'Three people,' he said. 'Three friends. But, why?'

'That's what we're going to find out,' said Kay. 'And we'll need to move fast because it's been four days since we interviewed Dominic and Liam and they've probably warned Isaac that we're onto him. So, once we're done here, make whatever arrangements you need to make back home or otherwise, because we're in for a late night. Task-wise, I want Dominic and Liam under arrest within the next two hours. They both work from home, so tracking them down shouldn't be a problem. Kyle, Laura – I'd like you to go with a uniformed patrol to arrest Dominic, and Gavin you can be the arresting officer for Liam. Given that we haven't been back in touch since we first spoke with them, I'm hoping their guard's down and they think they've got away with it. Ian, you and I are going to head over to Sittingbourne where Isaac works when he's not helping out his dad, and we'll make the arrest there. I don't want to wait until he gets home in case he hears about the other arrests.'

She waited while her officers updated their notes. 'While that's happening, I want all of you to turn your attention to Isaac Trimble. Social media, whether he's been arrested in the past – according to the Spencers, he's had a long history of drug abuse so there might be something there. He went to the same secondary school as Dean – track down the head teacher, find out if there were any issues between the two of them. Same with the university.

I'll need two of you to speak with his employers after we've taken him into custody too, to see if there have been any problems.'

Draining her coffee, she checked her watch. 'I'm assigning Debbie to collate as much information as you can within the time it takes me and Barnes to get to Sittingbourne and let me have an overview before we walk in there to arrest him. I don't want anybody getting hurt, including members of the public.'

'Sounds like a good idea, guv,' said Sean. 'Want me to come along then, given my experience in the Marines?'

'Yes please, just in case we need an extra pair of hands. Tim, I'd like you along with us as well.'

PS Wallace nodded. 'No problem.'

'Okay, everyone, that's it for now. We'll reconvene here after the arrests have been made.'

Laura stood outside the front door of Dominic Bridger's house and listened to the raised voices within.

Five minutes ago, Kyle's pool car and a liveried Kent Police patrol vehicle had swept into the cul-de-sac and parked in the shadow of the industrial unit that towered over the compact townhouses. She had seen a neighbour's living room curtain twitch back into place as they had approached Dominic's home and when Kyle rapped his knuckles against the door, the sound had reverberated off the surface and echoed around the other houses.

'Reckon that'll get him out of bed,' said Laura.

One of the uniformed officers had raised an eyebrow. 'It's the afternoon.'

'He's got international clients, apparently.'

They had all turned back to face the door as it opened, Kyle stepping in front of Laura in case of an attack but the man who peered around it at them was pale and haggard.

The stench of unwashed skin and clothes emanated through the gap and they took a step back.

'Afternoon, Dominic,' Laura said cheerfully, and then recited the formal caution.

'W-what do you want?' he managed.

'We'd like a word,' said Kyle. 'Not here, at ours.'

Dominic blinked. 'I need to get dressed.'

'Get a move on, then,' said Laura and pushed against the door. 'We haven't got all day, have we?'

The young man staggered backwards, and she saw he wore a pair of boxer shorts and nothing more. He blushed, then gestured to the stairs. 'I'll go and find some clothes.'

'No problem.' Laura gestured to one of the uniformed officers now standing in the hallway. 'But he's going with you.'

Dominic swallowed, then nodded and staggered up the stairs while Kyle made his way through to the living room.

It was gloomy, the light shut out by the closed curtains, and there was a distinct and greasy fat-heavy stench to the room.

Laura flicked the light switch.

'Bloody hell,' Kyle managed, covering his nose with his jacket sleeve. 'I thought it was a tip last time we were here…'

Laura nudged him forward and eyed the mountain of beer cans that had amounted on the coffee table since Thursday, some of which had fallen onto the carpet and rolled underneath. The pile of takeaway food cartons and pizza boxes had increased, and yet most of the food had been abandoned, partly explaining the smell that mingled with Dominic's lack of hygiene.

Laura raised an eyebrow at Kyle. 'So much for him doing the cleaning on Sundays.'

'Looks like the guilt's been getting to him, doesn't it?' He winked. 'Shall we get him into custody and start the interview?'

————

A duty solicitor was already waiting for them when Laura frog-marched Dominic towards the custody desk, the man failing to hide his disgust at the state of his latest client before he cleared his throat.

'I'll need a few moments to brief Mr Bridger. What are the details?'

Kyle handed him a thin file. 'We'll book him in, and then you can have a word. Take a seat in the interview room and we'll bring him down when we're done here.'

The man nodded and hurried after one of the uniformed constables who opened the security door for him, and Laura heard Dominic shuffle his feet.

Turning, she saw the fear in his eyes, and her heart turned cold. 'Harry, can you get this one processed quickly? I'd like to make a start.'

'No problem,' said the older constable, and held out his hand. 'Valuables first, please sir.'

Kyle led Laura from the custody suite and they wandered along the corridor to the vending machine. He swiped his card and selected a bag of crisps. 'Given that we missed lunch, I need something to eat otherwise the recording's going to hear my stomach rumbling. What would you like?'

'Chocolate, please. Thanks.'

They clinked the snacks together in salute, then leaned against the wall in companionable silence while they ate.

'So, what do you think?' Laura asked, keeping her voice low as two administration staff from another investigation walked past. 'Did Dean do something to piss off his friends, or what?'

'No idea,' said Kyle, licking salt from his fingers before walking a few paces away to throw the empty crisp bag into a rubbish bin. His expression was pensive as he turned back to her. 'Given how long the four of them seem to have known each other, it must've been bad in their eyes. Maybe he was blackmailing them or something?'

Laura frowned. 'I hadn't thought of that angle. Good point. Make sure you cover that when you speak to him, all right?'

'You want me to do the interview?' Kyle said, surprised.

'Makes sense.' She smiled. 'You need the practice, after all.'

'Bloody cheek.'

FORTY-FOUR

Kay gritted her teeth as Barnes accelerated along the dual carriageway that passed the Detling Showground, the scenery flashing past her window while she tried to steady herself against the car's motion and type a message to DCI Sharp.

In her peripheral vision, she could see the flashing blue and red lights of the patrol car driven by PS Tim Wallace in front of them, the vehicle's sirens silent for now as it carved a path through traffic and sped towards Sittingbourne.

'At least we'll get shot of the auditors,' Barnes mused, changing down a gear as the car met the hill's incline. 'That was close.'

'Too close. I've told Sharp what we're up to, so with any luck he'll have a word with the chief super and buy us some more time.' Her phone pinged once more. 'Good – Harry Davis has confirmed that both Dominic and Liam are now in custody. They're just waiting for Liam's solicitor to turn up – he's being kept in the cells while

Dominic's speaking with his legal rep before Kyle and Laura interview him.'

'It's all coming together, guv.'

'God, I hope so, Ian. I just want some bloody answers.' Kay's feet dug into the footwell as the two cars approached a roundabout and braked hard, the vehicles shooting out the other side before picking up speed once more, and then her phone rang.

Debbie's name appeared on the phone screen, and Kay switched it to speaker. 'What've you managed to find out so far, Debs?'

'Well, by all accounts Isaac was a right little toerag at school,' the constable replied. 'I spoke to his former headmaster, who recalls him being disruptive, disrespectful and belligerent.'

'A charmer, then,' said Barnes.

'Yep, and no stranger to fights, either,' said Debbie. 'He seems to have calmed down by the time he progressed through to university though. I spoke to some of his and Dean's lecturers there, and one of them told me that although there were rumours of Isaac taking drugs, it didn't affect his grades. He graduated with a two-two in business management. The company he works at is an advertising consultancy with several big-name clients in the south east and nationally. According to their website, Isaac is a key account manager responsible for onboarding new clients.'

'What's his social media like?' Kay asked.

'Silent for over a week,' Debbie replied. 'He was pretty active across two or three platforms until then, and suddenly – nothing.'

'Has he crossed paths with us before?'

'Nothing on record, guv. I'll keep digging around though, and I'm still chasing up a couple of outstanding leads from last week that might help us. I'll send over some recent photos of Isaac in the meantime.'

'I'll let you get on, then. Thanks.'

Kay ended the call and fell silent as they approached the outskirts of Sittingbourne.

The cars turned left into an industrial area and she spotted several well-known brand names on signposts at the end of each avenue that led from the main thoroughfare. Tim's car swept into one lined with two-storey units, each with a company's name above the individual warehouse doors, and parked outside the one belonging to the advertising consultancy.

Kay climbed out and led Barnes and the two uniformed officers to the front door, pushing against the chrome handle to find herself in a cool air-conditioned space that had been decorated to a high standard. A woman in a tailored business suit sat behind a reception desk, and her eyes widened at the sight of four police officers standing in front of her.

'Can I help you?' she managed.

'Detective Inspector Hunter,' said Kay, holding out her warrant card. 'I'd like a word with Isaac Trimble please.'

'I'll let him know you're here,' said the woman, reaching for her phone.

'Not necessary, thanks. Where's his desk?'

'Um, though that door there, but we don't let clients through there, we prefer—'

Kay didn't hear the rest of the sentence and followed

Sean Gastrell as he strode across to a door marked "private" and shoved it open. With Barnes and Tim Wallace at their heels, they walked along a short corridor, past a kitchen area and staff toilets, and through another door into an open-plan office.

Six men and eight women stared at them in shock, the youngest of whom emitted a squeak of surprise before a man in his late fifties emerged from an office at the end and glared at them.

'What the bloody hell is the meaning of this?' he demanded.

Kay ignored him, her gaze sweeping the desks until she spotted a man in his twenties as he ducked behind a computer screen. Striding over, she recognised Isaac Trimble from the photographs Debbie had emailed across to her.

Instead of the confident and gregarious man who posted his travel and partying escapades on social media, Isaac cowered away from her and raised his hands.

'Oi,' said the older man, stalking towards her. 'I asked you a question.'

Barnes stepped in front of him. 'Manners, please. Who are you?'

'Bradley Dankworth, the owner. Why are you hassling my staff?'

'We're not hassling him,' Kay explained, then turned to Isaac, who paled as she began to recite the formal caution. 'Isaac Trimble, I'm arresting you on suspicion of murder. You do not have to say anything, but it may harm your defence...'

Isaac bolted from his desk, pushing away his chair and

knocking over a young woman who was standing with an armful of magazine proofs that scattered across the floor. He ran along the length of the office towards the exit, pushing people out of the way in his haste to escape, and slid around a partitioned desk area sending the whole structure crashing to the carpet.

'Shit,' Kay murmured, then saw Sean Gastrell take flight.

The uniformed constable ran back the way they had entered the open-plan office, leapt over a stack of archive boxes and reached the door mere seconds before Isaac and stood in the way, his stocky build filling the frame. He gave a taut smile as Isaac stumbled to a halt, and reached into his stab vest for a pair of handcuffs that he dangled from his hand.

'Shall we try that again, sir?'

FORTY-FIVE

When Gavin led Kyle into interview room two, Liam Peyton looked like a sick man.

His demeanour had deteriorated since he had been processed through the custody suite and introduced to the duty solicitor who was representing him, and he now sat slumped in a chair beside him. His shoulder-length hair was greasy and unwashed and hung limply around a face with a pallid complexion. He kept his head lowered while he nibbled at a fingernail and contemplated the table surface, refusing to look up while Kyle checked the recording equipment and Gavin accepted one of the solicitor's business cards.

'Thanks for coming at such short notice, Mr Brackenridge,' he said. 'Have you had sufficient time to brief your client?'

'I have, thank you, Detective Piper.' The man inched the edges of his jacket together to offset the cold air conditioning that Kyle had set at a deliberately vicious temperature, and picked up his pen in readiness.

Gavin started the recording and repeated the formal caution, then sat back and waited until Liam lifted his head. The man's gaze was baleful, and he quickly looked down again and chewed his lip.

'Please confirm your name for the purposes of the recording,' said Gavin.

'Liam Peyton,' he mumbled.

'You'll need to speak louder.'

'Liam Peyton.'

'Right, Liam,' Gavin began, clasping his hands together on the table. 'Let's talk about what happened last Sunday when you, Dominic Bridger, Isaac Trimble and Dean Spencer decided to steal a van and drive it to a hop farm belonging to Justin and Cassandra Mallory. When did you get the idea to go there? Was it planned days in advance, or at the last minute?'

'I can't remember.' Liam sniffed.

'Why the hop farm?'

Liam's left shoulder lifted, then slumped.

'I need you to speak for the recording please.'

'I don't know.'

'But you were there, Liam, weren't you? Four of you stole a van belonging to Rex Trimble, last Sunday night, and then drove to a lay-by close to the farm. What happened then, Liam?'

The young man closed his eyes and shook his head, his face one of misery.

'I think you argued with Dean, didn't you?' Gavin persisted. 'Something happened, and the three of you waited until you were sure no one was looking before you dragged him from the van and one of you cut through a fence and manhandled Dean across a corn field before reaching a bridlepath that ran alongside the Mallorys' hop field, at which point you cut the fence and dragged Dean inside. Did he struggle the whole way?'

'I don't know.'

'I don't believe you,' Gavin said, sliding a photograph across the table. 'Care to tell me why you killed Dean Spencer and then carved these symbols into his skin?'

Brackenridge cleared his throat and quickly looked away, but Liam merely blinked, then shoved the photo away.

'I don't know anything,' he said.

'After you killed Dean, the three of you went back the way you came then decided to drive the van to a secluded location, where you poured petrol over the insides and set fire to it,' Gavin continued. 'Why was that? What happened inside the van? Is that where you overpowered Dean, or did you start torturing him while he was still inside?'

'I didn't kill him,' Liam blurted, leaning forward such that his spittle nearly caught Gavin in the face.

The detective ducked sideways just in time, and thanked Kyle for the paper handkerchief he held out. Wiping the shoulder of his jacket, Gavin eyed the man in front of him, and tossed the tissue to one side.

'Then, who did?'

Opening the manila folder that contained the evidence collated to date, Gavin pulled out the photograph Kay had found in Dean's flat and jabbed his finger on it. 'The four of you were always close, weren't you?'

A single tear welled up in Liam's right eye as his gaze flickered over the image, but he said nothing.

'What changed, Liam?' Gavin urged. 'What went so wrong between the four of you that Dean ended up being strung up amongst the Mallorys' hop bines before you took a knife to him and butchered him while he was still alive?'

'I… I can't.'

Liam's strangled cry was interrupted by a loud knock on the interview room door and Gavin spun in his seat as Debbie peered in.

'Sorry, I need an urgent word,' she said.

Gavin waved to Kyle to pause the interview and followed Debbie out into the corridor. 'What's wrong?'

'Nothing's wrong,' she said, giving him a tight smile. 'I've got some more evidence for you. Remember the leasehold agent that's selling the old pub that's up for sale? I've been chasing her all bloody week to send us any security footage from the cameras they've got dotted about the place.'

'And?' Gavin said, looking over his shoulder as Kyle slipped out of the room and closed the door behind him, the younger detective's face expectant. Gavin held his finger to his lips, then turned back to Debbie. 'Go on.'

She held up an enlarged photograph in reply. 'Nadine's been going through the footage for the past hour, and just found this. The pub's got a bright spotlight shining above the door that illuminates the road, which made her job a little easier. This is a freeze-frame, but in the footage the van's going past at quite a considerable speed – away from the hop farm.'

Gavin took it from her and angled it so Kyle could see.

In the picture, the frozen image of Rex Trimble's van could be seen, the liveried logo clearly visible across the panelled sides.

And, shirtless in the driver's seat, was Liam Peyton.

'Got you,' Gavin murmured. 'Thanks for chasing that up, Debs. And thank Nadine when you go back upstairs, will you?'

'No problem.'

Gavin and Kyle walked back into the interview room and while his colleague restarted the recording equipment and noted the time, he watched while Liam shifted his weight from side to side in his chair, the man evidently nervous.

'Liam,' he said, setting down his files once more and placing the CCTV image on the table between them, 'why were you driving away from the Mallorys' farm at speed last Sunday in Rex Trimble's van that you stole? Was it because you'd just murdered Dean Spencer and wanted to destroy any evidence linking you to the place?'

'No comment.'

Gavin swept the photograph from the desk, closed the manila folder, then leaned forward. 'Mr Brackenridge, I'd suggest you inform your client how precarious his current position is because whichever way you look at it, Liam, you know exactly what happened at the Mallorys' hop farm, and you're lying to us. Your future isn't looking too bright at the moment, is it?'

FORTY-SIX

When Kay followed Barnes through the security door leading to the custody suite, she spotted Laura and Tim Wallace deep in conversation with Debbie outside interview room one.

'How's it going in there?' she asked. 'Is Dominic giving us anything yet?'

'It'll go better after we put this in front of him,' said Laura, holding up the image from the abandoned pub's security camera. 'That was one hell of a find, Debbie.'

'Thank Nadine when you see her,' said the uniformed constable. 'Have you been given a copy, guv?'

Kay indicated the manila folder in her hand. 'Here. Have you spoken to Gavin?'

'He and Kyle have just gone back into room two with Liam.'

'Okay, thanks. Were DNA samples taken from all three suspects when they were booked in, like I asked?'

'They were, guv,' said Tim, 'and they've been couriered over to Harriet's lab for testing. Given the time, we probably won't get the results until tomorrow now.'

'Well, let's hope we get some answers in the meantime.' She glanced at Barnes and jerked her chin towards the next room on the right. 'Shall we make a start?'

'After you, guv.'

'All right, good luck with yours,' she said to Laura and Tim. 'We'll see you upstairs afterwards for a briefing.'

As she opened the door to room five, she saw Isaac Trimble and his solicitor, a man named Bernard Crossley, with their heads bowed while they spoke in low voices. They straightened when the door closed, and Kay saw a flicker of fear in the younger man's eyes as Barnes tested the recording equipment and then recited the formal caution and made the introductions.

That done, the room fell silent while she contemplated Isaac across the table.

He wasn't as good looking as his friends, that much was clear. He looked as if he had nicked himself shaving at some point during the past few days, and bore a deep cut on his jawline that had scabbed, looking angry and sore. His blue eyes were bloodshot, perhaps from lack of sleep, and sweat patches already appearing under his arms despite the cool air ventilating the small room.

Kay opened the folder. 'Tell me about Dean Spencer, Isaac.'

'What do you want to know?'

'Had you known each other long?'

'Since school.'

'Would you say you were close?'

'Spose so, yes.'

Kay slid the photograph taken in Thailand across to Isaac. 'Did you take this?'

'Yeah – we signed on to do a five-day hike away from the city.'

'Can you confirm the names of the other two men in this photo with Dean?'

'Dominic Bridger and Liam Peyton.'

'And how long have you known them?'

'Since our uni days.'

'And do you often do things like holiday together?'

Isaac shrugged. 'Now and again. Not so much these days because of work.'

'But would you say that you're close?'

'I guess, yes.'

'Whose idea was it to visit the Mallorys' hop farm over the summer?'

'I don't know. I didn't go.' Isaac sat back in his chair, a smug look in his eyes. 'I was on holiday with my girlfriend at the time.'

'And she'd say the same, if I spoke to her, would she?'

'We split up last month, but yeah. She'd tell you. We were in Cyprus for a week. One of those last-minute deals.'

'When was the last time you saw Dean?'

Isaac's brow furrowed. 'Last Saturday, I think.'

'Where?'

'I… I think it was at the supermarket.'

'The supermarket?' Kay glanced at Barnes, who raised an eyebrow, then looked at Isaac once more. 'Is that where twenty-somethings hang out these days? That doesn't sound very exciting.'

'No, I mean I was out shopping and saw him there.' Isaac scowled, and folded his arms across his chest.

'Did you fall out with him? Have an argument over something?'

'No.'

'Were you jealous of him?'

'No, why?'

'Because I'm trying to fathom why – for somebody who says he was Dean's best friend – you would do this to him.'

Kay tossed the photograph taken of Dean in the hop garden at Isaac and watched his expression as he first turned over the image, and then recoiled at what he saw.

She leaned closer, ignoring Crossley's look of dismay as he averted his gaze. 'You stole one of your dad's vans last Sunday, Isaac. You, Dean, Dominic and Liam. Why was that? Did you fall out with Dean and decide to murder him?'

'No.' He shook his head, his body rocking back and forth while he held a hand to his chest.

'You kidnapped Dean, didn't you, Isaac? You drove him to that lay-by near to the hop farm, you dragged Dean across the cornfield and cut your way through the fence before continuing across the bridlepath and through a second fence into the Mallorys' hop garden. Somewhere, one of you wasn't careful enough though and you caught yourself on the barbed wire. Is that where you got that nasty scratch from?'

Isaac raised his fingers to his jaw, then thought better of it and dropped his hand. 'No.'

'Remember the DNA swab we took when you first got here?' said Barnes. 'That's currently with our forensics team for testing.'

Kay watched as Isaac's Adam's apple bobbed in his throat, and sweat broke out across his forehead.

'When you reached the hop garden,' she continued, 'you murdered Dean Spencer, didn't you?'

Isaac pushed back his chair, and pointed at her. 'No! It wasn't me. All I know is that I… I woke up in my bed the next day, there was blood and vomit over my chest, and I was only wearing my underwear. I don't remember. Somebody else must've killed Dean.'

Kay took her hand away from the panic button under the table as Bernard Crossley ushered his client back to his seat and Isaac buried his face in his hands, and then she turned at a knock on the door.

'Pause the interview,' she said to Barnes, then opened it.

Gavin stood outside, his jaw set.

She stepped into the corridor and pulled the door shut. 'What's the matter?'

'Liam Peyton. I think you're going to want to hear this, guv.'

Kay nodded her thanks to Kyle who rose from his seat and indicated she should sit before he moved to the door and leaned against it, his arms folded across his chest.

Once she was settled beside Gavin and he had restarted the recording equipment and provided the date and time, she looked across the table at Liam Peyton.

Since the original interview had started next door, he had vomited onto the floor of interview room two and the investigation had moved to a smaller room that was usually used to interview juveniles. Harry Davis was the one who had to clean up afterwards, but the older constable had given Kay a stoical smile as she had walked past, and she nodded in response.

The room was different to the stark interior of the ones used for adult offenders. Bright colours covered the plasterwork walls and the lighting was softer, although it failed to disguise Liam's pallid complexion.

'I understand you have something to tell me in relation to the torture and murder of Dean Spencer,' she said, keeping her hands resting on the table while Gavin opened his notebook.

Liam nodded, then leaned forward, remembering the recording. 'Yes.'

'Go on.'

The young man looked at his solicitor, and once Brackenridge gave him a curt nod, he took a deep breath. 'I don't think he meant to murder him. It was meant to be a laugh, that's all.'

'Go back to the beginning,' said Kay. 'What were the four of you doing on the Mallorys' property last Sunday?'

'Dean's been seeing this girl, Ingrid, he met when he was travelling in Norway last year,' Liam said, his voice shaking. 'He's been spending most of his weekends over there, or in London when she flies over – he's doing all right for himself so he can afford the flights whenever he likes. He told us the other week that he was going to propose to her, but that we had to keep it a secret until he let his parents know first. They're… were really close, and he hadn't yet introduced them to her because she lives in Oslo. She's flying over later this week, apparently.'

'Right…' said Kay.

'Isaac phoned me and Dominic a day or so later and said we ought to celebrate, just the four of us, because everything would change once Dean was married. It wouldn't be the same ever again. Plus, he reckoned we could play a prank on Dean – leave him somewhere to be found, sort of like an early stag night was how he put it.' Liam paused. 'Could I have a glass of water, please?'

Kyle pushed himself away from the wall and out the

door, returning a few minutes later with a small bottle of mineral water that he uncapped and placed on the table.

'Thanks.' Liam drank half the contents, then wiped his mouth with the back of his hand. 'It was Isaac's idea to borrow his dad's van. He helps out over there every now and again, so we didn't see any harm in it at the time. We… we were meant to have it back there by the morning.'

He wiped at tears, then sniffed. 'Isaac… he's had problems in the past, with drugs I mean. He'd been clean for a while I think, but every now and again… Dean loved the farm. He'd told us that's where he wanted his wedding to take place, so we thought what better way to celebrate his engagement, right?'

Kay swallowed, her throat tight with emotion as she listened, but said nothing as Gavin's pen scratched across his notebook and the solicitor kept his gaze lowered to his own work.

'We had some booze with us,' said Liam. 'We had a few beers in the van on the way – we told Dean we were going to nick a couple of the pedalos on the lake at Mote Park when we picked him up, so by the time we left town and headed to the farm, he was already a few cans in and didn't realise. When we got him to the lay-by, it was too late. We pounced on him. It was still funny then – he had no idea it was coming. We bundled him through that field and into the hop garden. Isaac caught his face on the barbed wire, and it was then that I saw him stagger. Not like he'd been drinking, but like he was sky-high on something.'

He stopped, rested his elbows on the table, and put his

face in his hands. 'I should've known there was something wrong then.'

'But you didn't stop him.'

Liam shook his head. 'Dominic was laughing – so was Dean, although he was calling us every name under the sun while we strung him up. All we were going to do was take some photos. It was just meant to be a bit of fun before he got engaged next weekend.'

Gavin stopped writing and looked up. 'When did it all go wrong?'

'Whatever drugs Isaac had taken when we weren't looking must've messed with his head. I think – he must've been hallucinating. Dom and I walked off a bit to have a joint, and then...' Liam stopped and took another tentative sip of water. 'The first thing I knew something was wrong was when Dean screamed. We ran back and Isaac was standing there with a knife from the toolbox in the van. I had no idea he'd brought it with him. I thought he'd just brought the pliers to snip the barbed wire into the field. He... oh God. He'd stabbed Dean with it. He... he just ripped him open. There was blood everywhere, and...'

Liam broke off and started crying, his sobs filling the room.

Kay felt little pity for the man. 'Whose idea was it to carve the symbols into his skin to make it look like some sort of ritualistic murder?'

'Dominic's,' he said, his voice thick with emotion. 'He was panicking, we both were. Isaac was covered in blood, and after he'd... afterwards, he just sat there, crouched on the ground rocking back and forth, muttering to himself. I figured we needed to get him out of there, so we helped him back through the fence towards the van. We got him in the back and drove off. I couldn't think straight, Dominic was going on about how we needed to dump the van, and then we realised we had Dean's blood all over us too from where we'd dragged Isaac away. I... I'm not proud of it, any of it. But I told Dominic we'd have to set fire to the van with all our clothes inside – and the knife. So we did.'

'How did you get home after setting fire to Rex's van?' Gavin asked.

Liam's body shook and he hugged his arms to his chest. 'We walked... well, we managed to stagger along while we were holding up Isaac – he was still completely wasted – until we got to the outskirts of Marden. We reached the train station there, and then called a ride-share car and pretended we'd been duped into a drunken dare. We dropped off Isaac first, then I told Dom he was next. I figured that way, I could get the driver to stop at the end of my street so I could sneak back without mum and dad noticing.'

'You haven't told Isaac what happened that night, have you?' said Kay. 'All he can remember is waking up in his underwear covered in blood and vomit. It's why he wasn't expecting to be arrested earlier.'

'We didn't know how to tell him. I mean, he's murdered his best mate. What would you say to him?'

Kay looked at Gavin and gave him a slight nod.

'You should've reported him,' he said, turning to Liam. 'You could've told somebody what happened. Instead, you and Dominic chose to mutilate Dean's body to try and slow down our investigation by insinuating a satanic ritual or similar had taken place. You tampered with evidence, both by carving those symbols into his skin, and then by burning all your clothes and torching Rex Trimble's van. The list of offences the three of you committed last Sunday night are some of the worst I've seen in my entire career.'

'But it was Isaac's fault,' Liam insisted.

'You covered up a murder. You mutilated Dean's body. You deliberately destroyed evidence,' said Kay. 'I'll leave Detective Piper to explain the charges that are going to be laid against you.'

She pushed herself from the chair, nodded her thanks to Kyle as he opened the door for her and stepped out into the corridor.

Walking back to conclude her interview with Isaac, her legs wobbled and she leaned against the wall to steady herself.

Closing her eyes, she wondered how on earth she was going to tell Rowan and Maggie Spencer what had happened to their only child.

She sniffed, regained her composure, and squared her shoulders as she eyed the next interview room.

'Right, Isaac Trimble,' she murmured. 'Your turn.'

FORTY-EIGHT

Two hours later, the incident room was devoid of any administrative staff, and the last of the uniformed officers had left soon after.

It was dark outside now, rain pelting against the windows and a gust of wind from the direction of the River Medway shoving against the glass every now and again. Somebody within the maintenance team had finally turned the air conditioning to reverse cycle so that a warmth seeped through the ceiling vents, and most of the lights had been switched off, save for those above the whiteboard around which Kay and her team of detectives gathered.

Gavin had raced down the road to the mini-supermarket to find some cans of beer, and Kay's hair was still damp from the short walk she had made to collect pizzas for all of them. A weariness seeped through her bones, but as she looked around at the others' faces, she felt an overwhelming sense of pride.

'Here's to Dean,' she said, raising her can of lager.

'Dean,' the team chorused, clinking their cans against hers before drinking.

'Thanks for the pizza, guv,' said Laura, then smacked Gavin's hand as he tried to beat her to the last slice of the pepperoni one. 'Too slow.'

Kay laughed at Gavin's glare. 'You're welcome – Gav, there's another one of those, don't worry. I figured you two would be squabbling over it otherwise.'

He winked in response, then handed out extra slices to everyone. 'Has anybody had a chance to trace Dean's girlfriend yet?'

'I spoke to her mum,' said Kyle, wiping his lips with a napkin. 'Ingrid's distraught, as you can imagine. Her mum's asked me to pass on her contact details to Maggie and Rowan Spencer. She said Ingrid would still like to meet them, just not yet.'

'So many people have suffered,' Kay murmured, contemplating the carpet. 'Every time, not just the victims. It's everybody who's left.'

'What's first off the list tomorrow, guv?' Barnes asked, pulling her from her melancholy thoughts. 'Would you like me to liaise with the CPS if you've got to go over to headquarters?'

'That would be great, thanks Ian. Laura, could you work with Debbie to make sure all the statements are catalogued and reference the evidence we've collated?'

'Will do, guv.'

'Kyle, I'd like you to work with Ian on the CPS liaison if you could. It'll give you some more experience with that side of things.'

'No problem, guv,' said the younger detective. 'And

thanks for letting me do some of the interviews on this one, all of you.'

Gavin reached over and tipped his can against Kyle's. 'You did good.'

'As did you, Gav, working out we had two investigations on our hands, not one,' Kay said to him. 'Once the poisoning angle was taken care of, it became easier to separate out the evidence we had. It was overwhelming until then.'

'I still can't believe Dominic and Liam thought it was a good idea to mutilate Dean's body,' said Laura, shaking her head. 'I mean, all they had to do was report Isaac and explain what happened, and now…'

'Now they're looking at years behind bars,' said Kay. 'By the way, good work on eliminating Joseph Mallory from the investigation. I thought he might've been a suspect for a while there.'

'Thanks, guv, and me too,' said Laura, then shrugged. 'But I think he's just bitter because he's not in control anymore, and that's probably caused by boredom more than anything else. It's a shame.'

'Have you had a chance to talk to the Mallorys, guv?' Barnes asked.

'I gave Justin a quick call while I was waiting for these,' said Kay. 'And I've assured him a statement will be released to the media in time for the evening news tomorrow so the public know nobody at the farm was involved in Dean's murder.'

'Do you think they'll continue with the hop tours?' Kyle wondered.

'I doubt it. You can imagine the sort of people who'll

turn up just because they want to see where Dean was killed.' Kay shuddered. 'Justin reckons it's best they don't, and to be honest I'm inclined to agree with him. He did say the new crop variety is proving promising though, so hopefully that will help to keep them in profit.'

Barnes looked at the darkened windows as a fresh gust of wind sent raindrops scattering across the glass. 'Looks like they got everything harvested just in time, too.'

'No kidding. Okay, so who's going to Harry's retirement party on Saturday?'

Kay listened as her detectives shared their plans for the forthcoming celebration, grinning as Gavin and Barnes discussed what pranks they might get away with before the respected uniformed constable who had been such a huge part of their lives at the police station walked out the door for the last time, and then laughed as Laura berated them.

Soon, the beers were drained, the pizza was gone, and they started gathering up the empty boxes and discarded cans and napkins for the cleaners before wandering back to their desks.

'Right,' said Kay. 'Late start tomorrow given the hours you've all been working, so I don't want to see you before nine o'clock, understood?'

'Thanks, guv,' said Gavin, then frowned as he picked up his backpack and saw her sit in front of her computer screen. 'But aren't you going home now?'

Kyle and Laura paused at the door, their faces expectant.

'I will, in a minute,' said Kay, waving them away. 'But I've got a call to make first.'

Barnes waited until the others had gone, then looked at

her. 'Hope it goes as well as it can in the circumstances, guv.'

'Thanks, Ian. I'll see you tomorrow.'

'That you will.'

Kay waited until the incident room door closed behind him, then picked up her car keys and took a deep breath before leaving to tell Maggie and Rowan Spencer what had happened to their only son.

FORTY-NINE

Saturday

'The ride-share car's here.'

Adam's voice resonated up the stairs to the bedroom, where Kay stared in the wardrobe mirror and gritted her teeth while she pierced a silver earring through a lobe that last saw jewellery six months ago.

'I'm two minutes away.'

'You said that five minutes ago.'

'The car's early.'

Laughter reached her. 'He's early, yes.'

'Ah,' she said, the earring finally in place. She turned her head from side to side, admiring the silver threads dangling past her jawline. 'Then I'm in credit for a few minutes.'

'We're going to be late.'

'We'll be okay,' she said, reaching for her bag and

picking up a pair of heeled shoes. She headed downstairs to find Adam pacing the living room. Handing him her bag while she balanced on one foot, then the other, she looked at the dog bed in the corner. 'Will Poppy be okay on her own for a few hours?'

'She'll be fine.' Adam crouched and rubbed the dog's fur between her ears. 'Won't you? No loud parties while we're gone, okay?'

Poppy's tongue lolled so it looked as if she was smiling, and Kay laughed. 'We'll probably get back to find out she's ransacked the kitchen, knowing what Labradors are like.'

'Don't worry, I've closed the door.' Adam rose to his feet and handed back her bag. 'You look lovely.'

'Thanks, you tart up pretty well yourself.' She kissed him. 'Let's go.'

Twenty minutes later, their driver pulled to a standstill outside a village hall on the outskirts of Maidstone that had been decked out with streamers and balloons around its double wooden doors. Several cars were parked on the gravel outside it, and Kay's heels crunched over the small stones as she and Adam made their way over.

Music played from within, a mix of old and new, with a DJ's voice cutting through the tunes muffled by the building's thick walls. Every now and again, the door opened as someone left the party and walked to the far corner of the car park to have a cigarette, and the smell of food wafted on the night breeze.

'Evening, guv.'

She turned to see Barnes walking towards her, his

partner Pia holding his hand while she elegantly negotiated the driveway in three-inch high heels. 'I don't know how you do that.'

'Practice,' said Pia, then gave her a hug. 'I heard it's been a tough couple of weeks.'

'We'll get through it.' Kay smiled. 'Besides, it was something else to go over to headquarters and see the disappointment on the other detective inspector's face when he realised he wasn't going to get the chance to audit our investigation. The review is difficult, but necessary. I could've done better.'

'Bullshit,' said Barnes.

'It's just politics, that's all, Ian. It's just my turn.'

'Again.'

'Are you lot talking shop, or are we going to have a party tonight?' Gavin called.

Kay turned to see him and Leanne waiting by the hall's doorway and raised her hand in greeting. 'Party.'

'Good, because I can smell the food from here, and I'm starving.'

They laughed, and then Gavin opened the door for Leanne and grinned as Kay walked by him. 'Been too long since we've let our hair down, guv.'

'I know. Shame about the circumstances, though. I'm going to miss having Harry around.'

'Kay!' a familiar voice bellowed as soon as she entered the hall. 'You made it. Thought you'd be still at your desk.'

She looked to her left to see DCI Devon Sharp heading towards her, his wife Rebecca a short way behind, smiling. 'Perish the thought. I'm having a well-deserved night off.'

'Good. Kyle and Laura are around somewhere.' Sharp craned his neck over the assembled crowd. 'Have you met Laura's new boyfriend?'

'No… I didn't know she was seeing someone.'

'Seems all right compared to the last one.'

'Devon, shhhh,' Rebecca admonished him. 'Anybody would think…'

Sharp grinned in response, then turned back to Kay and Adam and handed them each a blue plastic token. 'Right, the bar's open. First drink's on me, and the food's over… right, okay, well Gavin's already found that by the look of it. We're just waiting on a couple more people to turn up, and then I'm going to embarrass myself and Harry by giving a short speech.'

'Where do we put this?' asked Adam, holding up the wrapped gift they had brought for the retiring officer.

'There's a table over near the buffet for those. You'll find it. Looks like a bloody Christmas tree,' said Sharp, then turned at the sound of his name. 'Looks like I've got to mingle some more. See you in a bit.'

Kay smiled as he and his wife walked away, then swept her gaze over the crowd until she saw Harry. She squeezed Adam's hand. 'Give me a minute?'

'Sure. I'll go and pop this present over with the others.'

'Thanks.'

Zigzagging between her colleagues and a number of officers she recognised from other departments within the West Division of Kent Police, as well as family members who had joined the party, Kay reached Harry just as another detective inspector was leaving. She smiled, and accepted the glass of wine the retiring sergeant handed to her, clinking it against his pint of beer.

He looked relaxed in jeans and a pale blue polo shirt, and some of the lines that had etched his features over recent years had already faded since he had left the police station for the last time three days before.

'Here's to you,' she said, raising her voice above the throng. 'And before Sharp beats me to it with his speech, I wanted to tell you that I really couldn't have done everything I've done without you, Harry.'

He smiled. 'Thank you, Kay. And you've come a long way since I first knew you when you joined us as a probationer from Tonbridge. I knew you'd do all right. I could see it, even back then.'

'Ah, you flatter me,' Kay said, blushing. 'You and I know full well that it's a team effort.'

His gaze drifted to the people in the room. 'And they're a good team, aren't they?'

'We're all going to miss you, Harry.'

'Careful,' he said, and winked at her. 'It's going to be hard enough making my speech as it is without you starting me off. Reckon I'll be a wreck by the end of tonight anyway. I'm certainly not going to have much of a voice by the morning.'

Kay laughed. 'Oh, you'll be all right. When do you leave for your holiday?'

'In a couple of weeks. The missus wants to spend some time catching up with long-distance family we haven't managed to see over the summer first, and I want to put out some feelers about some freelance consulting work so I've got something to get on with when we get back.'

'Well, you've got my number, so any time you need me, you call, got that?'

'Will do. And thanks again, Kay. It's been a pleasure.'

'Likewise.' Kay looked around the room. 'Right, I'd better go and find Adam and take a beer over for him. I'll catch you later.'

She spotted Adam talking with Aaron Stewart in a corner of the hall and started to weave between people to reach him, and then felt someone grab her arm.

'Got a minute, guv?' Barnes said, keeping his voice low.

'Sure. What's wrong?'

She followed him through the village hall to a stage at the far end that had been curtained off so that only the front wooden panels of the raised platform showed and placed her wineglass beside a row of empty plates that had been left by other partygoers. Barnes leaned against the stage and watched the celebrations with a pensive expression.

'What's going on, Ian?'

'I just wanted to let you know so you don't find out from somebody else,' he said. 'Headquarters got in touch with me three weeks ago. Well, the personnel department to be precise.'

'Is something the matter? Are you okay?'

'I'm fine, don't worry. Fighting fit.'

'So, what did they want?'

In reply, Barnes jerked his chin towards Harry, who was surrounded by four other colleagues, his laughter carrying across the crowd. 'The same as what they've just done to him.'

Kay's jaw dropped. 'You're not retiring, are you?'

'Don't worry, guv. I'm not going for a long time yet. The letter just said that if I wanted to, I was entitled to take early retirement.'

'What does Pia think?'

'She thinks they're just contacting a number of us to see if anyone will take the money and run. I'm ignoring the request, but at some point they're going to want to get rid of me to make room for new blood.' He winked, then pointed at Gavin who was standing with a drink in one hand and a canapé in the other, the detective's brow furrowed in concentration while he listened to another sergeant recounting a story. 'No need to panic though, you've got a good replacement for me right there.'

Kay followed his gaze, and frowned. 'I don't want a replacement, Ian. And I don't want you going anywhere for a long time, you understand? We wouldn't have solved Dean's murder without the pair of you, and I've made that quite clear to headquarters, so they can bugger off if they think they can make you quit.'

'Okay, okay.' Barnes held up his hands and laughed. 'I get the message. Like I said, they're just offering at the moment. Besides, at some point you're going to have to promote Gavin, aren't you? The clock's ticking as far as that one's concerned. We've said it before – if he doesn't get that sergeant promotion here, he's going to jump. Not from a lack of loyalty, Kay, but from necessity.'

'I know,' she said. 'And I've already told Sharp I want two detective sergeants on my team, especially as there are a couple of people who would make good candidates for probationary detectives over the next twelve months.'

'Oh? Who've you got in mind?'

Kay smiled, placed her hand on Barnes's arm and steered him towards the bar. 'Buy me another glass of wine, and I might tell you.'

THE END

ABOUT THE AUTHOR

Rachel Amphlett is a USA Today bestselling author of crime fiction and spy thrillers, many of which have been translated worldwide.

Her novels are available in eBook, print, and audiobook formats from libraries and retailers as well as her website shop.

A keen traveller and accidental private investigator, Rachel has both Australian and British citizenship.

Find out more about Rachel's books at: www.rachelamphlett.com.